PRAISE FOR

MURDER STRIKES A CHORD

"*Murder Strikes a Chord* hits all the right notes in this new cozy mystery by Heather Weidner."

— **Jackie Layton**, Author of the Texas Flower Farmer Cozy Mysteries and the Low Country Dog Walker Mysteries

"Ivy Springs is a fabulous setting for a cozy, full of quaint little shops and unique characters. Former social media manager Cassidy is the perfect modern-day Miss Marple, using her computer skills to hunt down the rock star's killer. Between Cassidy's smarts and the Pearly Girls fun, *Murder Strikes a Chord* is a winner all around."

—**Sue Minix**, Author of the Bookstore Mystery Series

"Cassidy Jamison's Groovin' Through the Decades concert series is heading for success when the popular if aging rock band, the Weathermen, give their first performance. That is, until the lead singer ends up face down in the koi pond. With the help of the four sixty-something Pearly Girls and her spunky chihuahua Elvis, Cassidy sets out to find the murderer and put things right. A fun, fast-paced, and heartwarming start to Heather Weidner's latest series."

— **Marilyn Levinson,** a.k.a. Allison Brook, author of the Haunted Library Series

"*Murder Strikes a Chord* is a fun read with curves and twists. Add to that the hilarious antics of the Pearly Girls and you've got a great book you won't want to put down!"

— **Ruth J. Hartman**, Bestselling Author of The Kitty Beret Café Mysteries

ALSO BY HEATHER WEIDNER

The Jules Keene Glamping Mysteries

Vintage Trailers and Blackmailers

Film Crews and Rendezvous

Christmas Lights and Cat Fights

Deadlines and Valentines

The Mermaid Bay Christmas Shoppe Mysteries

Sticks and Stones and a Bag of Bones

Twinkle, Twinkle Au Revoir

A Tisket a Tasket, Not Another Casket

The Delanie Fitzgerald Mysteries

Secret Lives and Private Eyes

The Tulip Shirt Murders

Glitter, Glam, and Contraband

Male Revues and Subterfuge

MURDER STRIKES A CHORD

A PEARLY GIRLS MYSTERY

HEATHER WEIDNER

KEYLIGHT BOOKS
AN IMPRINT OF TURNER PUBLISHING

Keylight Books
an imprint of Turner Publishing Company
Nashville, Tennessee
www.turnerpublishing.com

Murder Strikes a Chord

Cover design by Kent Holloway

Book design by William Ruoto

Library of Congress Cataloging-in-Publication Data
Names: Weidner, Heather, author.
Title: Murder strikes a chord / by Heather Weidner.
Description: Nashville, Tennessee: Turner Publishing Company, 2025. | Series: Pearly Girls mysteries
Identifiers: LCCN 2024017525 (print) | LCCN 2024017526 (ebook) | ISBN 9781684426508 (paperback) | ISBN 9781684426560 (hardcover) | ISBN 9781684426591 (epub)
Subjects: LCGFT: Cozy mysteries. | Novels.
Classification: LCC PS3623.E4257 M87 2025 (print) | LCC PS3623.E4257 (ebook) | DDC 813/.6—dc23/eng/20240419
LC record available at https://lccn.loc.gov/2024017525
LC ebook record available at https://lccn.loc.gov/2024017526

Printed in the United States of America

MURDER STRIKES A CHORD

A PEARLY GIRLS MYSTERY

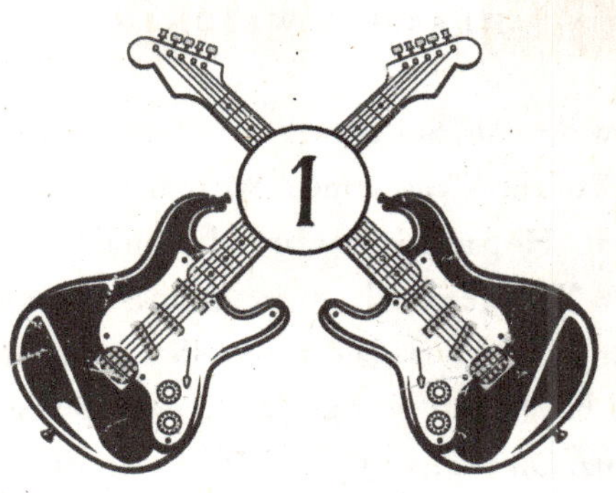

THURSDAY AFTERNOON

Cassidy Jamison glanced up from her laptop in the shared office space in the converted farmhouse on her property, Celebrations at Ivy Springs. Her sexagenarian bookkeeper, Ruthanne Carmichael, made a mad dash from her desk to the front window.

"They're here. They're here!" Ruthanne squealed in an octave so high it made Elvis, the brown and tan Chihuahua mix, scamper to the front room to see what all the excitement was about. Between Ruthanne's squeals and Elvis's barks, Cassidy couldn't tell what was going on. She slid on her shoes and tried to get a glimpse out the window behind Ruthanne, who continued to bob, point, and squeal.

Three large black and gray tour buses passed through the front gate and rolled to a stop near the porch. Gently nudging Elvis away from the door, Cassidy smoothed her long red curls and stepped through the door, pulling it shut behind her.

A rotund man resembling a professional wrestler stepped off the first bus, followed by a thinner guy with stylized salt-and-pepper hair. He pulled out a pair of expensive-looking sunglasses and slid them on before moving toward the porch.

"Good morning." Cassidy shielded her eyes from the sun peeking over the mountains. "Welcome to Celebrations at Ivy Springs and the Groovin' through the Decades music festival. We're excited you're here. This is going to be an amazing week."

After a few seconds, Sunglasses said, "Good morning. I'm Beau Cox, manager of the Weathermen. We're here and ready to headline the festival." He paused and glanced around like he hadn't been outside before. "Where exactly *are* we, besides in the mountains?"

"Ivy Springs, Virginia. We're near Staunton and Harrisonburg." When he showed no signs of recognition, she continued, "It's in Virginia. On the East Coast." When he still didn't respond, she changed course. "You all are going to set up between the grotto and the amphitheater, out of the way of the crowds, so you and the band won't be disturbed during your downtime. We have camper hookups. You should be all set. My facilities guy will meet you there and answer any questions." She turned to address the other man, presuming him to be the bus driver. "Follow this road around the bend, past the parking lots, then bear to the left. The turnoff is a gravel road through the trees to a meadow where you can park. If you get to a wooden barricade, you've gone too far."

The bus driver nodded. "Got it."

"Thanks." Beau peeked over his sunglasses. "Once we get settled, I'll swing by your office to go over details, and you can tell me what else is around here besides trees."

She pulled out her phone and tapped on a contact. After three rings, she heard, "Hey, lady. What's up?" Levi Jenkins, who had been the handyman and groundskeeper for as long as Cassidy could remember, sounded like he was outside with an engine running.

"Hey. The three buses with the band and their equipment are here. Can you meet them at the little meadow to show them the hookups and get them settled? I'm sure they'll have questions."

"I'm on it. Tell 'em I'm heading over there now." Levi's words were nearly drowned out by the idling of the engine.

Cassidy muttered "Thanks" to an already dead line. She turned back to the driver and Beau. "Levi Jenkins will meet you there. Please let us know if we can help in any way. You can't miss him. He's tall and thin, and he always wears a baseball cap."

THURSDAY AFTERNOON

Cassidy Jamison glanced up from her laptop in the shared office space in the converted farmhouse on her property, Celebrations at Ivy Springs. Her sexagenarian bookkeeper, Ruthanne Carmichael, made a mad dash from her desk to the front window.

"They're here. They're here!" Ruthanne squealed in an octave so high it made Elvis, the brown and tan Chihuahua mix, scamper to the front room to see what all the excitement was about. Between Ruthanne's squeals and Elvis's barks, Cassidy couldn't tell what was going on. She slid on her shoes and tried to get a glimpse out the window behind Ruthanne, who continued to bob, point, and squeal.

Three large black and gray tour buses passed through the front gate and rolled to a stop near the porch. Gently nudging Elvis away from the door, Cassidy smoothed her long red curls and stepped through the door, pulling it shut behind her.

A rotund man resembling a professional wrestler stepped off the first bus, followed by a thinner guy with stylized salt-and-pepper hair. He pulled out a pair of expensive-looking sunglasses and slid them on before moving toward the porch.

"Good morning." Cassidy shielded her eyes from the sun peeking over the mountains. "Welcome to Celebrations at Ivy Springs and the Groovin' through the Decades music festival. We're excited you're here. This is going to be an amazing week."

After a few seconds, Sunglasses said, "Good morning. I'm Beau Cox, manager of the Weathermen. We're here and ready to headline the festival." He paused and glanced around like he hadn't been outside before. "Where exactly *are* we, besides in the mountains?"

"Ivy Springs, Virginia. We're near Staunton and Harrisonburg." When he showed no signs of recognition, she continued, "It's in Virginia. On the East Coast." When he still didn't respond, she changed course. "You all are going to set up between the grotto and the amphitheater, out of the way of the crowds, so you and the band won't be disturbed during your downtime. We have camper hookups. You should be all set. My facilities guy will meet you there and answer any questions." She turned to address the other man, presuming him to be the bus driver. "Follow this road around the bend, past the parking lots, then bear to the left. The turnoff is a gravel road through the trees to a meadow where you can park. If you get to a wooden barricade, you've gone too far."

The bus driver nodded. "Got it."

"Thanks." Beau peeked over his sunglasses. "Once we get settled, I'll swing by your office to go over details, and you can tell me what else is around here besides trees."

She pulled out her phone and tapped on a contact. After three rings, she heard, "Hey, lady. What's up?" Levi Jenkins, who had been the handyman and groundskeeper for as long as Cassidy could remember, sounded like he was outside with an engine running.

"Hey. The three buses with the band and their equipment are here. Can you meet them at the little meadow to show them the hookups and get them settled? I'm sure they'll have questions."

"I'm on it. Tell 'em I'm heading over there now." Levi's words were nearly drowned out by the idling of the engine.

Cassidy muttered "Thanks" to an already dead line. She turned back to the driver and Beau. "Levi Jenkins will meet you there. Please let us know if we can help in any way. You can't miss him. He's tall and thin, and he always wears a baseball cap."

"Will do." Beau saluted with two fingers and climbed back on the bus.

Cassidy watched the buses inch slowly along the maintenance road and disappear around the bend. Before she had even closed the office door, Ruthanne and Elvis ambushed her. Ruthanne wanted details. Elvis wanted hugs. Gathering the wiggly dog in her arms, she nuzzled the soft fur on his neck.

"Did you see him? Did you get to talk to him? Is he still as dreamy as he used to be? He can still make my heart pitter-patter. Oh, my stars, I can't believe they're actually here. What's Johnny Storm like? What are they all like?" Ruthanne gushed. "Pinch me. I can't believe this is all real."

Surprised that the sixty-something—who was usually the austere one of the group—was this excited about the music festival they were hosting on the property for the next couple of weekends, Cassidy set Elvis down before answering the myriad questions. "No. Just the manager and a bus driver. Levi's meeting them in the space by the serenity garden to set up. I didn't get to meet the band yet."

"I may have to get my steps in this afternoon with a walk around the grounds." Ruthanne took one last peek out the front window then glanced at her wedged sandals. "These may not be the best shoes for a walk, but I'll take my chances if I get to accidentally bump into the Weathermen." She winked.

"The manager will be over in a bit to talk details. Maybe we can work out some sort of meet and greet." Cassidy winked in return.

"That would be amazing!" The color rose in Ruthanne's cheeks, and she made a beeline for her desk. "I need to finish payroll and the sales tax. This festival is going to be so much fun. Don't get me wrong," she said as she fanned herself with a manila file folder from her desk. "Weddings and receptions are wonderful, but this music festival is going to be the bomb. I have been a fan of Johnny Storm and the Weathermen since the seventies. Hubba-hubba. And he still has that rockin' bod and amazing deep voice. Not bad for a bunch of, well, let's say, seasoned guys." She did a shimmy in the chair while letting out another squeal.

An amused smile crept across Cassidy's face as she settled at her desk to check on her business's website. The Groovin' through the Decades festival was a coup for her small business in the heart of Virginia's Blue Ridge Mountains. She had been working long hours to keep her event calendar full. A multi-week festival was a phenomenal booking.

Life as a business owner was harder than her previous role after college. She left her frenetic position as a social media manager in Washington, DC, to move back to her rural hometown, Ivy Springs. Cassidy hadn't lived here since high school, and the culture shock of coming back to this small town was an adjustment. It was most definitely a change of pace—like going from eighty miles an hour to twenty-five, and skipping a couple of gears. Some progress had made its way to town while she was away, but life was still much calmer than what she was accustomed to. Most everything here closed by nine o'clock, and there wasn't any 24-7 city noise. Since she had been gone, the town had gained a winery, several cideries, some cool restaurants, and a second stoplight. But even while some things changed, others were the way they had always been. Nature provided the backdrop for everything. The mountains, trees, and wildlife replaced the noise and hurried pace of the city. Even the dialect here was a bit slower. There was definitely a drawl in the speech patterns. Even though it was only a couple of hours from the nation's capital, it felt worlds apart.

Cassidy had spent every waking hour trying to keep her business solvent after the world turned upside down in 2020. In addition to the global chaos that year, her grandmother—who had raised her after her parents' sudden deaths—passed away. The business and land had been in the family for over 150 years and had reverted to her. She was the last in the family line.

The property had originally boasted the Ivy Springs Saloon, but it burned to the ground in the early eighties. Instead of rebuilding the infamous honky-tonk, Cassidy's grandmother had decided to create a peaceful garden near the property's grotto and cave for weddings and special events. She turned the dairy barn into an event hall and built a huge amphitheater for meetings and concerts to showcase the beauty of the landscape.

The slamming of the front door jarred Cassidy from her memories. She shook off the melancholic feelings and trotted after Elvis to greet the new arrivals.

"Good morning again, Beau," she said as she stepped into the restored farmhouse's former parlor, which housed a cozy seating area for clients and guests. The old dining room across the hall now served as their conference room for event planning, and the back half of the first floor was the shared office, workroom, and kitchenette. The second floor had been converted into Cassidy's apartment.

"I think we're all settled in. I have a list of things to do for the band, as usual. Can you catch an Uber around here?" Beau pushed his sunglasses on top of his head.

"Yes, but it's not like larger cities. It may take a while for them to arrive, depending on whether both drivers are on duty today."

Beau wrinkled his nose and looked at his phone. "Meals? Is delivery available out here?"

Cassidy rummaged through a stack of pamphlets about local attractions and pulled out several menus. "We have quite a few eateries in town, and several also provide delivery services." She offered him the brochures.

"Thanks." He pocketed them inside his blazer without looking at them. "We have security with us, but our contract said you also have it on the property. You can never have too much these days. Fans and wackadoodles get out of control sometimes. Here's my guy's contact. Have your team reach out to him. He'll go over all the protocols and what the band does and doesn't like." He flipped two business cards in her direction.

Taking the cards, Cassidy pasted on her best customer service smile. "We contract with Domingo Private Security. They'll have at least two guards on the property around-the-clock during the festival. We've also arranged to have a police presence here to direct traffic before and after the concerts. I'll make sure Mateo Domingo gets your information."

"Very good. And one last thing, Any issues with the band or staff coming and going at will? I mean, you don't have gates or passkeys they'll need? They're a free-spirited bunch who don't do a lot of advance planning."

"The property has fencing and cameras around the perimeters, but there's no gate or locks preventing entry. One security guard is usually stationed at the front entrance," she said.

"Good. Steve Owens—you know, the concert promoter, right? He's supposed to meet me here this afternoon to go over logistics. We're also going to do a sound check. If he stops in, please send him over to the buses. He can't miss us. We filled your little meadow with all our stuff. The guys are making themselves at home." Beau flashed his megawatt smile and strode toward the door.

When the thick door shut firmly behind him, Cassidy let out a sigh that sounded like air escaping from a balloon as Ruthanne squealed again from the back. "A real live sound check with the band. Be still my heart. I'm definitely heading over there the minute I finish here. I need to let the other gals know. This is so incredible." She whipped out her phone and sent a flurry of texts. "There. The rest of the Pearly Girls know. They'll be here lickety-split." Ruthanne winked and returned to her desk.

Cassidy smiled at the image in her head of her grandmother's lifelong friends rushing over like teenagers to get a glimpse of the rock stars. Sometimes, their advice was a bit over-the-top, even smothering, but the baby boomers meant well. Herself a millennial, Cassidy spent most of her time bringing her business into the current century while bridging the generation gaps on a daily basis.

LATER THURSDAY AFTERNOON

The front door slammed again, sending Elvis into attack mode until he realized it was Roxie, Aileen, and Kate—the other three Pearly Girls—who must have dropped everything to respond to Ruthanne's flurry of texts. As a young woman during the heyday of Camelot and the threats of the Cold War, Cassidy's grandmother Evelyn had made some lifelong friends who now kept a watchful eye on Cassidy in her absence. All of the ladies loved the music and popular culture of the fifties, sixties, and seventies and still sported their signature pearls like Jackie O. The gang, now retired and widowed, all worked part-time in some capacity to help Cassidy keep the business solvent—and to attempt to fix her up with any eligible bachelor who unwittingly crossed their paths.

"What's shakin'?" Roxie Matthews asked as she dropped her red Coach bag onto the coffee table in the sitting area. "Ruthanne, I brought my camera and autograph book."

"You still have that?" Kate, the former nurse, took a seat on the teal love seat in the reception area. "Who collects autographs anymore? Is that even a thing?"

"I do. And photos for my IG account. I like to know who I've met. Sometimes it's hard to remember all of them," Roxie quipped, rummaging through her purse. Her leopard-print blouse and skintight, satiny pants accentuated her figure, making her look ten—if not fifteen—years younger than she actually was.

"Glad you all could get over here so fast." Ruthanne shut her laptop. "I am so excited to meet *the* Johnny Storm and the rest of the band. I still have all their albums, and even some of the forty-fives, and I got to see him in concert in Richmond and Roanoke. Dreamy. Just dreamy." She pulled out a pink lipstick and mirror from her purse and retouched her makeup.

Cassidy half expected cartoon hearts to appear in Ruthanne's eyes as she waxed on about the singer.

"We are unprepared. We should have gotten them a fruit basket or something." Aileen, the former elementary school teacher, dressed in a flowing pink and aqua tunic, fretted. "I feel like we're arriving empty-handed. My mother would be appalled. Her rule was to always make a good first impression and never arrive without a gift." Today her silver bob was tinted pink to match her outfit.

Roxie waved her hand dismissively. "Our adulation and undying love will be enough. Where are they anyway?"

"Over in the meadow. They're staying here on the property since they're headlining the concert's big shows on multiple weekends," Cassidy said.

"And our little town doesn't have any luxury accommodations nearby, nothing rock star worthy." Roxie smirked.

Cassidy considered the two drive-up motels on the outskirts of town that were relics of the Eisenhower years. "I'm sure they'll be comfortable in their Megabuses."

"It'll be nice when Dot and Jim finish their restoration of that old Victorian near the Baptist Church. That'll be a perfect location for a bed and breakfast." Aileen winked. "And if I know Dot, everything will be top notch. Ivy Springs needs something fancy. Sid "Pro Quo" Proctor's no-tell motels went the way of the dinosaurs years ago. It's much better that the band is staying here—for them and for us."

"They get to hang out with us. They don't know how lucky they are." Ruthanne grinned with a dreamy-eyed expression.

Kate, the tallest of the Pearly Girls, joined in. "Oh, lots of opportunities for us to run into them." Turning to Aileen, she added, "A fruit basket, Aileen? These are hard-living, whisky-drinking, bar-fighting kind of guys. It should be a beer and bourbon basket if anything. Next thing you know, we'll be baking them cookies."

"Cookies are nice," Ruthanne said. "Everyone likes fresh-out-of-the-oven chocolate chip cookies or brownies. That would be a lovely gift."

Roxie rolled her eyes. "If you want them to think you're a grandma. I don't bake cookies."

Kate waved her hand dismissively. "Cassidy, everything else going okay here? You don't need us to do anything, do you?"

Cassidy shook her head. "We're all set. The festival people are taking care of the concerts and equipment. And security's in place. We're good to go."

"Oh, goodie." Ruthanne clapped. "And we'll definitely have all kinds of access. You never know how many times I may conveniently run into them on my walkabouts. If you had told me about being this close to the band in my teen years, I never would have believed it would be possible. Up close and personal with the Weathermen...I can't wait!" Ruthanne's silver curls bobbed as she wriggled her whole body and waved her arms in an arc.

"We better dig out some cigarette lighters for the concert. Not sure if I still have any. I threw a bunch of them out when I quit smoking," Roxie said.

"Nobody uses lighters anymore." Aileen snickered. "They wave their phones at concerts now. You know, with the lights on."

Ruthanne raised a finger. "Maybe we should get some glow sticks."

"Less of a hazard," Kate agreed, nodding.

"But not as cool." Roxie wrinkled her nose. "What are we waiting for? I rushed over here to see those heartthrobs. Let's get a move on before we—or they—get any older. I hope I'm not disappointed."

Cassidy pocketed her phone and snapped Elvis's leash on his collar. "Come on, baby. Let's go meet these rockers the gals are so enchanted with." She locked the front door, and the tiny group marched out the back and past the barn to the gardens surrounding the rocky grotto. Cassidy slowed her pace a bit when she realized not all the ladies were power walkers.

"I'm coming," Ruth huffed. "I should have worn my Chucks this morning. These sandals are definitely not for hiking. But they do show off my new shade of va-va-voom red from my pedicure. That could always come in handy."

"Hey, Cassidy, the lilies and lotus in the koi pond are doing well. What's that?" Kate pointed to the black netting draped artistically over the water feature.

"Levi helped me hang those. We had a little bit of a bird problem. A couple of hawks thought this was a new fish buffet."

Ruthanne wrinkled her nose. "Poor goldfish. Levi has such a tender heart. I'm glad he found a solution to protect the fish besides his pellet gun. We had to take it away from him last spring when that woodpecker kept tapping on the side of his house."

"We had to do some restocking, but so far, the netting seems to work. Levi's been keeping an eye on it. He does a daily inventory of the fish." Cassidy slowed as Elvis decided to smell every blade of grass on the path.

"Levi always knows how to fix everything. He was Evelyn's right-hand man. After the saloon burned, he was the foreman who oversaw all the construction on this place," Kate said.

"Levi is a miracle worker. He saved my Christmas cactus last year, and he recommended the right light for my orchid that was on its way to the plant graveyard. He's a jack-of-all-trades," Ruthanne agreed.

Levi, who was about the same age as the Pearly Girls, was a fixture around the property and was always willing to take on any new project. His clever remedy at the pond had solved the problem of the disappearing koi. Cassidy called him the Lawn Ranger because mowing the acres of grass and tending the facility's gardens were his favorite things to do.

The women and the adventurous dog made their way along the wooded path to the meadow area. A shriek echoed across the grassy field and bounced off the trees. The five women and the Chihuahua froze in their tracks.

"What is wrong with you? Did you see a snake again?" Roxie asked Ruthanne, who was gasping and pointing to the area on the other side of the tree line.

"Did you turn your ankle?" Kate rushed forward to help.

"No. Look. It's them. Not sure my heart can take it, but if I have a heart attack and die, at least there will be a smile on my face. Come on, girls. Let's go meet the Weathermen." Ruthanne led the charge to the three buses parked in a *C* shape in the grassy meadow.

It hadn't taken the band and its entourage long to settle in. They had established a camp next to the mammoth buses with patio awnings, lawn chairs, a grill, a meat smoker, and a row of coolers. A tailgate party had already begun.

"Hello, y'all," Roxie drawled as she waved at the men seated in fancy stadium chairs under the awnings fluttering in the breeze.

The manager rose as she sashayed over. "Hello, ladies. I'm Beau. The Weathermen are just getting settled in. The guys are working on some snacks before their sound check and tour of the facilities this afternoon. Can we get you anything? Ice-cold drinks? An adult beverage?" He bowed toward Roxie and held the hand she offered long after he was done shaking it.

Ruthanne and Aileen giggled. "We're fine." Roxie spoke before anyone else. "We at Celebrations at Ivy Springs wanted to stop by and welcome you all. You know Cassidy, the owner. This is

Ruthanne, Aileen, and Kate, some of your biggest fans. And I am Roxie Matthews."

Beau smiled. "It's a pleasure to meet you. The guys always love to talk to their fans."

All heads turned to the doorway of the nearest bus as Johnny Storm climbed down the steps with a can of beer in his hand. He wore an open red silk kimono and a pair of black leather pants. Despite the gray hair, he still had six-pack abs. *Not bad for a seventy-something rocker.* Ruthanne gasped. Cassidy glanced over in her direction to see if she needed to grab her elbow to steady her.

"Somebody make sure I'm not dreaming," Ruthanne whispered. "And if I am, don't wake me. I want to see where this goes."

"Ladies," Beau said, "this is the one and only Johnny Storm."

Johnny belched and took a swig from the can. "Good afternoon. Where are we by the way?" He squinted around at the blueish-green mountains in the distance.

"You're in Ivy Springs, Virginia," Kate volunteered.

"It's between Roanoke and Staunton." Aileen eyed the newcomer.

"*Where?*" The singer's nose scrunched up in apparent confusion.

"On the East Coast near DC. Don't worry about it. Just smile and do your thing." Beau patted him on the shoulder. "And this is the rest of the band, Karl Schultz, Dirk Lawrence, and last but not least, Jack Simon."

"I'm always last," Jack muttered under his breath.

"It's because you're last alphabetically by real names." Karl smirked.

Ignoring the peanut gallery, Ruthanne said, "We are so thrilled to meet you. Can we get some pictures? I'm going to want to remember this day forever."

"Here. I'll take them," Beau offered, extending his hand for the phone. "You all get in close around the chairs. Johnny, make sure you're in the shot. You need to be front and center. Ladies, gather around him. Everybody look sexy."

All the women handed Beau their phones, while Roxie maneuvered next to Johnny Storm.

"Say 'lots of money,'" Beau said.

A chorus of voices rang out as he snapped photos with the different phones. "Stay still. I'm almost done. Okay, last one. Here you go, ladies. Make sure you tell all your friends. We want all the shows packed while we're here. The Weathermen came a long way to see you all."

"Finally," Dirk muttered as he rose. "That's enough for a while. I've got things to do."

"What makes you so special? We're all busy and have things to do." Jack glared at him.

Dirk returned the glare and stepped closer to Jack.

Jack raised both hands and flashed a fake smile. "But right now, I'm going to chill after that freakin' long ride and enjoy the sunshine and really nice view of the mountains over there. You could use some downtime, Dirk. You seem a little tense. Maybe some meditation or yoga. Something eating at you?"

Dirk lunged forward and shoved Jack, who stumbled backward and fell, almost hitting his head on the ground.

Beau stepped in between them. "Enough. I suggest you two take a break from each other. But don't go too far. We meet with the show's promoter at two. We will do a mandatory sound check and rehearsal to measure the outdoor acoustics. And that means *all of you* will be there and on time." He extended a hand to Jack and pulled him to his feet. "Got it?"

Jack, the guitar player and backup singer, dusted himself off. Without saying a word, he walked toward the bus parked behind them.

"Well, too bad I don't get to stay with you all here at the lovely facility. I'm hopeful the show's promoter will take me to my accommodations at the Ivy Springs Motel and Resort after our meeting. If not, I'll have to find a taxi." Beau flashed a smile at the ladies.

Roxie wrinkled her nose at the mention of the motel. The owner, Sid Proctor, made it look and sound way better than the broken-down old roadside motel on the outskirts of town that it really was. "If you don't catch a ride, I'll be glad to take you. Taxi service is slow around here, like everything else. Everything in the south is slower, but hotter," she cooed.

Beau winked and reached for her hand, making a production of kissing it. "Thank you for the offer. I may take you up on it. It's always great to be rescued by a pretty lady."

Ruthanne let a giggle slip and clasped her hands together, drawing them toward her like she was trying to contain herself.

"Well, I don't know about you guys, but I'm going back to bed. Someone wake me before rehearsal. This is way too early for me." Johnny Storm belched and stumbled toward the bus.

Not quite the dreamy rock stars I imagined. Maybe they will be more charming on stage. So far, I don't see why everyone is so crazy about the Weathermen, Cassidy thought as she scanned the faces of the starstruck Pearly Girls. None of them seemed fazed by any of the band members' real-life behavior.

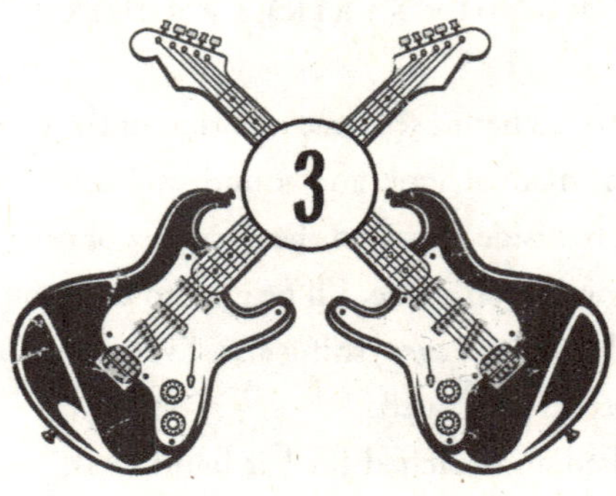

FRIDAY MORNING

Aileen sat at the conference table between Kate and Ruthanne and reached for a coaster to place beneath her mug. Her silver bob with today's teal highlights shimmered from the glow of the penlights dangling above the oval table. Aileen changed her hair color almost as often as other people changed their minds.

"Nice blouse," Ruthanne said. "Where'd you get it?"

"Thanks." Aileen grinned. "My niece gave it to me for my birthday. I don't wear lavender that often, but it goes with these." She raised a strand of purple and black pearls.

The front door swung open. Roxie waltzed in with Levi on her heels. Cassidy entered, bearing a tray of bagels and spreads, which she placed on the end of the conference table. "Good morning, all. I swung by Bake It to the Limit last night, and I couldn't resist fresh bagels. They smelled so good. Help yourselves. Anyone need coffee?" When the crowd around the table shook their heads, she settled in at the end of the table and opened her portfolio.

Elvis scampered in to check out the snacks and greet everyone before he curled up at Cassidy's feet.

"So, did our favorite rockers behave last night?" Roxie settled herself in the seat beside Levi.

"Not a peep out of them, and the contract security had no reports of any problems or oddities." Levi reached for a bagel and the cinnamon and brown sugar–flavored spread.

"That's good. Knowing their bad-boy reputations, I was expecting a rip-roaring party," Roxie said. "And at least one police visit. We'll have to make sure we get an invitation if they do have one of their famous shindigs."

"It's early." Kate shook her head. "I'm sure they won't disappoint as the week goes on. Maybe they're getting situated and catching up on some much-needed rest. It sounded like they're on the road a lot."

"It's nice to have some free spirits around here. This town gets a little stuffy at times." Aileen grabbed an asiago bagel from the platter.

"Glad the first night went well." Cassidy checked her agenda. "Thanks everyone for coming in early to go over the schedule. It's going to be a busy few weeks around here. Are y'all ready for Groovin' through the Decades? This is our first multi-weekend event, and I'm both excited and nervous. I'm really hopeful that the ticket sales will make it worthwhile and we become a stop for other shows."

Ruthanne let out a "woo hoo!" and clapped. "Can't wait. It's going to be great."

"Y'all have copies of the schedules in front of you. We don't have much to do in the front office except to provide support and answer questions that pop up. All the planning and marketing are done. The promoter and his assistant are stopping by this afternoon to make sure we've covered all the open tasks. Most everything is now on the security and grounds teams. Levi, that's you. You ready?" She looked at the lone male at the table.

"I'm good to go. Mateo and his security guys have the schedule, and he's got guys staffed round the clock." Levi wiped a dab of the spread off his chin with a napkin.

"Good." Cassidy made a check mark on her agenda. "And we've contracted with the sheriff's office to have a police presence during the concerts and to handle traffic. Now we wait to see how things go. Please mingle at these concerts and be great ambassadors for the property. Hopefully, folks will see our wonderful facilities and amenities and want to book other events with us. We could use a few more in the fall to round out our calendar." After a long pause during which her mind wandered to what else she could plan to bring guests to the property, she added, "Anything else we should cover? It seems like we're not doing much, but all the planning you all put into this has really paid off. Let's hope this event is memorable. And take lots of pictures for our social sites and the newsletter."

The front door banged open, and everyone turned to see who had arrived. Elvis jumped immediately to DEFCON 3 and scurried for the door. Karl Schultz, the stocky bass player, stomped in and looked around. "Uh, good morning. I'm Karl. I'm with the band. I was wondering if there was a place in town to get bass strings. You know, guitar strings? I can't find my stash...of extra strings." He blinked several times like he wasn't used to being out in the daylight.

"You may try Russell's on the far side of town," Aileen volunteered. "It's where all the kids go to rent instruments for band class. I'm sure someone there can help you."

"Uh, Russell's. Thanks. I'll get one of the drivers to check it out." He paused and ran his hands through his wavy brown hair that was graying at the temples and roots. "Cool. Thanks." He turned and disappeared as quickly as he had arrived.

"Anything else you guys want to talk about?" Cassidy asked as her team started shifting in their chairs.

"That was Karl Schultz," Ruthanne whispered, waving both hands in front of her face.

"I'm going to hang out here and work on some design combinations for the wedding coming up," Aileen piped up. "I had some ideas last night I want to explore. I saw some cute braided ivy garlands that would work on the trellis and the pergola."

"I'll be here, too," Ruthanne nodded. "I've got to finish some monthly admin tasks. Maybe we can take a walk later." Her eyes darted to where Karl had stood just a moment ago.

"And spy on the band." Roxie winked. "I've got a lunch date, so I'm going to do my spying now. Anybody up for a healthy jaunt that might swing by the buses? Though I thought musicians always slept until at least noon. Karl must be the exception."

"I'm meeting my book club in town for lunch." Kate frowned, obviously perturbed at the prospect of missing out on more band member sightings. "I've got to run home and get the book. I forgot it this morning."

"I wouldn't worry about it," Roxie said. "Most of my book club meetings are about wine and gossip. It's rare if we actually get around to talking about what we were supposed to have read." She turned and finger-waved over her shoulder as she headed out the back door. "See you all later. I'll let you know if anything interesting happens."

Levi stood. "I'm going to check on the grass at the amphitheater. But I won't rev up Ole Betsy or the blowers until after lunch. Don't want to disturb any late sleepers with mowing and leaf removal. Those'll be my after-lunch activities."

"Well, thank you again for all the hard work. Y'all take the bagels with you. Don't leave them for Elvis and me."

Aileen helped Cassidy tidy up, and Kate carried the tray back to the kitchen.

"Why don't you take some of these for you and your book club later?" Cassidy encouraged her friend.

She shook her head. "We're good. There's always plenty of food and wine, or mimosas if it's before noon. I'll put the bagels in the fridge in case anyone wants one later. Anything else you need?"

"I don't think so. Keep your phone handy in case there are any surprises. Who knows what the guys might need besides bass strings? And y'all might have to rescue the band from Roxie."

Aileen laughed. "She's certainly a force to be reckoned with. Johnny Storm may not stand a chance against her Southern hospitality and feminine wiles."

"I don't think his standards are sky-high," Kate muttered. "It probably won't take much to charm him. The Southern drawl usually does it."

"Roxie is definitely fierce when she sets her eyes on something. My money's on her," Aileen added. "Those naive rock stars won't stand a chance against any of us."

"Call me if you need me. After I do a couple of things here, I'm heading home and then to book club." Kate patted Elvis and walked to the front. The pup ran behind her with a soulful whine.

Cassidy shrugged. "I'm glad y'all are on my side. Those poor rock 'n' roll guys won't know what hit them." She turned to Elvis. "What's up, baby? You want to see the Weathermen, too?"

Elvis continued his sad whimper and bounced around in circles until she fastened his leash in place.

"Come on. It's a lovely day. Let's have a walk."

The early summer blooms mixed with the woodsy smells reminded Cassidy of why she loved the mountains. There was no prettier view, and each season brought new surprises. A june bug caught Elvis's attention, and he bounded off after the slow-moving insect.

Suddenly, loud, muffled voices caught their attention. They both paused and then headed in the direction of the noise.

Cassidy stepped cautiously along the trail, not sure of what she'd find at the buses. She hoped Roxie wasn't in the middle of some dustup, but it wouldn't surprise her if she was. She tended to be at the heart of any controversy in the tri-county area. With three ex-husbands and a slew of beaus, Roxie had never been the shrinking violet of the group.

Scooping Elvis up, Cassidy increased her pace and scooted around the nearest bus. No Roxie in sight. She exhaled in relief.

"I told you *no* yesterday. I told you *no* this morning. The answer is still *no*!" Karl bellowed. "Stop hounding me. I'm not going along with your latest scheme. Enough already. I need this gig."

Johnny Storm, this time dressed in faded jeans and an unbuttoned white dress shirt, stood next to a barefooted Jack in a Metallica T-shirt and ripped jeans.

Before Cassidy could figure out which rocker Karl was talking to, he shook his beefy fist at the pair. "I came along because the money was good. I'm not interested in your stupid ideas that take money out of my pockets. Leave me out of this." He stomped toward the bus parked behind the meat smokers and the cluster of coolers. Then he stopped and turned around. "And I will kill you if you mess this up for me." His face reddened, and his mouth twitched into an almost evil sneer.

Jack plopped himself down in a stadium chair and feigned like he had just noticed Cassidy and Elvis standing there. When no one responded to Karl's threat, Jack said, "Cute dog. You've got a lovely place here, too. I can see why they call them the Blue Ridge Mountains now. I don't think I've ever seen them up close before. Usually, I never pay attention to the places we go. But it's nice here. And all those trees in the distance really do look blue. Splendid views." He reached into the cooler next to him and grabbed a beer.

Johnny simply grunted and headed for his bus.

As the bus doors made a sucking sound behind the lead singer, Cassidy spoke in a low voice so the grumpy singer wouldn't overhear. "Is he okay?"

"He's fine. He's coming to grips with his own mortality—and he's not a morning person." At Cassidy's puzzled look, he continued to explain. "None of us are as young as we think we are, and life didn't turn out quite like we expected for some of us. I guess we thought we'd ride the roller coaster of fame and fortune until we drifted off into some eternal slumber or Shangri-la. Or the end would be something tragic like Morrison or Hendrix, and we'd become legends." He pulled out a cigarette and a lighter. The smoke curled around his slicked-back, jet-black hair as he fidgeted in the stadium chair. "The music business has changed a lot, but here we still are. We seem to fit best on the nostalgia tours with the rest of the geezers who haven't had a hit in thirty years. I guess Johnny's getting tired of life on the road."

Not knowing how to reply, Cassidy stammered, "Uh, please let me or my team know if you need anything."

"The nearest liquor store? Do they deliver? If not, Beau will have to make a beer run later. Our stock is running low already." Jack leaned back, closed his eyes, and exhaled a puff of bluish smoke. "He's out getting breakfast now. Though most of the guys don't usually eat until the afternoon."

Cassidy nodded her head. "There are a few places in town, but I don't think any deliver breakfast."

He rolled his eyes, and she continued, "See you all around." Cassidy waved and carried Elvis back the way they came.

Wow. Lots of different personalities and short tempers in that group. I just hope they're still friends after this tour. They all seem to have hair-trigger tempers. The rock star lifestyle is going to take some getting used to.

Cassidy picked up her pace and headed back to the normalcy of her office.

"Oh, there you are," Ruthanne said as Cassidy climbed the back steps, and Elvis bounded inside. "Kate's up front with the promoter and his assistant," she whispered. "It's Steve Owens and Bianca somebody or other."

Cassidy nodded and made her way to the lobby area.

"And here she is now," Kate beckoned her toward the group. "Cassidy, this is Steve Owens and Bianca Carpenter with Way Cool Entertainment." Turning back to Steve and Bianca, she added, "It was nice to meet both of you. I need to head out for an appointment."

"Good morning." Cassidy shook both of their hands. "My team met this morning to go over all the details. We're very excited to be part of your tour."

"And we're excited to be here," Steve said. "The schedule is finalized. The Weathermen, our headliners, will be the only ones staying on your property. They have their own security. And their manager is around if you need him. They are all pros, so you shouldn't have any problems. If you do, let one of us know, and we'll take care of it. Here's the official schedule. If it changes, Bianca will send you an update."

The pixie-like assistant, whose platinum hair had bright magenta tips, whipped out a packet and handed it to Cassidy. "Here, this is an old-school paper version. I'll text you any updates from now on. Somebody likes to have handouts." She nodded her head toward Steve.

"It's all in there." Steve ignored his assistant. "All our contact information is at the bottom. We're staying in town, but we'll be here most of the time to keep an eye on things. Don't hesitate to call us if anything goes sideways."

"You've got my numbers, too," Cassidy said. "I've contracted with a local company for additional support. I'll text you the contact's information. Also, the sheriff's office is handling crowd and traffic control."

"Crowd control," he snickered. When he realized Cassidy didn't respond, he continued, "For a smallish venue, your ticket sales have been great. Lots of music fans in the area. But when we say crowds, we're thinking in the tens of thousands."

"We've had good activity on the socials. There's lots of interest here," Bianca added.

Cassidy brushed off the venue size comments. "Levi has installed temporary fencing, and we'll funnel everyone in through the main gate. There's a welcome gazebo there you all can use for tickets or an information booth."

"That'll be my spot. We may have some people who still need tickets," Bianca said. "Here are festival lanyards for your team, so they won't get hassled." She pulled out a handful of neon yellow Groovin' through the Decades lanyards with all kinds of psychedelic artwork in bright colors.

"We'll be doing sound checks this afternoon with the first opening band and the Weathermen. I want to talk to your security folks." Steve glanced down at his phone and then back up at Cassidy.

Taking the cue, Cassidy pulled out her phone again and tapped out a text. Steve's phone dinged. "Just sent you Mateo's information. This is more activity than the town's had in a while, so you should get lots of attention from our local police, especially if nothing else is going on."

"I think that's all we need. Bianca will reach out if I think of anything else. Don't hesitate to call, day or night, if anything comes up. We want to take care of the little things before they turn into big, hairy things." He rose, and Bianca gathered the folders and followed her boss. Then he turned suddenly, causing Bianca to almost plow into his back. "I don't anticipate any trouble. We don't do repeat business if there is trouble."

"We're hoping for a jam-packed, fun event." Cassidy smiled, hoping she didn't show too many teeth. When the promoters finally closed the door, she let out a long puff of air.

"That almost sounded like an ominous warning," Ruthanne commented from the doorway. "Don't fret about it. Things will go off without a hitch. You've done all the planning and preparation for any contingency. We've got this. What could go wrong?"

FRIDAY EVENING

"Who's ready for some fun?" echoed from speakers surrounding the amphitheater. "I'm Rocky Parker, from Mornings on WBLU92 in beautiful Staunton, Virginia. And I don't know about you, but I'm ready for a party! In a minute, we're going to welcome the Rhythm Cats, known for their *purrrrfect* renditions of all your favorites from the rowdy years of the 1960s. And after they get you revved up and rockin', the Weathermen who never fly under the radar are going to take this stage by storm and shake these mountains louder than any thunderclap you've ever heard. Whadya say?" He held the mic toward the audience, and the crowd's roar drowned out any other sounds. "I can't hear you, Ivy Springs!" Rocky yelled, egging them on. The crowd roared even louder.

When the noise subsided to a low rumble, Rocky continued. "Okay, all you cool cats and kittens. Put your mittens together and let's give a hearty Virginia welcome to the Rhythm Cats! Show 'em some Southern hospitality." Rocky waved his arm around and five baby boomers in peasant blouses, maxi dresses, and crocheted ponchos took the stage. They could've stepped off the set of *Laugh In* with all the groovy designs and headbands. The gal in the back with the long, straight hair must have flat ironed her entire head to get that Marcia Brady look.

Cassidy made her way to the back of the stage as "Jeremiah Was a Bullfrog" blasted from every direction. Peeking around one of the speakers, she spotted Kate, Roxie, Aileen, and Ruthanne in the front row, hooting and hollering. Ruthanne and Aileen had daisies in their hair, and they were showing off their Woodstock-esque dance moves with six or seven hundred of their closest friends.

A strange noise interrupted her musing. She paused and took a couple of steps toward the backstage area behind a long black curtain. There it was again—a crash, muffled by the pulsing music. She hurried up the cement steps to the stage in time to witness Karl kicking at a metal folding chair near him. Then he turned and lunged at Johnny. Cassidy stepped closer to hear what was being said.

These guys argue all the time. What is with all the drama?

"Don't play innocent! I know you sabotaged my stuff. You're always trying to mess things up for us. What happened to all-for-one? I thought we were a team. You know, a band, friends... Man, I was stupid." Karl spat out the words like bad sushi.

"I don't know what you're talking about. I offered you some strings. I was trying to help you out, man." Johnny adjusted the waistband of his leather pants and straightened the long white shirt with the puffy collar and sleeves—like something out of a swashbuckling film, though most of the film pirates buttoned their shirts. From a distance, he was the epitome of the Johnny Storm from his album covers. But up close, the crow's feet and parentheses surrounding his mouth gave away his age.

"It was another of your passive-aggressive attempts to pretend to be helpful." Karl glared at the rocker. "Not helpful. You knew they wouldn't work."

"Any port in a storm. They were better than nothing." Johnny ran his hands through his long, shaggy hair. With it sticking up all over, it looked like he used more hair spray and product than all the Pearly Girls combined.

"I got some bass ones. The kind I really need. No thanks to you. I know you did it to throw me off my game. And I know what you're up to. I'm not going to slink out of here feeling sorry." Karl lunged at him again.

Johnny stepped back as Dirk Lawrence, the Weathermen's drummer, stepped between them and pushed Karl away. "Settle down. It's nerves and whatever's hyping you up. Go take a walk and clear your head. It's not worth it. We've got a gig and a whole audience full of fans. You know, the thing we get paid to do."

"Be sensible," Johnny said. "We've got something good. Don't screw it up."

"You're one to talk. You've done nothing except profit any way you can from the band without bringing us along with you," Karl hissed. "If I remember correctly, when we started this journey, we all sat in Jack's kitchen and agreed we would share everything equally. Now you're the one running off doing a book tour without us."

"Come on, let's take a walk." Dirk stepped in between the feuding bandmates. "We don't need to discuss this here or now. Bad timing. We can take it up with Beau later. Let's go." He nudged Karl toward the cement steps.

"This isn't over, John. Last time I checked, there are four of us in this band!" Karl yelled over his shoulder. "You'll be sorry you cut us out. This isn't a one-person band. You can't do this without us."

Dirk shook his head at Johnny while leading Karl to the other side of the stage.

I hope they get it together before showtime. Lots of short-fused tempers around here. Should I call Beau or Steve? Maybe it's opening night jitters.

Cassidy took a deep breath and decided to take her own walk around the perimeter of the amphitheater. Maybe things would calm down on their own.

Most of the crowd had gathered near the front of the stage, where fans sat on wooden benches or on lawn chairs they brought from home. A sea of blankets covered the grass where the land leveled off at the top of the hill.

Cassidy paused to wave to Levi who sat in the golf cart. "How are things?" She hoped she didn't sound out of breath from climbing the incline.

Levi smiled and nodded as he pulled out his earplugs. "We've got a good crowd. Looks like everyone's having fun. All's quiet here. Well, sort of. Everyone within ten miles can definitely hear the music. But these babies help." He held out his fluorescent pink and yellow earplugs.

"Let me know if you need anything. We'll see if the Weathermen live up to their reputation. The Pearly Girls really like them." Cassidy waved and continued her walk until the Rhythm Cats did their encore, and Rockin' Rocky took the stage again to hype the headliners. She hurried to find a spot away from the speakers near the stage.

Rocky waved his arms around and bounced across the stage like a giant bird. "Okay, okay. How was that? Did y'all enjoy the Rhythm Cats?" He paused a beat and waited for the noise to subside. "Well, here's what you've all been waiting for. Let's not waste any more time. Put your hands together for the always bright and sunny Weathermen!"

The four rockers bounded onto the stage and found their places. The crowd went wild. The roar seemed to go on forever before Dirk pounded out the first few notes of their hit "Rock Me Like You Mean It," and the crowd went crazy again.

Cassidy decided to walk farther up the hill to watch the rest of the show.

I definitely need a pair of Levi's earplugs.

* * *

After the last guests meandered to the parking lot and security took care of the cars and trucks trying to squeeze out of the property's sole gate, Cassidy hurried home to give Elvis some love. Her ears rang from the pulsating music, and she hoped the dull ache behind her eyes would go away.

Opening the residential entrance and stepping into the foyer, she headed up to her apartment on the second floor of the farmhouse. Elvis bounded out and smothered her with puppy kisses. "Hey, boy. Let's do one more check of the property and get some steps in." She grabbed the leash on the coat rack near the door and snapped it to his collar. "You missed quite a show. I hope the gals enjoyed it. They seemed to be in their element earlier. And the Weathermen pulled off a good performance, despite their earlier scuffles."

Elvis, more interested in his walk than the band members' squabbles, took off at a steady trot to explore any new scents.

Tree frogs, cicadas, and other night noises had replaced the pulsating drumbeats and bass chords from the concert. An occasional lightning bug lit the dark spaces in the nearby woods. Happy to be outside, Elvis wandered the perimeter in search of anything new. As they approached the meadow, voices filled the night air, and Elvis yipped.

Cassidy picked him up and carried him closer to the buses. The Weathermen, their manager, a couple of the Rhythm Cats, and all of the Pearly Girls sat around a bonfire that had been made in an old oil barrel. Dirk passed out drinks, and Jack strummed on an acoustic guitar.

"Hey, Cassidy," Aileen said, waving. Then she turned to the group. "That's Cassidy, the owner of this place, and her sidekick, Elvis." She called out to Cassidy, "Come on over and join the party."

"Hi. Great show. The audience loved y'all," Cassidy said.

"Pull up a chair and relax. Karl, get her a beer." Johnny draped his arm around her.

"Thanks, but I've got an early morning. Elvis and I were out for his evening stroll before turning in. Y'all have fun."

Elvis sniffed Johnny's hand as he reached out to pet him.

"Young people these days." Johnny shook his head. "Your generation doesn't know how to have fun. If you change your mind, you know where we live. I'm sure the party will be rockin' into the wee hours. You don't know what you're missing." He walked toward the cooler as Roxie sidled over to him.

SATURDAY MORNING

"What?" Cassidy moaned, rolling over to determine the source of the beeping. Undeterred, Elvis hopped around her pillow to rouse her from her deep sleep. "Okay, okay." She pushed a clump of long curls out of her eyes. "Let me get a quick shower, and then we'll do a walk before breakfast."

Elvis bounced around some more and settled on the other pillow while Cassidy dragged herself out of bed and into the shower. When she remodeled the upstairs of the farmhouse, she had splurged on the bedroom suite. A pulsating multiheaded walk-in shower was exactly what she needed after all of yesterday's excitement.

I wonder when the gals got home last night. They have way cooler social lives than I do.

After the steaming shower and a jolt of caffeine, Cassidy felt herself perking up. "Come on, Elvis. Let's get this day started." She picked up her phone and messenger bag and hunted for his leash.

Elvis trotted down the back stairs and waited impatiently at the door. She barely had his leash clipped before he tore out after a panicked rabbit who had been enjoying his breakfast nearby.

With no hope of catching the long-gone hare, Elvis settled into his take-three-steps-and-stop-to-sniff-something routine. Cassidy enjoyed the cool mountain air and the light rustle of the breeze through the trees. The leaves and the occasional creak of the pine trees lent a musical quality to the air. Smiling, she hustled after Elvis who had decided their walk included the grotto this morning.

The little dog paused and turned his head to listen. Cassidy did, too. Something crackled in the distance. Could it be the wind through the tree canopy? Elvis whined and tugged on his leash. He pulled her to the edge of the grotto where the thick grass turned into the rocky side of a cave, rumored to be part of a long-ago relative's bootlegging operation during Prohibition. It used to be a fun place to explore when Cassidy was little. Now it was just another part of the property she didn't know what to do with. "What's up, Elvis? There's nobody here."

Not interested in the cave, Elvis continued his sniff-fest around the mulched beds full of tea roses and rhododendron. The flower beds, planted by her grandmother and tended lovingly by Levi, rivaled any botanical garden. It was a perfect site for special occasions and photo shoots.

This was Cassidy's favorite part of the property. The ancient cave had always been a place of wonder and excitement that she loved to explore as a kid. Despite not ever providing any dinosaur bones, Native American relics, or pirate treasure, it was still a place of great childhood memories. The grotto was a huge natural stone entrance to the enchanted garden that had been used for weddings, an anniversary celebration, and a memorial service. The white pergola had a breathtaking view of the valley below—the perfect picture or selfie spot—and the gardens and koi pond created a serene atmosphere. If she closed her eyes, she could almost see fairies and gnomes, along with a variety of woodland animals, all frolicking in the whimsical garden.

Cassidy stared at the white pergola.

I wonder if local photographers would want to rent the space for outdoor photo shoots. Maybe I'll put out some feelers and see if there is any interest. That might be a new revenue stream when we're not hosting events.

After exploring all the flower beds, Elvis moved on to greet the fish. Cassidy quickly scanned her screen to see if there were any issues needing her attention first thing this morning. Not finding anything yet, she pocketed her phone and glanced over at the fish that swam to the edge to see if anyone was going to feed them.

She did a double take and walked closer to the water. Someone had left trash in the pond. *Didn't we have this area roped off to discourage concertgoers from wandering around? People tend to explore and leave their junk everywhere. Levi will have a fit if they messed up his roses or hurt any of his fish.*

Cassidy stepped closer to survey the damage and to see what was floating in the koi pond. Leaning closer, she squealed.

She squeezed her eyes shut and opened them again. Yes, there was a body face down with her fishes.

Reaching out, she tugged at the body to turn it over. A bloated and pale Johnny Storm stared back with lifeless eyes. Some kind of necklace or wire dug tightly into his neck. Cassidy screamed. Not to be left out, Elvis growled and barked at the body floating on the lotus and lily pads.

After what seemed like an eternity, she was finally able to calm the sick feeling in her stomach and the pounding of her heartbeat. Cassidy took several deep breaths until her heart rate felt somewhat closer to normal.

Still shaking, she tapped 9-1-1 on her phone and waited for the call to connect.

"Ivy Springs nine-one-one, what's your emergency?"

"Good morning. This is Cassidy Jamison. My dog and I found someone floating in the koi pond on the back of the property here at Celebrations at Ivy Springs at 4585 Ridge Road."

"Is the person breathing?" the dispatcher asked.

"No. I turned him over. He's definitely dead." Cassidy sunk to the ground, and Elvis climbed in her lap.

"Okay, stay where you are. Don't let anyone else touch him. Police and rescue are on their way. Where are you located on the property?" The dispatcher spoke calmly.

"We're near the cave at the back. Tell them to enter at the main gate, go past the farmhouse and the parking lots, keep going around the bend, and they'll see a barn. There's a short incline, and the road levels out again. There's a grotto with a lot of granite near the cave, and a garden we use for weddings. We're in the garden."

"I've let them know. They should be there in a few minutes. Are you safe where you are?" Radio squawk rang out in the background.

"I'm okay. Elvis—that's my dog—and I are the only ones here. Most of my team starts work later. We do have a band and their entourage staying on the property for a music festival, but I haven't seen any of them this morning." She closed her eyes and said a silent prayer for Johnny.

What happened out here after the party?

"You should see the deputy's car and the ambulance soon. They are nearing your property." The dispatcher interrupted Cassidy's moment of silence.

"I hear them. I'm going to disconnect now and flag them down. Thanks for your help." Cassidy scooped Elvis into her arms and jogged toward the maintenance road. She waved with one hand at the ambulance as it crested the ridge.

The ambulance stopped at the end of the road, and a police cruiser followed with its lights flashing. It kicked up a tiny dust storm when it drove off the road into the grassy area and parked. The car's lights continued to flash as Deputy Zac Turner slid out from behind the wheel and said something into his shoulder mic.

He sauntered over to Cassidy, surveying the body as he passed the pond, while a pair of EMTs pulled a gurney and something resembling an orange tackle box out of the back of the ambulance.

"Hey, Cassidy. You okay?" She nodded and the deputy continued, "What happened?"

"Elvis and I were out for our morning stroll, and we found him."

She pointed to the rock singer in his waterlogged open kimono and black leather pants. "It's Johnny Storm."

The deputy stared at the body in the koi pond and nodded. "I was here last night for the concert. Any idea how he ended up in your pond?"

She shook her head.

"When was the last time you saw him?" Deputy Turner pulled out a pen and a small notebook from the front pocket of his uniform.

"Last night. The band and some folks were out by the buses after the show. I think some of the members of the other band that opened for them were there, too."

"When was that?" He stared at her.

"I guess around ten-thirty. I was home and in bed by eleven. I remember because I set my alarm, and I looked at my phone."

"Anything else?" He continued to focus on her.

She nodded slowly. "He was with the group around the bonfire after the show. Everything seemed fine when I left. I ran into the band several times yesterday before the show. They seemed to squabble a lot. Not sure if that's important or not. Some of it seemed petty, but Karl, the bass player, was involved in several of the altercations. He seems to be a little hotheaded." She sighed deeply, putting her hand over her heart. "This isn't what I expected to see first thing this morning."

"Did you touch him?" Deputy Turner rooted around in his utility belt for a pair of rubber gloves.

She nodded weakly. "I flipped him over to see if he was breathing. But he was bloated and bluish-white. And he was staring back at me. That's when I called y'all."

"And no one else was around here?"

"Not since Elvis and I have been here." At the mention of his name, the dog's ears shot skyward. His little head swiveled around to ascertain what he was missing.

Deputy Turner pocketed his notebook and pulled out his

phone. While he was snapping photos of the pond and Johnny, she pulled out her phone and sent a group text to the Pearly Girls about there being a situation at the grotto.

This is going to break their hearts. What will this do to the festival?

Her stomach flip-flopped, and she closed her eyes for a moment to quell the building anxiety.

Her phone started pinging immediately with responses. Ignoring them, she watched as Deputy Turner made some calls and the EMTs huddled around the gurney.

"The medical examiner's office and the sheriff should be here soon," Deputy Turner said to the EMTs. One repacked the big orange box while the other jotted notes on his clipboard.

The deputy turned toward Cassidy. "Forensics will be here soon. It definitely looks suspicious. Any idea if anyone would want to kill him?"

She shook her head. "I mean. I told you about the dustups with his bandmates while they were checking in or getting set up, but at the time, it didn't seem to be any big deal. Maybe just creative differences. They seem to keep to their own schedules, not really like normal people who tend to start their days in the morning. The party was getting started when I headed home last night. Johnny Storm was kinda brash and maybe a little demanding, like he was used to being the star," Cassidy said. "The Pearly Girls were so excited to meet him and the band. They've been fans since their late teens."

At the mention of the foursome, a slight smile crossed his face. "I bet," he muttered. "If you think of anything else, let me know."

"What's next? I mean, I don't want to sound callous, but there's a concert scheduled for this evening. Do you think I need to cancel it?" The dull ache behind Cassidy's eyes seemed to worsen as she mentally ran through the mountain of tasks that she would need to quickly accomplish if she had to shut down the evening's events.

The deputy paused and looked at the mountains across the

valley. "We'll see what forensics and the sheriff say. We should be wrapped by this afternoon, so I don't think it will affect your evening plans, but let's wait for the sheriff's official word." He turned as a dark police SUV and a panel van bumped along the maintenance road and parked next to the ambulance.

Two forensic technicians descended on the garden and pond and took over the space. With all the equipment scattered along the grassy area, the garden took on a far more sinister look.

I hope I can get the calm vibe back after all this is over.

Sheriff Asa Howell spent several minutes rummaging through the trunk of his car. Pocketing whatever he had been searching for, he sauntered over to the pond. Nodding several times at what the technicians said to him, he watched them photograph and measure everything in sight. The forensic guys had tented off the edge of the pond, so Johnny's lifeless body was no longer visible.

Cassidy picked up Elvis to keep him from getting in the way. She shifted her weight from one foot to the other as she watched the methodical work.

The sheriff paused midway between her and the deputy. "Morning, Cassidy. We'll be out here for a couple more hours. The deputy and I are going to talk to the band members. We'll head over to the office before we leave to give you an update."

Cassidy nodded and her mind flipped through a series of things she needed to check on. "We'll be in the office. I'm going to refer any questions or media requests to your office. I need to get in touch with the concert promoter and make a few other phone calls." Her stomach flip-flopped again.

"We should have some updates for you soon," the sheriff assured her.

"We have coffee in the office if you need it." She hugged Elvis closer for a bit of comfort. When the little dog wiggled, she made her way across the grass to the farmhouse.

Almost as soon as she had the back door to the office open, Elvis tore through the room to see who he might be able to score a treat from.

"There she is," Ruthanne said in her singsong voice.

The Pearly Girls surrounded Cassidy like a flock of seagulls going after a french fry and fired off random questions with no chance for her to get a word in edgewise.

Roxie put two fingers in her mouth and let out a whistle that echoed through the office and made Elvis whine. "Okay. Good morning. Kate, get her some coffee. Now, tell us what is going on. Your text was cryptic. Who is it? And what is going on around here? This can't be good."

"It's so sad." Ruthanne shook her head. "Someone died on the property in your beautiful garden."

Cassidy took a deep breath. "Elvis and I found Johnny Storm floating in the koi pond this morning. He wasn't responsive. Police, EMTs, and a forensics crew are out there now."

"Oh, my stars." Ruthanne covered her mouth with her hand and sank into the nearest chair. "He was so, so alive last night. We were just with him. This can't be true! It's all so surreal. Not Johnny Storm! Not Johnny!"

"Was it an overdose? Or alcohol poisoning? I lost count last night of all he consumed, but it was a lot. That group had a rip-roaring good time, and they liked the party scene. They were knocking drinks back like Kool-Aid." Kate handed Cassidy a steaming mug of tan-colored coffee. "I wonder if he had some kind of medical condition. Death is death, but somehow, we rationalize natural causes as better than something malicious."

"Or maybe it was his time to go." Aileen wiped away the tears leaking from her eyes.

"I'm not sure if they have any theories yet. The sheriff said he'd be over later to give us an update about whether we can go on with the concerts tonight." Cassidy wasn't sure what had been around his neck, but whatever it was, she was certain that he hadn't died of natural causes.

"Of course we can keep our schedule. The grotto is nowhere near the stage," Aileen said.

A slight frown crossed Kate's brow. "We'll have to see what Sheriff Asa says. He kinda has the final word on this one, regardless of how inconvenient it is for us."

"I hope he doesn't get on his high horse and shut us down." Aileen frowned.

"Maybe you should do some sweet talking." Kate winked at Aileen. "He's always had a soft spot for you."

Aileen waved her hand dismissively, but a slight blush crept from her neck to her cheeks.

Cassidy sank into her office chair. Thoughts of the disaster ping-ponged around her brain. *This concert is a huge windfall for the property. If we have to cancel or if we get a lot of bad publicity, it could also be our ruin.* She let out a breath that fluttered her bangs.

Ruthanne patted her shoulder. "Don't worry until we know something. It could have been a horrible accident. We know it's not your fault."

Cassidy's thoughts reeled back to the wire around Johnny Storm's neck. *This was no accident. Who would want him dead that badly? One of his so-called friends or maybe a crazed fan?*

Kate picked up her purse. "As much as I want to hang out with you guys, I have an eye appointment in town. Text me if anything changes. Hey, Roxie, at least this isn't like the last dead musician you encountered. What was his name? Buzz Something?"

"Buzz McMichaels," Ruthanne said quietly.

Roxie's countenance turned stormy. She chewed on her bottom lip. "It wasn't that big a deal. Just a bunch of tongues wagging not knowing the whole story."

Aileen stared at her with bug eyes. "Not that big a deal?" Buzz McMichaels was a pretty famous country and western singer, who was in town for a show at the saloon back in the day. He died in one of Sid 'Pro Quo's' seedy motels of a heart attack doing the deed with a hot young thing who was much younger than him." She pointed with both of her index fingers at Roxie. "It made all the tabloids, and for one hot minute, Roxie, you were famous."

"Not one of my best moments. We all had a few too many tequila shots, and the guy's sweet talking got to me. I was single and in my late twenties, and he was a mature, handsome guy. Hey, it was the Big Eighties, the Decade of Excess."

Kate cleared her throat and glared at Roxie. "We can all do basic math."

"Okay, my early thirties."

"That's ancient history." Ruthanne tried to change the subject. "At least, you weren't with Johnny Storm when it happened."

Roxie's lips formed a straight line, and she picked up Elvis and stroked the fur on his neck. A flush flooded her cheeks.

"Roxie, you weren't with Johnny Storm last night after we left, right? I thought you were heading out, too, especially when the band started to get sloppy drunk." Kate's eyes had grown the size of tea saucers. "Tell me you didn't. Not again. What happened? What do you know?"

"Spill it!" Aileen scooted closer to Roxie.

Remaining unusually quiet, Roxie continued to pet Elvis, who loved being the center of attention.

"Oh, mercy. The tabloids are going to have a field day with this. Come on, you have got to tell Asa what you know. You're going to be the black widow when it comes to old musicians. What a reputation." Kate grabbed Roxie by the arm and pulled her toward the door.

Handing Elvis to Cassidy, Roxie shrugged. "It's not really a big deal. He was living, breathing, and talking up a storm when I left around two thirty. I have no idea what happened afterward. I was home, safe and alone in my own bed, by three. My doorbell cam can attest to that."

A sinking feeling started in Cassidy's spine and inched to her stomach, creating a sour taste in her mouth.

The autopsy had to clear Roxie. The sheriff couldn't possibly think she had anything to do with Johnny Storm's death. Roxie may have earned her reputation around town as a cougar, but she was no killer.

LATER SATURDAY MORNING

It felt like an invisible pallet of bricks pressed down onto Cassidy's weary shoulders. "I probably should check with the night attendant. Hopefully, we haven't received a ton of calls yet."

"It'll take the grapevine a bit to get revved up, but I'm sure you'll get some calls after folks wake up and have had their coffee. It's so sad he died after such a great concert. He will be missed. You know the national media is going to descend on us. He was really popular in his heyday," Aileen said. "Rockers and their tortured lives and untimely deaths make great TV. And then there is the Roxie angle. I'm sure the sheriff is going to want to ask her and the rest of us some questions."

Cassidy let out a long puff of air that sounded like a leaky beach ball. "I checked social media. No mention of it yet, but it's only a matter of time until it's everywhere. I'm all about free publicity, but the tabloids and gossip sites were not what I had in mind when I booked this concert. I've got to call the promoter. Hopefully the sheriff has notified the band and the manager by now. And Johnny's next of kin."

"His real name is John Mason from Tampa, Florida. He has a couple of sisters and two ex-wives. And despite all the tabloid rumors, there are no kids." Ruthanne busied herself at the desk across from Cassidy's. "What? I used to keep up with my favorite singers, and I still get *People*."

Thoughts of the dead singer and the damage this news could do to her business whirled around in Cassidy's head. "The sheriff can't seriously think Roxie's a suspect, can he? He's known her forever, just like everyone else around here."

Ruthanne pursed her lips. "We can vouch for her until about twelve fifteen or twelve thirty. It was way past my bedtime, and I headed out with Kate and Aileen. Roxie was engrossed in some conversation with Johnny and Dirk, so she told us to go on without her."

"Sometimes that gets her in trouble." Aileen shook her head. "We should have insisted she leave with us."

"But you know her. She's always got to be in the middle of everything. And she said her camera will show when she made it home. Hopefully, it was before Johnny died. Do you think it was medical, like a heart attack?" Ruthanne whispered. "If it was, the tabloids are going to have a field day. Roxie's going to get cast as a jinx. This'll be the second singer to die after an evening with her."

"I don't think it was a medical condition," Cassidy said.

"What? You saw the body. Did you take pictures?" Ruthanne jumped out of her seat, and Kate and Aileen leaned forward, hungry for more details.

"What? No. Eww. But I'm pretty sure he didn't die of natural causes," Cassidy said quietly.

"Why are you whispering?" Ruthanne asked.

"I don't know. It seemed like some kind of secret. How bad was the Buzz McMichaels thing?" Cassidy squeezed her eyes shut.

She opened her eyes again and typed his name in Google. Several results immediately popped up. Scanning the first one, the writer described him as a fifty-two-year-old crooner, a Nashville favorite, who died near Staunton, Virginia. "This doesn't mention Roxie," Cassidy muttered.

"Keep looking," Aileen said. "It even made *Entertainment Tonight* and *Inside Edition*. She got her fifteen minutes of fame out of this."

"I saw her face on some grocery store tabloids. I bought a copy," Kate said quietly.

Ruthanne shook her head, and her silver curls bounced back in place. "I'm sure Roxie was embarrassed by all the publicity, but you know her. She goes through men like the rest of us go through handbags. She got caught that time in a public way with someone who used to be famous. And who says lightning doesn't strike twice? But this time with a more famous musician." Ruthanne's eyes widened, and her mouth formed a tiny *O*.

The front door opened, and Elvis darted into the lobby before Cassidy could stop him.

After some scuffling on the wood floor, the sheriff took off his Smokey Bear hat and cleared his throat. "Good morning, ladies. Do you all have a minute?"

The tall concert promoter, Steve Owens, stood sullenly behind him.

"Can I get you coffee or something to drink?" Cassidy motioned for them to be seated.

Neither man moved. "No, thanks," the sheriff said. "My team is wrapping up here. They're still talking to the manager and the band, and going through Johnny Storm's bus. We should be out of your hair in an hour or so. Like I told Steve and the manager..."

"Beau," Cassidy interjected.

"Yep, him," Sheriff Howell nodded. "Like I told them, it's okay to go on with the concert. When word really gets out, you're going to want to prepare to be bombarded with reporters' questions. Make sure your security is ready. It could be an onslaught with the media and curious fans."

Cassidy nodded her head slowly. "I'm so sorry about what happened to Mr. Storm, but I'm glad we can go on with the show. I'll talk to my security guys after we're done here. Is there anything you need from us?"

"Nope," Steve said. "Bianca's out in the car working the phones. You'll definitely start to get press questions. Anything death related should be directed to the sheriff's office, and anything about Johnny personally should go to Beau."

Cassidy continued to nod. "If you need us, please let us know. I'll let my team know and get with Beau to see if he wants me to put out any kind of statement."

"Bianca's got one on the concert socials. You may want to use it as a guide." Steve turned toward the door. "It's probably good to be consistent in the messaging."

"I'm going to talk to Roxie to schedule a longer interview, and then I'll head out," the sheriff said, running his hand through his steel-colored hair. "Let me know if you hear anything that might be helpful."

The door shut firmly behind the men before Ruthanne said anything. "I hope Roxie's okay. Oh, my stars, he thinks she knows something. And what if she really does?" She wrung her hands and pulled out her phone.

Cassidy tapped Mateo's contact on her phone as she walked to her desk.

"Hey, Cass." He sounded more chipper than she was.

"Hi, Mateo. I hope you're doing well. We had a situation here."

"What's up?" It sounded like he was chewing on something.

Cassidy lowered her voice. "The sheriff and his team just left. We found Johnny Storm dead in the koi pond this morning."

"I'm guessing it wasn't natural causes."

"Doubtful. He had a wire around his neck. The sheriff and the promotions guy wanted you and your team to know. They've wrapped their search of the site, but they're pretty sure we're going to get bombarded with reporters and paparazzi."

"Thanks for the heads up. I'll let my guys know. We'll be ready."

"Any questions about the death should be directed to the sheriff's office."

"Gotcha. Anything else?"

"That's about all I know. I'll text you if I hear anything. The sheriff wanted your guys to call in anything suspicious they encounter."

"Ten-four. I'm on it." The call disconnected.

Cassidy slid into her desk chair and skimmed more of the Buzz McMichaels search results. There was a lot of information about his country western career in Nashville in the fifties and sixties. By the late eighties, he was on a series of country jamboree concerts that snaked their way up and down the East Coast. On the second page of the results, she found several stories about his demise. It seems his heart—abused by years of smoking, drinking, and carousing—couldn't take several rounds of whoopsie-doodle with one Roxie Matthews. Cassidy's cheeks warmed.

Poor Roxie. How embarrassing.

Roxie tried to hide her face in some of the pictures, but it was definitely her, sporting a platinum Lady Diana hairstyle and a lime green blazer with shoulder pads to rival any NFL lineman.

Bored with the Buzz McMichaels articles all seeming to repeat the same story, Cassidy closed her laptop. "I'm going to take Elvis for a walk. We need some fresh air. I'll be back in a bit."

"I'm good here," Ruthanne said. "I'm going to work on a few things, and then I'm heading out, too. There's nothing on the calendar this week except for the concerts. I've got some errands to run, but I'll be back in time for the show tonight." Ruthanne wiggled her fingers. "But let me know if you hear anything good."

Cassidy and Elvis trotted out into the warm sunshine. The day was almost perfect, except for the crowd of law enforcement combing over every inch of her gardens and meadow. Ivy Springs didn't have that many cops. *They must have imported a few from surrounding departments to help.*

This is not what I had in mind when I booked this music festival. It was supposed to be a big draw to the facility, a way to get our name out as a concert venue. Taking a couple of cleansing breaths to calm the jitters, Cassidy followed Elvis toward the barn.

Spotting Roxie near the flower beds overlooking the valley, Cassidy guided the spunky dog down the sidewalk.

"Hey, how are you?" Cassidy moved closer to Roxie. Her grandmother's friend's expression made her appear ten years older than she did yesterday.

"I've been better. The sheriff worked me over again. I think he's trying to see if my story from earlier varies. It doesn't. He's wasting his time trying to get me to crack. All I know is the great Johnny Storm was alive and crowing about all his successes when I headed home. Up close and personal, he was boorish and a braggart. He didn't seem to care that much about others, so I could see why someone might have been out to get him. But our plucky sheriff wants me to come in for more questioning. I mean, really. How many times can he ask me the same questions? I'm beginning to think he's got a crush on me or something. If anyone's counting, I've spent more time with the sheriff than I did with Johnny Storm. People are going to start talking."

"They probably already are. Any ideas on who would want the singer dead?" Cassidy asked.

Roxie shook her head. "No, the band seemed to fuss and snap at each other all night. If I didn't know better, I'd think they disliked each other. They focused on money and publicity. It sounded like no one wanted anyone else to get more than what they had. Not as dreamy or noble as the Weathermen of my teen imagination. Instead, they were nothing more than a bunch of old men grousing and complaining. Grumpy old men."

"The sheriff can't think you had anything to do with it." Cassidy put her arm over Roxie's shoulders.

Roxie raised both sculpted eyebrows. "Who knows, but he still wants me to come by the station. He said not to talk to the press either. But I am going to call my lawyer. Asa has always been out to get me since I shot him down in high school and went to prom with his best friend. That fragile male ego. You'd think we'd all be past that since it's ancient history, but obviously not. And our past has nothing to do with the dead rock star."

"I saw the body," Cassidy whispered. "What a horrible way to die. I know you didn't do that."

Roxie patted Cassidy's arm. "But I'm probably going to have to convince the sheriff and his task force I'm innocent. He's bringing in a team from the state police to help. Can't wait to have a sit-down with all of them. I'll probably get to tell my side of the story at least three more times."

Cassidy's eyes widened. "I wish he was pursuing other leads. There is no way you could have killed Johnny that way."

"Sheriff Asa told me not to leave town." Roxie gave her head an exasperated shake and headed toward the farmhouse.

Johnny Storm is a foot or more taller than Roxie, Cassidy thought. *She couldn't have strangled him unless he was seated or on the ground. Physically, there is no way, and I'm going to prove it. This is not going to ruin her…or my business.*

7

SATURDAY AFTERNOON

Trying to figure out what to do next, Cassidy paused as heavy footsteps approached. Deputy Turner was on a mission, and she was the target. Might as well see what he wanted.

Sheriff Howell walked at a slower gait and veered off in the other direction. "Roxie! Hey Roxie!" The sheriff picked up his pace to catch her.

Pausing to watch the pair on the farmhouse's patio, Cassidy wished she could hear what they were saying. From Roxie's facial expressions, she wasn't thrilled at having to talk to Sheriff Howell again. He led her to one of the lounge chairs on the patio.

Uh, oh. He motioned for Roxie to take a seat. *It's definitely going to be a longer conversation than she wants.*

Before Cassidy could figure out how to get closer to eavesdrop, Deputy Turner interrupted. "Ms. Jamison, may I have a word?"

He stepped in front of her, and she couldn't peek around him to see Roxie without being too obvious about it.

I bet he did that on purpose.

She flashed her best customer service smile. "Cassidy's fine. We don't have to be super formal. What can I help you with?"

"I want to get you to clarify a few facts for my timeline. Some of the events from earlier aren't clear. When did you see Johnny Storm last?"

"In my koi pond when Elvis and I went for his morning walk."

He appeared to struggle not to crack a smile. "Alive. When did you last see him alive?"

"Last night. I attended the concert. Then I saw him again later when I was walking Elvis before bedtime. I ran into Johnny Storm, his band, and some others outside their buses. They were celebrating after the show."

"Who were the others and when was that?" He looked up from his notebook.

She closed her eyes for a minute and tried to picture the bonfire party. "Um, it was the band, their manager, and their drivers or security. Not sure who those guys are. Maybe they're roadies. Steve and Bianca were there, too. Oh, and some of the members of the Rhythm Cats were there. Anyway, I guess I left after ten thirty. I wasn't really paying attention to the time. I did watch a bit of the late news when Elvis and I got back home, so it was definitely before eleven or eleven fifteen."

"Okay. How long did you stay at the party?" Deputy Turner asked.

"Not long. They were hanging out after their performance. Oh, the Pearly Girls were there, too. All of them, Roxie, Ruthanne, Aileen, and Kate. The band had a bonfire going in an old oil drum. I'm guessing there were about fifteen or twenty people there. It was dark. I didn't really pay attention to all the faces."

"Did you stay to celebrate?"

"No. We talked for a few minutes, but I was tired. I took Elvis home." She shook her head.

He paused for a few beats, and Cassidy wished she could see what was going on at the patio. Trying to be discreet, she took a couple of steps to her right to see if she could catch a glance of Roxie and the sheriff. Roxie stood with her feet planted and one hand on her hip. The sheriff was doing all the talking.

"So, the Pearly Girls hung out and partied with the band until the wee hours?" The deputy raised one eyebrow and stared at Cassidy.

What is he implying? Cassidy tried to think of a reason to extricate herself from his questions. "I have a business to run. I usually turn in early because my workdays start early. That happens when you live where you work. The gals are all retired, so they do pretty much what they want and keep different hours."

"I thought they all worked for you." One of the deputy's eyebrows arched almost to his hairline.

Cassidy nodded. "They do, technically. The four of them were childhood friends of my grandmother. When she died, they stepped in to help me keep the business going. Ruthanne is my accountant. Aileen, Kate, and Roxie help with event coordination and decorations. It's nice to have an experienced support team."

"It looks like you've done well for yourself." Deputy Turner abruptly snapped his notebook shut and stuffed it in his front pocket. "If I have any more questions, I'll call you." He strode off without another word toward the parking lot.

She finger-waved and made a sassy face at his back. Tired of all the talking, Elvis led her to the now empty patio.

Where did the sheriff and Roxie go?

"Woo hoo. Hey, Cassidy," Ruthanne hollered from the back door.

Elvis considered it an invitation to play a game, and he raced Cassidy to the door.

Cassidy untangled Elvis's leash from around her ankles. "Hey, what's up?"

"Sorry to bother you, but the phones are ringing off the hook, and I locked the front door after the third reporter wandered in and got a little mouthy with me." Ruthanne sighed heavily. "No manners."

"Rats. I guess word is out about Johnny Storm. I was hoping we'd have more time. Thanks for taking care of it. Let me get something on our website and an auto-attendant message out there." Cassidy hustled to her desk and pulled up Bianca's message to figure out what to say.

After a few tweaks, she posted a similar statement on her website, blog, and social media sites. Clearing her throat, she punched in her voicemail code and read the message she crafted. After listening to the recorded message in her own childlike voice, she hung up the call. "There. Hopefully that will take care of some of the questions. I'm going to leave the answering service on. I'll go through the calls later to see if any of them are real business. My message told reporters to contact the sheriff's office, so I don't feel obligated to call them back if they don't listen."

"Sounds good. I'm getting ready to head out. I didn't want to leave you with a crowd of hyped-up reporters. I know I don't like surprises like that. And some of them weren't very nice." Ruthanne picked up her bag and oversized pink purse. "They kinda act like sharks who've smelled blood in the water."

"You didn't happen to see Roxie before she left, did you? She was talking to the sheriff, but she was gone before I could get over there to see what he wanted," Cassidy said.

Ruthanne's usual smile dissolved into a pained look. "Nope. This whole Johnny Storm thing is bothering her more than she's letting on. I wish Kate and Aileen hadn't brought up Buzz McMichaels. Old wounds."

"I'm worried the sheriff has her in his sights for what happened to Johnny. And maybe he's trying to use the Buzz McMichaels story to show a pattern. Roxie said she left and had proof on her door camera of when she arrived at home. But what if the autopsy findings about the time of death contradict her alibi? This could be trouble and turn into something really bad."

"I'm going to check on her. I'll find out what the sheriff asked her." Ruthanne headed to the door. Her normally good-humored countenance was somber. Pausing, she patted Cassidy's shoulder. "Don't worry. It will be okay. I hope."

"I hope so, too. Let me know if you need me."

"Okey dokey. Watch out for those rabid reporters. I'm going out the back and taking the long way around to my car to dodge them. See ya at the show. Toodles."

Cassidy settled in at her desk and searched the news sites for any updates on Johnny Storm's demise. A few stories with sparse details popped up. Most had reused stock photos from the Weathermen's heyday and rehashed the history of the band. Nothing mentioned her property yet. "When that happens, we'll get even more media attention," she informed the uninterested dog.

IIIIIIIIIIIIIIIIIIIIIIIIIIIIIIIIIIIIIIII

Stomping and noises out front caused Cassidy and Elvis to hurry to one of the front windows and peek out from behind the curtains. The Chihuahua mix let out a low growl at a crowd of hundreds of people milling around in the grass and the parking lot outside. Satellite TV trucks from Harrisonburg and other nearby towns were camped out in her parking lot.

It looks like we're surrounded.

"Oh great!" She nudged Elvis out of the way. She slipped outside and scanned the crowd. Spotting Steve Owens near the crape myrtles lining the main entrance, she power walked in his direction. Before she covered ten feet, the reporters seemed to zip like a school of fish to the far side of the lot.

What is going on?

Steve shrugged his shoulders and trotted after them with Cassidy hot on his heels. The pair edged around the reporters and camera and sound technicians until they found a spot where they could see what was happening. Karl Schultz stood on a plastic milk crate and waved his arms around in circles. "Attention. Attention. May I have your attention?" He bounced and continued to wave his arms and hands. "Can you guys in the back hear me?"

Karl's plea went on for several minutes until someone in the front started making shooshing sounds like an elementary school librarian. Finally, the noise dropped to a dull roar, and Karl scanned the crowd. Even with the milk crate, he had to stretch to see over the first few rows of reporters and technicians.

"Thanks for coming over. I'm Karl Schultz from the Weathermen. We had a tragedy recently in our music family, but I met with the guys earlier, and we have an update for you. Johnny Storm was loved by so many. We are so sorry to announce his tragic death to you all. I don't have any details, so please don't ask. Let's have some respect for his family and friends who are grieving his passing. We all need to find ways to honor his memory. But as much as we loved him, Johnny was all about the music and the show. The remaining members of the band have decided to continue the scheduled shows for the rest of the Groovin' through the Decades tour. He would have wanted us to. We will miss him every single day. And we want to honor our fans who bought tickets and drove here to see us. So, we'll be performing the rest of our scheduled shows. And you can download our albums wherever you get your tunes. If you listen to it and like it, buy it and tell all your friends."

When Karl paused, the reporters shouted questions over one another. The noise level rivaled one of their concerts. Karl waved his arms again. In a huff, he hopped off the milk crate and stalked toward the barn. He yelled over his shoulder, "If you want to see us, get a ticket and come to the show!"

The reporters milled around for a few minutes, but when no one else came forward to make a statement, they drifted back to their cars and trucks to wait for more sightings or anything else that might be deemed newsworthy.

"Well, that was weird. Why would the bass player make the announcement?" Steve Owens asked.

It was Cassidy's turn to shrug. "Maybe they were close friends. Or maybe he felt like he needed to say something. But honestly, to me, it kinda sounded more like a commercial for their shows and songs than a tribute to their friend."

"They are always in marketing mode. Some of the guys didn't invest their earnings from the banner years, and they need this show more than the others." Steve shook his head. "This is how they earn money during what should be their retirement years. Johnny had a heart of gold. He didn't need to tour anymore, but he did it to help the other guys."

Cassidy frowned slightly, not sure how this related to Karl's announcement.

"Karl thinks of himself as the new leader in Johnny's absence, and he probably believed he needed to let the world know they were still performing. He's had a tough go of things lately. But I'm glad they decided to go on. I was heading over to see what else they're up to. I kinda hoped they would have waited to make their announcement, but it is what it is. We could have released a more polished joint statement. Some of these artists do their own thing whenever the mood hits them. I hope Beau was aware of their decision. It's not good when you read or see news about your clients you knew nothing about. And you'll probably have to do some damage control to contain the bad buzz."

The promoter fell silent, and Cassidy increased her pace to keep up with his long strides. Near the barn, the pair spotted Beau Cox on his cell phone near the buses. With a quick nod of recognition, Beau ended his call and headed toward them.

"Hey, man. Heard your boy's press conference out front," Steve took Beau's extended hand.

A puzzled look crossed Beau's face, but he recovered quickly. "How did he do? He's usually a better bass player and backup singer than a spokesman. Please tell me he didn't leak any details of the murder. The state troopers and the sheriff were pretty adamant with us about not sharing any details until they notified his next of kin, and they especially didn't want photos leaking out." A pained look inched across Beau's face.

Steve raised both eyebrows. "Did the police give you any more information?"

"Nope. They were pretty tight-lipped. But I overheard the techs talking when they didn't know I was behind them. They were discussing how Johnny was strangled. He had a wire wrapped around his neck."

"He was strangled?" Steve lowered his voice. "I figured it was some kind of accidental overdose or a heart attack or something. I guess he did have some enemies. That's disturbing."

"Oh, he had his detractors. He got hate mail, and some band members weren't too happy with some of his decisions. They believed he didn't do enough for sales like new albums and bigger concert tours. He told them the other night this was his last tour. He's tired and didn't want to perform anymore. That went over like a lead balloon. The others want to do a new album and, of course, a new tour."

Cassidy pursed her lips.

Would Johnny's decision to quit have caused someone to lose a sweet deal and a cash cow?

8

SATURDAY EVENING

Cassidy leaned on the metal railing next to the cement steps leading to the amphitheater's stage. The state and local police seemed to be everywhere tonight. Reporters and TV crews lined both sides of the stage. Between law enforcement and reporters, the crowd size had doubled since last night. Food and beverage trucks were doing brisk business. At least sales were good, even if most people only came to see the site of Johnny Storm's tragic death and to glean any new details.

Sensing someone approaching, Cassidy craned her neck to peer over her shoulder. Bianca, Steve's assistant, stood inches away with her fancy earpiece and clipboard. The younger woman's magenta hair seemed to glow under the stage lights. The walkie-talkie clipped to her jeans chirped from time to time with updates about the evening's preparations.

"Hi," Cassidy said. "Y'all ready for tonight?"

"About as ready as we'll ever be. I've been working the phones and our socials all day. The reporters definitely turned out. I wish it were for a better reason. It's too bad these artists can toil all their lives, and they really don't get this much press attention until one of them dies. But Steve and our investors are really happy the show's going to continue, so that makes me happy." She glanced at several sheets of paper on her clipboard while Cassidy scanned the crowd.

Spectators were packed in so tightly she couldn't see any grass on the hillside. It was nothing but a sea of blankets and beach towels behind the bench seating. Had everyone in the tri-county area come out for tonight's show?

"That's good. Who's performing tonight?" Cassidy was a little embarrassed she hadn't checked the schedule.

"The Disco Funksters, a seventies cover band, is opening. They probably haven't seen this big of an audience *ever.* I hope it all goes smoothly. I had to silence my phone today because of all the media requests. Too bad for Johnny, but it hasn't been all that bad for us. We take our wins where we can get them." She shrugged and continued to jot notes on her clipboard.

Cassidy raised one eyebrow as the twentysomething whipped out her phone and walked backstage.

So, murder can be profitable. I bet Johnny Storm souvenirs jumped in value.

Looping around the perimeter, Cassidy paused when someone she didn't recognize took the stage. He introduced the Disco Funksters, and the crowd went wild. Beach balls suddenly appeared and bounced through the audience. "Boogie Wonderland" pulsed through the speakers. Most of the crowd was on its feet, gyrating to the disco beat.

The smell of grilled meat made her stomach rumble and reminded Cassidy that she had skipped lunch. She found a taco truck with a short line and sidled behind a couple in matching white disco jumpsuits. Both outfits were bedazzled, and they sparkled when the setting sun glinted off the tiny jewels. When it was her turn, she ordered a shrimp taco with guacamole, several sides, and a large iced tea.

After paying the woman in a tie-dyed T-shirt at the tiny window, Cassidy found a spot where she could sit and enjoy her dinner and the show. The taco, Spanish rice, and Mexican corn were the best she had eaten in a while, and she devoured every morsel. After wiping the excess guacamole off her fingers and disposing of her trash, she trekked along the maintenance road to the sound booth, which was more like a wooden shack with a huge glass window facing the stage. Leaning against the green structure, Cassidy allowed herself a few moments to rest and enjoy the seventies music, pleased with herself for recognizing several of the tunes. Her head bobbed, and she tapped her feet. The audience was having fun with all the crazy dance moves.

During the short intermission, she succumbed to the wonderful smells and splurged on dessert. She took her funnel cake to a spot closer to the stage to watch the Weathermen. Karl took over as the lead singer, and suddenly, the mild-mannered bass player turned into a bombastic lead singer who had the crowd on their feet. Cassidy couldn't tell much difference in the sound or the format of the show. The lifelong fans didn't seem to mind the change either. Most danced throughout the entire show that was as high in energy as the one the night before. If Cassidy hadn't known about Johnny's death, there would have been no indication something tragic had happened.

The lights dimmed after the second encore, and the crowds swarmed up the hill and funneled out the exit. She watched as several guys in black packed equipment. With nothing needing her attention, she hustled to the farmhouse to check on Elvis.

The little dog hardly waited for her to get the back door open before he bounded out with a joyful greeting. "Come on, bud. You deserve an extra-long walk, and maybe two treats when we get back."

Elvis did a full body wiggle at the mention of a treat. He waited for the click of his leash and then took off toward the grotto. Not ready to relive memories of the dead rock singer, an image she had to keep pushing out of her mind, Cassidy led him toward the barn and the almost-empty amphitheater. Mateo's guards outnumbered the fans.

That was a quick exodus for so many people. They've got the traffic control down to a science.

The night sounds echoed in her ears, and she flipped on her phone's flashlight as they made their way along the edge of the grass toward the maintenance road. The darkness and the sounds from the woods seemed to close in around them after all the pulsating rock music and the stage lights. She took a deep breath of the cool night air. Some of the stress from the day melted away. Cassidy pushed her to-do list to the back of her thoughts and enjoyed being outside. Elvis trotted along like any other evening walk. No worries at all for the little dog.

Cassidy paused when she heard what sounded like footfalls. Elvis didn't react, so it could be nothing. *Girl, you're letting your imagination get the best of you.* She took a deep breath and trailed behind the Chihuahua mix.

A twig snapped, and she froze. This time, Elvis let out a low growl that sounded like it was coming from a much bigger dog, and he lunged toward the tree line. Pulling him back gently, she doused her light and blinked several times to force her eyes to adjust to the darkness before she ventured farther.

Something moved near the trees. Picking up Elvis, she stepped closer to the woods. Leaves crunched. Someone in dark clothing darted along the edge of the grass and ducked into the trees. Cassidy stood frozen in her tracks for several seconds to see if the mysterious figure reappeared. Who was running around the property after dark? The woods went on for almost a mile down the ridge with no nearby roads. It's not the best place for an escape unless someone was looking for a dark place to hide.

Willing her heart to slow its snare drum rhythm, she hustled back to the farmhouse and locked the door behind them. When she unleashed Elvis, he did zoomies in the foyer while she pulled out her phone and sent Mateo a text detailing what she'd witnessed. Hopefully, his team would keep an eye out for trespassers or anyone lurking in the woods.

Within seconds, Mateo responded.

> Still have guys on the property. Sending two to walk near the woods. Lots of reporters still in the parking lot. Could have been one of them.

A few minutes later, Mateo added, It could also have been one of the guys from the buses. My guys didn't see anything, but they'll keep an eye out. Nothing out of the ordinary right now.

Calm down, girl. Your imagination is on overdrive tonight. It could have been anyone. Someone in all black doesn't necessarily have to be the murderer or a marauder.

Elvis turned his head and led her up the stairs for his treats. "Okay, buddy. I know I promised good treats. I'm trying to process all the weirdness that's been going on around here lately. I feel like I have to keep looking over my shoulder to see what's next. And so far, everything seems to be centered around the Weathermen."

And now I'm on the lookout for the creepy man in black. Too bad it's the standard uniform of all the roadies and stagehands.

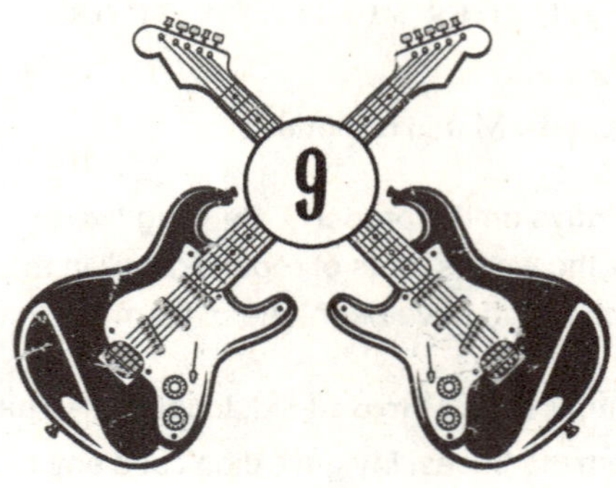

LATER SATURDAY NIGHT

Cassidy settled on her couch and flipped through the news channels to check out the coverage of the Johnny Storm story when Elvis whined at the door. He hopped around and let out a mournful whimper.

"What's up, puppy?" Cassidy opened the door.

Elvis tore down the steps and stood barking at the back door.

Slipping on her shoes, Cassidy followed. "You've been out already. Are you okay?"

The little dog whined again and jumped on the door.

"Okay, okay." She attached his leash to the collar. "One more quick one, and then we're hitting the sack."

Elvis darted out the door before Cassidy had a chance to open it completely. She took a couple of deep breaths to ward off scary images of the guy in the woods. Clutching her phone, Cassidy looked around in all directions before they stepped off the patio. Nothing was amiss, but even the typical night noises seemed magnified, which unsettled her.

Elvis trotted past the patio and into the grassy area leading to the grotto. Nosing around near the mulch, the small dog froze and let out a growl that turned into a barking jag. "Shh. Sound carries at night. Let's not disturb anyone." She scooped the attack dog into her arms and tried to calm him, but he wriggled and bucked until she put him back on the ground. He shot down the path toward the grotto and the garden.

"Elvis, come on. It's bedtime."

The little dog had other ideas, pulling on his leash. He let out another growl, and Cassidy flipped the flashlight on her phone. She let out a gasp. Beau Cox was headed her way.

"Is everything okay, Mr. Cox?" She tried to cover the quake in her voice as he strode toward her.

He reached to pat Elvis, who turned from security K9 to a friend in less than three seconds. "I was out for a walk. Your property is really pretty. I was hoping to clear my mind. You know, with all the stuff that's been going on."

In the dark with no flashlight.

"It is a peaceful spot." Cassidy tried to think of something to keep him talking. "The band sounded good tonight. How is everyone doing? Karl did well on lead vocals."

He paused and took a deep breath. "Karl was in his element. He finally got out from under Johnny's shadow and was able to shine. We'll have to see if they want to keep going after this tragedy. But for now, they seem okay. They've been together for a long time. I mean, it's tough when your friends are your coworkers. Their lives have been intertwined forever. It's hard to untangle all the feelings." He paused to light a cigarette. "I'm pretty sure they're going to want to continue touring."

She decided against reminding him of the no-smoking policy. "I guess there will be a lot of estate work sorting out the music and the business end of things for Johnny."

"Yep." He inhaled a long drag. "Sales, media requests, interviews, and memorabilia prices are soaring right now. Hopefully, the band will make the right decision to capitalize on all of this. Who knows how long it will last."

"Have you had any updates from the sheriff's office?"

"They've talked to all the guys a couple of times. I'm not sure how much progress they're making. I guess it's not like the TV shows. They did show us gruesome pictures of his injury and the so-called weapon." When Cassidy wrinkled her nose and didn't respond, he continued, "They showed us a picture of what they found near the body, too. They passed the picture around. It looked like ordinary stuff to us. Here's the funny part, if you can call it that. Dirk immediately identified a drumstick. The cops thought he was being smart, so I'm sure he's on their radar now. And it was probably his, even though he didn't admit to it. Anyway, it's not like he signs his name on his drumsticks. I think they wanted him to say it was one of his. Actually, he didn't say much of anything. He couldn't say for sure it belonged to him. The band goes through so many picks, sticks, and strings, they buy them in bulk. Nobody keeps track of them. Maybe someone can get prints off them. We'll see. I'm not holding my breath, but since it's a drumstick, he looks like a likely suspect."

"A drumstick in the flower bed?"

"Yep, they said it appeared damaged. The cops kinda insinuated it was used with the wire as part of a garrote. You know, someone wrapped the wire around the stick to get better leverage when they attacked Johnny."

An icy shiver jolted down Cassidy's spine.

Could the killer have discarded or tossed the stick as he escaped? Or was it something a fan or someone dropped by accident?

"That is terrible." Cassidy shuddered. "Why would someone want him dead? He was a talented singer with lots of fans."

Beau took another long inhale from his cigarette. "He had a darker side. He had some bad breakups in his personal life and some issues with the band."

"Like what?" Cassidy stared at the glowing ember from his cigarette that gave his face a surreal, shadowy look.

"There were always artistic struggles about credits and what goes on the album. I've had to break up many a fistfight over the years. Johnny was rabid about his song credits and what should go on each album. He was too hands-on for some of the record companies. Often, he overshadowed the other members, and they didn't like it, but they always seemed to work through their differences eventually. There were lots of spats. That was normal for them." Beau paused and took another drag on his cigarette and blew out the smoke.

Cassidy tried to stifle a cough. She turned her head, wondering what else to ask.

Before she could reply, Beau continued, "The fight generating the most publicity was over a guitar player named Eddie Merritt. He was in the band at the beginning, and he sued Johnny and the guys a couple of times over royalties. It was a big to-do back in the day. It made all the gossip mags."

"What became of all of it? I've never heard of him."

"Nobody has. He was with the band for a couple of months. The guys voted him off the island and decided they needed only two guitars to get the sound they wanted. He was a hothead who everyone walked on eggshells around. He was Dirk's roommate for a short college stint, so it wasn't like he was a longtime friend. But when he saw the guys' success, he and some flimflam lawyer brought several suits against everyone and his brother for his share of the money he really didn't deserve. Eventually, the courts decided he wasn't entitled to anything from the Weathermen." Beau took one last puff on his cigarette and dropped it on the ground, crushing it with his shoe. "I know. I'll get that before I leave. It's a bad habit, but I can't seem to kick it. It's worse when I'm stressed." He paused again. "Thankfully nothing came out of all of Eddie's threats, and the press died down. Our publicist at the time made a big deal about Eddie being a washed-up junkie who would try anything to squeeze money out of his more successful friends who tried to help him."

"What happened? I don't remember seeing anything about it when I searched the bands online," Cassidy said.

"Nothing. The publicist worked really hard to push the story out of the limelight. And it worked. The bad stories and the negative publicity ended, like it never happened. You gotta love the professionals. They can work some magic." His phone beeped an alert. He pulled it out of his pocket.

While he scrolled through something, Cassidy wondered if this Eddie could be involved in Johnny's death. Could a grudge last that long? And why act on it now? It's probably a long shot, but the killer could be someone from the singer's past.

Hoping to get more information, she waited impatiently for Beau to finish. Elvis, bored with where the conversation was going, danced around their feet.

"Like I said, it ended. Like poof. Got a letter from the courts one day. Cases dropped. No more problems." He shrugged. "I need to go check on something. Got a text from Jack. See you around." Beau turned and quietly disappeared in the darkness.

That was odd.

Cassidy scooped Elvis up and walked as fast as she could back to her place. This Eddie Merritt guy sounded like a bigger deal than what Beau made him out to be.

A jolt of excitement arced through her. This could be a missing piece in all of this. She whipped out her phone and texted Deputy Turner.

> Talked to Beau Cox this evening. He mentioned a long-running feud between Johnny Storm and a former bandmate, Eddie Merritt. Not sure if he told you all. I thought you might want to know.

When there was no response, Cassidy picked up her notebook and laptop and settled in on the couch. Elvis snuggled next to her and made a nest in the lap blanket. "Okay, Eddie Merritt, what have you been up to? And have you been to Ivy Springs lately?"

Elvis opened one eye and closed it again, definitely not interested in the band's past feuds or lawsuits.

After what seemed like hours of searching, Cassidy had recorded two notes. Eddie Merritt had no song credits on any of the band's albums. And she found a blog post on a fan site portraying Eddie as a liability who had to leave the band. The blogger concluded the band and their music were better off without the third guitarist.

After some more poking around on the web, she found about three sentences on the ex-guitar player and bandmate. They must have had a really good publicist.

Eddie Merritt, what happened to you? It's almost like you didn't exist.

Letting out a heavy sigh, she was determined to chase this lead. She refined her search. Perhaps he had gone by another name.

"Eureka," she yelled, startling Elvis. He gave her a side-eye and snuggled deeper into the blanket.

"I think I found something, Elvis. Look here. It's an old newspaper article from Atlantic City." She skimmed the article, including several concert photos of the original Weathermen—younger, thinner, and with lots of shoulder-length hair. The look that had charmed the Pearly Girls all those years ago.

Cassidy continued to read. A sinking feeling turned into a lead weight in the pit of her stomach. Eddie's girlfriend at the time found him dead one night in a hotel bathroom at an after-concert party in Atlantic City. Cassidy used the byline to search for the newspaper site. "Yep, there it is. That answers my question about Eddie's whereabouts." She let out a long puff of air that fluttered her bangs.

She did a quick search on a site called Find a Grave. The result was nothing but a picture of a bronze plaque, surrounded by grass. Edward "Eddie" Merritt was buried in 1985. His final resting place was the Silverbrook Cemetery in Wilmington, Delaware.

Well, that's a dead end...quite literally. At least it's someone to mark off my list.

After a glass of milk and several well-earned chocolate chip cookies, Cassidy discovered that the New Jersey medical examiner had ruled Eddie's death as an accidental overdose. That seemed to confirm Beau's side of the story, but it was strange there was no mention anywhere of the lawsuits or the dustups leading to his exit from the band before they truly made it big.

Cassidy let out another sigh when she read Deputy Turner's reply.

> Yep, but we crossed him off the suspect list since he hasn't been around since 1985.

Then, You aren't poking around in our investigation, are you?

She took a deep breath to prevent herself firing off a sassy retort she might regret later.

> No. Just heard it mentioned and didn't know if it would help you all.

Take that, Mr. Smarty Pants. She hoped her text sounded like she was trying to be helpful and share information. *He always gives me attitude. So annoying.*

Calling it a night, Cassidy shut her laptop and padded to her bedroom. Elvis watched from the foot of the bed as she went through her regular nighttime routine. Johnny Storm and his murder kept creeping into her mind, and what seemed like hundreds of possibilities of who wanted to kill him danced around her mind.

"Okay, who profits the most from his death?" she asked her reflection in the mirror.

Elvis rolled over and sighed.

"I know, puppy. But his murder could affect my business. I don't want to be known as the owner of the place where a rock star died." She brushed her teeth, turned off the light, and flopped on her pillow. Her bed seemed to draw her in, but other ideas crashed around in her head.

She tossed and turned for hours, finally slipping into a fitful sleep full of dreams about rock stars, drug overdoses, garrotes, and a smart-aleck deputy.

SUNDAY MORNING

The alarm buzzed way too early. Cassidy rolled over and tried to drown out the noise with her pillow. But when Elvis joined in with his whine, she turned off the alarm. "Come on, buddy. Let's get a move on and see what's going on at the office. I wonder if we're still getting media calls."

She hustled into the bathroom for a steamy shower while Elvis stretched out under the covers in the still-warm bed.

A few minutes later, she towel-dried her hair and worked gel into her long curls. She applied a few swipes of mascara and some blush and then headed for the kitchen to see what was in the refrigerator.

Staring into the almost empty fridge, she made a mental note to get groceries soon. Home delivery at any hour was one of the perks she missed about living in a big city. She'd have to make time to stop by the corner market.

Cassidy found some grapes and vanilla yogurt behind something she could no longer identify. Along with a jolt of espresso, she was ready to face the day, even though a dull headache throbbed behind her eyes.

She gathered her things, slipped on her shoes, and readied Elvis for their short walk downstairs. "Hey, puppy. At least the commute is way better than it was in Washington. The traffic's not bad either.

The only pileups are when you stop short on the steps." He gave her a side-eye and continued his march.

She settled into her office and by the time her laptop booted, she was ready to tackle her inbox and a second cup of coffee. Deleting over sixty interview or information requests about Johnny Storm, she jotted down the contact information of two legitimate business requests and popped a pod of extra dark roast in the coffee maker. While the magic java machine hissed and spit out steam, she thought about all the requests. Johnny Storm was more popular in death than life, and his band was basking in all the attention.

Why did someone want him out of the picture? And what an ugly way to kill someone.

After pouring a cup of piping hot coffee and putting in enough creamer to turn it beige, she pulled out her notebook and wrote down what she knew. Then she made a list of all the players and drew arrows in pink highlighter to show the relationships. "A lot of people benefited from Johnny Storm's death," she said aloud.

"And I'm not one of them." Roxie dumped a shopping bag and her pink Kate Spade classic purse onto the desk next to Cassidy.

"Hey, good morning. I didn't hear you come in. How are you? Any more from the sheriff?"

"He said he wants to talk to me again later this morning. That's why I'm here early—to see if you need me to do anything before I head over and grace him with my presence. I definitely need caffeine before another one of his rapid-fire question-and-answer sessions." Roxie made a beeline for the counter in the corner and sorted through the coffee and tea pods in the drawer.

"He can't still suspect you of killing Johnny Storm. That's ridiculous. Everyone who knows you knows you couldn't have done it."

Roxie wrinkled her nose as she removed the expended coffee pod from the coffee maker, selected a pod of tea, and popped it in. "I don't think I'm a serious suspect. Johnny Storm is way taller than me. If I were to get a good enough grip to strangle him with a wire,

I would have needed a stepladder or for him to be seated. And then how would I have dragged his body to the koi pond? The other gals would have had to help me. It's sad. The sheriff's clinging onto an ancient story about Buzz that has nothing to do with present day. Sheriff Asa and his team are grasping for anything to prove they can handle a murder case here. We haven't had one in at least ten years. We're going to look like some little, bumbling hick town when the press gets hold of this and they don't have a suspect."

"Maybe if you remind the sheriff of the height difference and the brute force it would have taken to transport the body..." Cassidy suggested.

"I'm not doing his job for him," Roxie snapped. "Plus, if I sound too defensive, he'll poke around more and maybe suspect Kate, Aileen, and Ruthanne. They had nothing to do with it. They all left even before I did, so they couldn't have even been around when it happened. I'm not dragging their names into anything or giving the police any ideas." Her voice faded as she stared at her mug.

Cassidy changed the subject. "Kate started some design boards for the August wedding. The bride and her mother are coming in next week to finalize everything and to look at our floral options."

"Kate said something about that. I'll see if she left me anything. If not, I'll catch up with her later. I was on Pinterest last night when I couldn't sleep. I saved some pictures of floral arrangements I'd like to try." Roxie rummaged through the files on top of the desk and then slid into the chair. "I'm curious what the sheriff wants now. I have told him my story at least twelve times. I have half a mind to take my lawyer to this session."

"Do you think you need a lawyer?" Anxiety rose from Cassidy's core.

"No, because I'm innocent. And I've already told him that, but Asa and one of those state troopers are fixated on the fact I was with Buzz McMichaels all those years ago. And I was with Johnny before he died. They said they don't believe in coincidences. They're looking for any scrap of evidence, and anything resembling a pattern. I'll be glad when they find the real killer, and we can go back to our normal business. I have way too much going on right now to worry about being accused of killing a heartthrob. I can see the headlines now: 'Black Widow Strikes Again.' I'll be infamous when some streaming service or true crime podcast gets hold of it." She rolled her eyes and took a swig of her tea. "Just what I need."

"I deleted all the media requests. Most wanted some kind of reaction to Johnny Storm's death or details of how he met his end. I don't feel obligated to return the calls. The sheriff's team is better equipped to wade through all the requests." Cassidy stared at her inbox.

"That'll serve him right. I hope his office gets slammed with calls. Then maybe he'll be too busy to bother with me. I think I may call my lawyer. If he's going to keep dragging me in there for questioning, he can certainly listen to my attorney give him an earful about wasting everyone's time. Even if it does cost me, it'll be worth it." Roxie let out a huff and slammed her mug on the desk. "I'll see you later." She gathered her bags and stomped out the front door.

Before Cassidy could settle in for more internet research, the front door shut again. Racing Elvis to the greeting duties, she zipped into the other room and almost slipped on the hardwood floor. Catching her footing and trying to look graceful, and not klutzy, she caught Deputy Turner's eye. She hoped she didn't make a face at him. He turned his head and scanned the front room. His gaze landed on the seating area.

Saving the day, Elvis pawed at his pants leg, and the tall deputy leaned to pet the dog. Deputy Turner had the physique of a football player, a giant next to the brown-and-black Chihuahua mix. Cassidy pushed away the flutter of excitement when she noticed his still damp hair curled at the base of his neck. The smell of soap and citrusy cologne distracted her for a second and made her more self-conscious.

Cassidy regained her balance and tried to look cool. She had known Zac Turner since he moved here from Charlottesville. He wasn't much older than her, but he was always aloof, and she never bumped into him on his nonworking time. Maybe he didn't live here. Every time she was around him, he made her feel like she had to justify what she was doing or explain every little action.

He's very judgy. Why do I even care what he does in his spare time?

Shaking off the anxious feeling continuing to build inside her, she cleared her throat. "Good morning, Deputy. How can I help you?"

"Just saying hello to your ambassador here. He's a good greeter." Pulling out his notebook, he flipped through several of the pages. "I'm following up on a couple of things. Did you or your grounds people find anything near the gardens and pond after the murder?"

"No. I don't think so, but I can check with Levi." She pulled out her phone and scrolled through her contacts.

After four or five rings, she heard Levi's voicemail message. After the beep, Cassidy said, "Hi, Levi. I'm here with Deputy Turner. He wants to know if you found anything in the garden after the forensics team left. Please give him a call when you get a minute."

"It's 525-3280," Deputy Turner said.

She repeated the number and disconnected. "Thanks. I thought your forensics team scoured the area thoroughly."

"They did. I'm following up to see if you found anything else." A frown darkened his countenance.

"Like what?"

"Like anything. Cigarette butts, litter, clothing, weapons, unusual trash..." His tone sounded slightly annoyed.

I've done it again. I always seem to set him off.

Trying not to let her face give away her feelings, Cassidy replied in the sweetest tone she could muster. "No. I'm sure there was a lot of trash around the amphitheater after the concerts, but I haven't heard anything about the grotto and the gardens. We tried to corral all the guests away from that area. I'll let you know if I hear anything. Levi would have said something if he found a weapon or something of value."

He nodded. "What about the Eddie Merritt lead? Where did that come from?"

Cassidy could feel the heat rising in her cheeks. It didn't take much with her pale complexion to look like she was full-on blushing. "The sheriff said to let him know if we heard or saw anything. I was talking to the band's manager last night, and he mentioned some lawsuits Eddie filed against the band. I wanted to make sure you all knew about it."

"We've discounted him. That happened a while back."

So did the Buzz McMichaels and Roxie thing, but the sheriff's still pushing that theory.

When Cassidy didn't reply, he added, "But thanks for reporting it. You never know what bit of information might be important. And that's the reason I'm here. The sheriff wanted me to talk to you about the case."

A spark of excitement bounced around inside and turned into butterflies. She took a breath to calm the fluttery feeling. "What do you need help with?"

His eyebrows squished together, and the collaborative tone was gone in an instant. "He wanted me to thank you for any information your team provided. We always appreciate tips and ideas that could help us, but he wants you and the Pearly Girls to be careful and not to get any more involved in this. If you come across anything or any strange things happen, call the sheriff's office immediately."

"We're already involved. It happened on my property." Cassidy fisted her hands on her hips.

"We know, and we're sorry you all are having to go through this. We hope to wrap this investigation as soon as we can. I know the influx of the media hasn't been easy. They've been crawling all over town like coyotes looking for any scrap they can snag. The sheriff wanted me to remind you not to play investigator with this. It's serious."

His glare bored straight through Cassidy. Whatever butterflies were there had turned into bricks and had fallen to the pit of her stomach. She closed her eyes for a beat. When he cleared his throat, her eyes fluttered open, and she locked on his stare, determined he wasn't going to make her second-guess herself about trying to find out who killed Johnny. She stared back at him. "I'll let the ladies know. They're all concerned about the business and Roxie's reputation."

"We have to follow every lead to see where it takes us. Report anything suspicious, mind your business, and don't play Nancy Drew." He jammed his notebook in his uniform pocket. "Got it?"

"Got it," she muttered to his back as he trekked out the door. His heavy footsteps grew fainter as he descended the porch steps. She stuck her tongue out after she closed the door. "I am minding my business." Her voice rose to a snarky, high pitch. "It's my job to make sure nothing damages my business. And I'm not investigating. I'm only asking questions. There is a difference."

SUNDAY AFTERNOON

Cassidy did several yoga poses to ease the kinks in her back. "Elvis, I think that's enough work for the day. I got the newsletter draft done, updated our socials, and deleted about a million requests for interviews from reporters. Let's go freshen up for the show tonight, and then you and I will take a walk around the property. We need to see what's going on."

Elvis yipped his approval and dashed for the door.

Cassidy dug through her closet for a quick change into aqua capri pants and a gauzy white camp shirt. Deciding against strappy sandals with wedged heels, she pulled out a pair of white sneakers for trekking the hilly landscape. "Come on, let's see what's happening in the big world around us."

Outside, she had to increase her speed to keep pace with the excited dog who jogged toward the faint sound of voices near the parking lot. The number of TV trucks had decreased exponentially from earlier. The fickle bunch must be off to the next hot story or out looking for other, more talkative sources.

I hope they don't run into any of the Pearly Girls. They won't be able to help themselves if reporters start asking questions or shove a camera in front of them.

Shaking off the worry of how the reporters might portray her property as the scene of the crime, she tagged along behind Elvis to the back of the farmhouse. Loud voices distracted both of them, and they hurried around the corner. Near the woods, Dirk Lawrence was yelling at a lanky guy with shaggy hair wearing a khaki fisherman's vest with lots of pockets. He had a camera hanging on a strap around his neck and another one in his hand.

When the guy said something Cassidy couldn't hear, Dirk lunged at the man and pushed him hard enough for him to lose his balance. The guy teetered, dropping one of the cameras.

Cassidy hoisted the wiggly Elvis into her arms and hurried toward the men. She needed to defuse this before the police, or the press, got involved. Another incident with the band would send the reporters flocking back to the property when she was trying to avoid more bad publicity at all costs, not to mention any injuries or bodily harm.

Before she could intervene, the guy on the grass picked up the camera, examining it for damage. "You're going to pay for this if it's broken. I will sue you." The unfamiliar man snarled at Dirk. "You have no right to attack me. I'm just doing my job, man."

"It's what you get for poking around in my business and sticking that stupid camera in my face. I'm done with your ridiculous questions. Leave me alone." A spray of spit accompanied Dirk's harsh words. "I have nothing to say. I already told you that. And you need to find a less loathsome way to earn a living. Get out of my face."

"Says you. I like my job. And for your information, I can be here. This is public property. Haven't you heard of freedom of the press?" The reporter wiped off the lens with his sleeve and pushed a few buttons on the back of the camera.

Cassidy decided it was time to intervene. "Yes, we all cherish that as one of our rights, but this isn't public property. This is a private facility, and the media area is over there." Cassidy held on tightly to the wiggly dog with one hand and pointed with the other toward the parking lot.

"Ha!" Dirk bitterly chuckled. "You have no business being here. You've been harassing me all day and for that matter, my entire adult life. Take your slimy tricks and leave, or I'll have her call the police. You're trespassing and being a general nuisance. She's the owner. She can kick you out."

"Wouldn't you like that?" The reporter was unrepentant as he sneered at Dirk. "I'm here to get the truth, and I'm not leaving until I know more. You guys live the rock star lifestyle even though you peaked decades ago. I'm going to expose all of you for what you really are. You're living off of success from the past. This little nostalgia tour has been fun, but I'm still going to follow the money. There's a story here. Not to mention the drugs. Your beloved lead singer was known for his coke habit, and the rest of you have your own issues. I know you guys are concealing the cause of his death."

"We've all been clean for years. The hard-rocking life is an act. We're too old for all that these days. The strongest thing we take on any given day is Tums or Metamucil. Oh, and our multivitamins. And they were perfectly legal last time I checked. So, mind your own business and stop spreading lies. Have some respect for the dead and grieving." Dirk's words were spoken in a calmer tone, but his face still flushed red with anger.

"That's not what my sources say. I've got a bunch of stories and pictures from all kinds of girls. I heard Karl even had a scam where he lured them to private parties with the promise of a record contract. You guys are a piece of work."

Dirk emitted a low, guttural growl seconds before he lunged again at the reporter. The camera went flying again and landed with a thud on the hard ground.

If it wasn't damaged before, it is now, Cassidy thought, sighing.

Elvis tried to spring toward the fight, but Cassidy tightened her grip. She took a couple of steps back and tried to calm him. There were too many arms flying for her to put an end to the ruckus. She pulled out her phone but didn't know who to call.

Before she could decide what to do, the lanky Weathermen guitarist, Jack Simon, jogged over. "What is going on here? Dirk, you're missing the sound check." He waded into the fracas, trying to pull the two men apart. "Enough! He's not worth the hassle."

Dirk had the reporter around the neck. The man, now covered in dirt and grass, strained to pull Dirk's hands away. He coughed, sputtered, and kicked, not connecting with anything.

"Dirk! Don't cross a line." Jack pried Dirk's fingers off the gasping reporter. "It's really not worth it. Let him go. Now." Jack said something Cassidy didn't catch as he pulled Dirk to his feet and stood between him and the reporter.

The drummer's face flashed scarlet with the veins bulging at his temples and neck. Dirk glared at the reporter, his eyes raging with fury. His stone-cold silence was eerie, and he continued to stare as Jack led him toward the amphitheater. Cassidy shuddered.

When the bandmates were out of sight, Cassidy approached the reporter. "Are you okay?"

"I've been better." He rubbed his neck. "I didn't think he would fly off the handle like that. I was hoping to get him to say something I could use in my story."

"Do you need an ambulance? Maybe you should get checked out." She turned, hoping to escort him back toward the parking lot.

"I'll be okay. I've been in worse situations. It's part of the job." He sat up, trying to get his bearings. "People usually aren't very happy to see me. Most of my pieces highlight their sins and misery or reveal their dirty little secrets."

"Are you sure you're okay? Can I get you something to drink, or maybe you should sit here for a while. You look a little woozy." Thoughts of this man fainting and the flashing lights of an ambulance sent butterflies dancing in her stomach again. *I don't need another injured guest.*

"I'm fine. I'm on a deadline, and I was hoping to get something here from some of the band to add to my story. They're still trying to act like they're on top of the charts, and there's always some kind of drama swirling around them. I'm Xander, by the way. I work freelance for a bunch of online news and entertainment sites."

"Interesting. Would I have seen any of your stuff?" Cassidy really didn't want to make small talk with the man, but she couldn't find a polite way to get herself out of the conversation now.

"Maybe. It depends on how much you're into fan sites. I've sold stories to *Entertainment Tonight*, TMZ, and a bunch of the tabloids. But I'm also working on a book. It's full of lots of tales of woe and broken dreams in the music industry."

Cassidy's eyebrows shot up under her bangs. "I'm sure you've encountered a bunch of folks with tragedies in your line of work. I'm Cassidy Jamison. I own the property, Celebrations at Ivy Springs."

"It's pretty here. I got some good shots of the trees and the valley. That is, if my camera's still working." He paused and looked around. The silence became uncomfortable. "So, what other celebrity events do you have planned?" The color started to return to his cheeks. He reached for his camera and pushed more buttons on the panel on the back.

"This is the first. Well, for me anyway. There used to be an old saloon on the property. It was built in the 1920s, and it served as a stop for singers making their way to and from Nashville. The honky-tonk hosted the top names of the country and western circuit, but the building burned in the eighties along with most of the memorabilia. My grandma's friends have lots of stories about the musicians and their antics."

"Interesting. I'm going to be around for a couple of days. Can I come back and talk to you about it? It might turn into something." Xander flashed a flirty half-grin.

"Sure. I'll be around." Cassidy fished out a business card from her phone case and handed it to the reporter.

He pocketed her card and then rummaged around in one of his many pockets. "Here, this one's mine. Who's your friend?"

"This is the one and only four-legged Elvis. He's a spunky Chihuahua with 'tude who's the greeter and director of security with a hunka burning love for everyone he meets."

Xander laughed. "Great name. He kinda looks like the King." The reporter cracked another smile and rose to leave. "Don't worry. I'm headed over to the media area. I'll stay with my kind. I think ole Dirk bruised something when he attacked me. I should have recorded his outburst. That would have made the shows: 'Weathermen's drummer attempts to strangle photojournalist.' I could have been the story. Hey, what time do the gates open?"

"Four." She watched him walk gingerly toward the parking lot.

When he was out of earshot, she relaxed. "Elvis, it might be nice to get some good publicity for a change. Let's see what comes out of talking to Xander about the area's musical roots. We all know the Pearly Girls will entertain him for hours with their stories. But, come to think of it, he'll probably get way more than he bargained for if he chats them up. We may have to rescue him again!"

LATER SUNDAY

"Oh, hi!" Cassidy was delighted to find Ruthanne in the office as she pulled the back door shut. Elvis ran over to provide an official Ivy Springs greeting with bouncy moves and a few yips thrown in for good measure.

"Howdy. I'm going to work on some little things while I wait for the gals. We're headed over to the show in a little bit. How do you like my outfit?" Ruthanne modeled her getup straight out of the days of Reagan, Gorbachev, and Pop Rocks. She patted her headband and large bow corralling her recently crimped hair. Her black fishnet vest covered a neon pink T-shirt. Black, studded boots rounded out the outfit. When she waved both hands, bunches of black rubber bracelets jiggled on her arms. "I had to dig out my blue eye shadow and hair crimper. I couldn't find my leg warmers or any true stirrup pants, so I had to settle for a pair of black leggings. Gone are the days of stirrup pants, shoulder pads, and economy-sized cans of AquaNet. We were probably responsible for the hole in the ozone because of all that hairspray."

"Who's on tonight?" Cassidy did her best to hold in the giggle building in her chest.

"There are two cover bands before the Weathermen. It's going to be a big eighties extravaganza with the Purple Dragon and Abracadaver." She giggled at the band names. "I love the eighties. The movies and the music were great."

Before Cassidy could comment, the door flew open. Kate and Aileen barreled in. "Hey, y'all. Ready for a raucous night? I bet there will be some 'Dancing in the Streets!'" Kate twirled around with one arm raised.

"Or 'Dancing on the Ceiling.' Or maybe 'Dancing in the Dark.'" Aileen giggled. "I found my collection of big earrings from the Decade of Excess. Check these babies out." She pointed to a pair of hoop earrings that could have doubled as cuff bracelets.

"Oh, what fun we had. Tonight will be a blast. Where's Roxie?" Kate dug around in her purse.

"You say that about every decade." Aileen fluffed her hair and rifled through a beach bag until she found a barrel brush and hair spray. She feathered and teased her teal-colored hair until it stood several inches above her head. Then she let loose with a steady stream of scented hairspray that hung in the air.

"Okay, you just took out another big chunk of the ozone. Not sure I miss all the hair products." Kate coughed and fanned the air with a magazine she found on a nearby desk. "And by the way, when you get to be our age, we have lots of decades to choose from."

"We had a lot of fun then." Ruthanne paused and lowered her voice. "But, speaking of *not* much fun, Roxie texted me the sheriff wanted to talk to her again. What is he thinking?" She stomped her boot on the hardwood floor. "He's out of his gourd if he thinks she's the killer."

"He's grasping at any lead he can right now," Kate added. "I talked to Hazel in his office. He has nothing. No leads. No killer. He's feeling the pressure to solve this."

"And he's trying to look like he knows what he's doing in front of all those state troopers." Aileen pulled out a compact and applied a layer of sparkly blue eye shadow. Then she capped off her eye look with teal mascara. As always, her look coordinated with whatever hair color she was currently sporting.

"He needs to stop bothering Roxie and find the real culprit. And we need to do something about this," Ruthanne said.

Before anyone could reply, Roxie strode in sporting a black leather miniskirt and thigh-high patent leather boots. Her skin-tight magenta blouse with a plunging neckline was accentuated with more jewelry than a rack at Claire's in the mall.

"Great costume," Cassidy said.

"What costume? This is what I went clubbing in back in the day." Roxie twirled a chain with an oversized cross. She sported a long strand of pearls and several other silver necklaces. Her honey-blond hair was spiked in all directions, and she had enough blue eye shadow and eyeliner on to make an eighties hairband jealous.

"How are you?" Ruthanne ran to hug her.

"I'm fine. It was nothing to worry about. I took my lawyer this time, and she told Asa—in no uncertain terms—to stop harassing me. He needs to put up or shut up. Hopefully, that will cool his jets for a while. Hey, has everybody eaten already?"

"No, we were going to see what food trucks showed up tonight," Aileen smeared on another layer of bright-pink lipstick and puckered to wipe off the excess.

"Cassidy, wanna come with us?" Ruthanne asked.

"We're going to have a blast." Kate pulled out a flask from her giant bag and wiggled it in the air. "We're prepared this time."

"I brought mine, too," Roxie jiggled her oversized bag. "Ten dollars for a watered-down beer was outrageous. Skunky beer was all we could afford in the seventies. And we didn't know any better. We have refined our tastes over the years. And we've all learned we don't have to settle."

"I have some peanuts and Junior Mints if anyone wants any. I wasn't sure what food trucks were coming, so I brought emergency snacks." Ruthanne rummaged through her bag and held up an assortment of junk food.

Observing all of this, Cassidy was reminded of her days of sneaking candy and drinks into the movie theaters. She smiled fondly at the memory and these women reliving their own youth. "I'll be over in a bit. I want to check on a few things here and get Elvis tucked in at home. Save me a seat."

The Pearly Girls stashed the snacks and flasks in their bags. The chatter increased as they headed toward the door with a chorus of goodbyes and giggles.

After the door shut, the silence in the room was overwhelming. It seemed to fill the void with a pressing immediacy that was stifling. Cassidy found a streaming station on her phone and played some smooth jazz to keep her company. She scanned her social media sites for comments about the festival. Most of what she found were tags from attendees who'd had a great time. *Nothing negative, thank goodness.* Cassidy let out a long stream of air. She did a couple of quick Google searches about Johnny Storm. Nothing new popped up. *I guess that's good news for now.*

On a whim, she searched for Xander and pored over a variety of articles about Britney Spears, Chris Pine, Dave Chappell, and some older ones about Michael Jackson's doctor and Lindsay Lohan. *Xander's been around a while.* All his articles focused on scandals and sudden falls from grace. "What an interesting way to make a living. Elvis, maybe we should get his book when it comes out to see what he says about the Weathermen. And to see if he mentions any of us. All right, that's enough. Let's get you fed and settled in for the evening. I need you to guard the house while I'm gone."

The pair made their way upstairs to the residence. She refilled Elvis's food and water bowls, giving him a new focus.

Resisting the urge to create a quick costume, Cassidy decided it would pale in comparison to what the Pearly Girls had on anyway. She pocketed her keys, phone, and wallet; kissed Elvis on top of his head; and jogged down the stairs. Realizing she had forgotten her all-access lanyard, she retraced her steps and grabbed the pass.

Outside, the crowd noise echoed across the property. Glad for a good turnout again, she walked to the gate, where the guard waved her around the ticket-check line.

The smell of deep-fried food made her stomach rumble. With all that had been going on, she'd forgotten to go to the grocery store—again. And she hadn't eaten all day. Cassidy walked the lengthy line of colorful food trucks and checked out all the offerings before settling on a Coney dog with mustard, a side of onion rings, and a root beer.

After paying the hot dog vendor, she wandered over to a quiet spot near the sound booth to people watch. She sat against the wall and dug into her meal. As she reached for a napkin in her pocket to wipe off a stray glob of mustard from her top lip, someone touched her shoulder, and she almost dropped her drink. Letting out a little squeak, she grasped her cup tight enough to pop off the plastic lid.

"Sorry about that. I didn't mean to startle you. You're a bit jumpy today." Deputy Turner stepped back. Cassidy could see her reflection in his mirrored sunglasses. Snapping the cup lid back in place, she wiped the glob of mustard off her face.

How embarrassing.

"I didn't hear you approach." She desperately hoped there wasn't any stray mustard smeared across her face. "So how are things going with your investigation, Deputy Turner?"

"It's Zac. And the investigation continues. The task force is fully staffed and operational, so we have lots of folks working on it."

I guess we're on a first-name basis now. Maybe he's offering an olive branch. I guess it's better than his normal bull-in-a-china-shop routine that tends to set me off. Cassidy was embarrassed to realize she hadn't replied as he stared at her. "Oh, good. I'm glad to see you're looking at lots of suspects, besides Roxie."

His lips formed a straight line for a moment. "Like I said, we have lots of resources dedicated to finding the killer and bringing him or her to justice. We follow every lead, wherever it takes us. It's a long and exhaustive process."

"Good to hear that, and I'm sure Roxie and her lawyer will be happy about it, too." When he didn't reply, she sensed he was preoccupied. "Let me know if my team can do anything for you."

He scanned the crowd. "Enjoy your evening." He turned and blended into a sea of spectators.

Cassidy stared after him. It had been a strange encounter. But then again, most of her conversations with the deputy up to this point had either turned into one of his lectures, a scolding session, or some heated discussion that made her blood pressure rise. He could be so annoying, and he always turned up whenever she wasn't expecting him. And calling him Zac felt weird, too. Every time Cassidy thought they'd turned a corner, he did something to aggravate her.

Shaking off the odd feeling from their conversation, Cassidy focused on enjoying some classics from the era of the Rubik's Cube, Live Aid, and Hands Across America. She tossed her plate and napkins in the nearest can and headed toward the stage to find the gals.

Making her way through the crowd was like swimming upstream. She finally found a break in the throng and jogged across the path to the benches near the stage.

A sharp wolf whistle echoed from the VIP area. Turning, she found the Pearly Girls waving their arms and pointing to the empty seat at the end of the row.

"We saved you a seat." Kate gathered her beach bag to make room for Cassidy.

"That nice promoter guy, Steve, moved us here after Roxie worked her flirty magic," Ruthanne gushed. "We're so close. We can see every detail. It feels like they're singing to us."

Roxie raised her perfectly manicured hand in a lacy, fingerless glove and waved off the comment. "It was nothing. He was being friendly."

Kate and Aileen both rolled their eyes.

Before they could chat further, Rocky Parker, a local DJ, rushed out on stage and introduced the members of the Purple Dragon. Laser lights pulsated in sync with the sounds of drums and a synthesizer. The band stormed the stage and launched into a Prince tribute.

Cassidy settled in her seat, waving off the offer of Kate's flask. She closed her eyes. The young lead singer did sound a lot like the Purple One. "Little Red Corvette" and "Let's Go Crazy" would always be her favorites. The eighties definitely had great songs and interesting clothes—even if they did look like costumes.

After the fun pop hits from the Purple Dragon and the louder heavy metal vibes from Abracadaver, Cassidy stood and stretched to ease the kinks in her back.

"I'm going for dessert." Ruthanne hopped up. "Anyone else wanna join me?"

"No," Roxie said, "but bring me a Diet Coke, will you?"

Ruthanne nodded as Aileen followed her toward the food trucks.

The local DJ popped out on stage again as Dirk pounded out a slow beat on his drums. "Who's ready for our headliners this evening?"

The crowd noise increased.

Karl stumbled out on stage and tried several times to pull the microphone out of its stand. Giving up, he slurred, "Maybe I'll play drums this time." Teetering back toward the risers where Dirk pounded out the beat, he tried to step onto the platform and slipped.

Dirk struggled to continue the rhythmic drumming and scowled at Karl. "What are you doing? Get it together. Now!"

The audience couldn't hear the unsteady Karl's reply as he tried to wrestle Dirk for the drumsticks.

Then the mic picked up Karl's voice. "Come on, it's my turn. Don't be a jerk." The cymbal stand teetered and crashed onto the stage.

Beau and a burly guy in all black rushed out and guided Karl backstage.

Dirk ignored the interruption and continued to pound on his drums like he was doing some big solo. Jack jumped in with matching chords. They acted like Karl hadn't caused a scene. They continued to play a long interlude with seemingly no end.

By the time the audience started getting restless, Rocky jogged back out on stage. "Hey, guys. Sorry for the technical difficulties there. We seem to have them under control now." Peering over his shoulder, he nodded at someone backstage. "So, without further ado, here is Karl Schultz, Jack Simon, and Dirk Lawrence—the Weathermen!"

That didn't look like technical difficulties. What else is going to happen with this band? First Dirk's dustup and now Karl's antics. I'm sure Xander's having a field day snapping photos.

A few boos emanated from the back. Cassidy looked around. The lines at the food truck were almost nonexistent. She sucked in a bit of air when she realized the crowds were filing out the front gates. *Beau and the promoter aren't going to like this. Has the interest worn off already? Or is it not the same without Johnny Storm?*

SUNDAY EVENING

Cassidy hurried home where Elvis waited for his evening walk. Mateo's security team had made quick work of the crowd control and the almost-empty parking lot. She'd have to check with the Pearly Girls to see if anything else happened after the Weathermen's performance. Hopefully, there were no other dustups or technical difficulties. Cassidy crossed her fingers the concert went off without a hitch. But if anything did happen, the gals would know the scoop.

The crowd size hadn't been as large this evening.

I wonder if the Weathermen have maxed out on the nostalgia craze and interest is waning. Trying to push worries of bad publicity and lost revenue out of her head, Cassidy ticked off the list of possible suspects in Johnny's murder as Elvis breathed in every scent on every blade of grass they passed. Thinking of their crew, family, and friends, her list grew to twenty-five names before Elvis finished his sniffing quest.

She tugged lightly on the leash and led the little dog back home. Somehow, the walk energized him, and he zoomed around the apartment while Cassidy poured a glass of peach tea and settled with her laptop on the couch. First she had fretted because she had no suspects, and now she was overwhelmed with a list of too many. *Time for a different tactic.*

Not finding anything on the local or national news about Johnny Storm, she landed on an entertainment channel in hopes they were still covering the story. But the gossip channels had moved on to the next hottest celebrity scandal, too. *It looks like the band's fifteen minutes of fame are already over.*

Cassidy opened her spreadsheet and listed everyone she perceived could be a potential suspect, including Roxie. She quickly deleted Roxie's entry. There was no way Roxie had anything to do with Johnny Storm's murder. Absolutely no way.

She added the reporter, Xander, in the spot where Roxie's name had been. He was on the mission to find a story, but maybe he was more involved than he let on.

Girl, you are grasping at every little possibility. It could have been aliens or Bigfoot, too, for that matter.

She added four question marks next to Xander's name. He'd probably get scratched off the list later.

Cassidy racked her brain for anyone from the festival who could be involved in the crime. *What if it was some random person? They could be anywhere by now, or they could be hanging around, waiting to find another victim.* A shiver slid down Cassidy's spine. *Wait a minute. Your imagination is running wild. You've watched way too many stalker and true crime shows. Who has a motive?*

Most of the band members seemed to have blown through their earnings quickly and needed this tour as a source of revenue. Beau made his money on the band's success. Those sounded like solid reasons and dollar signs for them *not* to kill the lead singer. Could it be something other than money? Drugs? Jealously? Revenge?

"Elvis, I need more information, and since Asa and my pal Zac aren't sharing, it's going to be up to me and my contacts to see what we can uncover. There has to be a reason behind all of this." Cassidy returned to her online searches, in hopes of finding even a scrap of new information. Changing tactics, Cassidy googled the term *garrote.*

"Interesting." She tapped her bottom lip with her pen. "This was originally used as a method of execution. Elvis, it's called a silent execution. One could kill someone with it in as little as fifteen or twenty seconds. It was usually death by strangulation, but it could also cause a broken neck or decapitation. Hmm." Cassidy learned that special forces trained with these for years and often used them behind enemy lines because it was a stealthy weapon that didn't make noise or attract attention.

Elvis looked at her and turned around several times in his bed. He faced the wall and buried his head under his blanket.

"I know. I know. It sounds like a horrible way to die," she muttered to the dog's back.

Cassidy read more about the process of making and using a garrote. "Elvis, it's really kind of simple. It's a strong wire wrapped around two things that can serve as handles or grips." She stared at the pictures ranging from sticks to pieces of pipe. She closed her browser and her eyes for a few minutes to try to wipe the gruesome images from her memory.

"Oh, puppy. That's what the police found in my serenity garden. Drumsticks and a guitar string. What did Johnny Storm do to make someone kill him that way? Or was it a crime of passion, and someone used what was nearby? That would seem to point to someone with access to the band's equipment. But Johnny seemed to be worth more to the band alive than dead. Okay. Here's my theory. It's someone who wanted it to look like one of the bandmates. Or it happened in a fit of rage. Or maybe it was some lunatic fan or ex-girlfriend. Great. Now I'm back to aliens, Bigfoot, or a crazy maniac running around." The little dog turned his head but offered no suggestions.

Cassidy laughed at her dog's response. "This is harder than it looks. There are so many people with opportunities. I've got to narrow this down. I know the sheriff's team doesn't want me involved, but who else is this close to the band every day? I'm going to keep asking questions and looking for possibilities."

She opened her browser again, determined to find something in the band's past to explain Johnny's murder.

IIIIIIIIIIIIIIIIIIIIIIIIIIIIIIIIIIIIIII

A shrill whine resounded through the apartment. Cassidy sat up and winced when her laptop jabbed her in the ribcage. "What's up, Elvis? I must have drifted off. Surprise, surprise. I didn't find anything new. I guess I'm not the greatest sleuth. But we have to keep trying. This business is all I have." The brown and tan dog continued to whimper at the door. "Okay, let's go out one more time." She stood and slipped on her shoes.

Elvis continued to dance until she led him downstairs and out near the patio. He paused and listened for a second then darted toward the barn. Neither the early morning chill nor the woodland sounds seem to bother him. He heard something and led the charge to see what it was. *Maybe Elvis should be my model for success. If you want something, go for it. Step out of your comfort zone, girl. You need to protect your business and your reputation. Stop worrying about what others think. Follow your nose or your instincts.*

Two male voices echoed in the stillness of the mountain air. Cassidy picked up Elvis to try to keep him from barking as she crept closer to the barn. "Shhh. Let's see what's going on," she whispered. Still in the darkness away from the barn's floodlights, she tiptoed to the corner of the building and peeked around.

Under the barn's exterior lights, Dirk stood against the wall with one foot propped on the wooden siding. Jack, standing in a patch of gravel, faced the drummer. He blew on his hands and stuffed them in the pockets of his jeans. "Man, it got cold fast. I'll be glad when we're done here. After this tour, I'm taking a break and heading somewhere warm to recuperate. I've had enough. We're getting too old for all of this."

"Speak for yourself. I'm as good as I ever was. And things were going fine until Karl started pulling his stunts again. I thought he had kicked all that after his seventh or eighth stint in rehab. He knows better than to get messed up before a show. I know Johnny and the promoters laid down the law before we all signed on. What was he thinking?" Dirk asked.

"It's not the same anymore. I know we were all a part of creating the sound and recording the songs, but the energy and the soul aren't there without Johnny. I miss him." Jack shifted his weight from one foot to the other and kicked rocks with the toe of his biker boot. "We may have reached the end of this journey. Maybe we should have a band meeting and talk through what we want to do. It's probably time to call it. People'll understand after what happened to Johnny. I don't know if any of our hearts are truly in it anymore."

"Karl won't understand, and real rockers don't retire," Dirk argued. "What are we going to do after music? It's all we've ever done. None of us are going to be good retirees. And none of us can remember our last real job."

"I think Karl's taking Johnny's death harder than we anticipated. We may need to check on him. I mean, have a real convo with him. Something's not right. He's not right." Jack shook his head then stared down at his feet.

"Like an intervention?"

"If he needs it." Jack continued to fidget.

"What if it isn't grief? What if it's guilt?" Dirk's voice trailed off with that last word. "What do we do if we find out something we don't want to know?"

Cassidy sucked in a mouthful of chilly air, and Elvis decided at that moment to let out a series of yips. Thinking fast, she put him on the ground and let him zip around the corner toward the two men, whose faces reflected surprise as they approached. The little dog distracted Dirk and Jack, while Cassidy made a lot of noise as she drew closer to the duo. "Good evening, gentlemen. We're out for his evening stroll. How are you all doing?"

"More like morning, but hey, who's being precise? We tend to be vampires most nights anyway." Dirk released a nervous-sounding chuckle. "I can't tell you the last time I had breakfast when normal people eat their first meal."

"Sorry to intrude on your conversation. Elvis got excited when he heard y'all, so here we are. He's very nosy." Cassidy racked her brain for something else to say that wouldn't come across as a made-up excuse.

"Great name." Jack leaned to pet the bouncy dog. "It's getting chilly out here. I don't know about you all, but I'm ready for bed. I've had enough for one day." He nodded and headed off toward the buses.

"Me too." Without waiting for a response, Dirk followed his bandmate.

When the musicians disappeared in the darkness, Cassidy whispered, "That was close. Come on, baby. We need to get some sleep. Tomorrow's a big day."

On the way back, Cassidy's thoughts revved up again and clicked through her head like an old View-Master. *Did they suspect I was eavesdropping? They both hurried off pretty quickly. And what did Dirk mean Karl could be guilty? It sounds like Karl's demons haven't been tamed.*

After checking the back door twice to ensure it was locked, Cassidy bounded up the stairs with Elvis. Too wired to sleep, she woke her laptop and stared at the extensive list of names. She added Dirk's question about Karl's guilty behavior with a string of question marks. "It doesn't make sense that someone making money off the band would want to ruin the revenue stream by killing the lead singer. I mean, why kill him unless you get something else from it?"

Elvis, not interested in revenue streams or murder, snored softly from the other end of the couch.

"Okay, think about this. Why would a coworker want Johnny Storm out of the picture?" She tapped her hand on the laptop. "Was someone jealous? Why would someone be happy he was gone? Or could it have been an accident?" Cassidy shook her head. "No, it didn't look like an accident."

Cassidy spent the next half hour listing possibilities and any wild idea that popped into her head.

She googled Karl Schultz and pored over hundreds of articles on him and the Weathermen. He had spent most of his adult life with the band. Their successes and hijinks had been chronicled in tons of newspaper and gossip stories. Everything about his two messy divorces, four kids, and several stints in rehab was out in the open on the internet. "What's that?" she asked out loud. "This site lists all the arrests and bad-boy behavior of the Weathermen." Cassidy spent the next hour writing down facts from the rockers' pasts.

When her eyelids began to sag, she yawned and stood. "Come on, Elvis. Let's drag it to bed. We're going to have to go to work tomorrow, and at this rate, I'm going to look like a raccoon. I'm kinda bummed we didn't find anything new except Dirk's statement about Karl, and a list a mile long, cataloguing all their bad behavior. I still have a ton of unanswered questions. Swell. I guess that means our goal for tomorrow is to find out more about Karl and how the guys in the band really feel about each other. There's got to be more than meets the eye. They argue and squabble like siblings."

Elvis yawned and trotted behind her to the bedroom. Cassidy flopped on the bed and tried to blank everything out. She knew the remaining band members were key to this, but how could she get them to open up to her?

I've got to find a way to wriggle in and get them to answer some awkward questions. Maybe it would be easier to start with Beau.

MONDAY MORNING

Before Cassidy and Elvis had time to settle in and plow through the pile of administrative tasks, a rat-a-tat-tat came from the front. *No client appointments today. Somebody's awake early.*

Before she could get to the door, the knocking repeated at a steadier pace.

Nudging Elvis out of the way, she opened the door to see the back of the entertainment reporter. Xander waved one arm around and cradled his phone on one side. "I need more time. I need a couple more days. I'm onto something huge. It'll definitely be worth it. I won't let you down. Be patient." His tone was quite whiny for an adult. He glanced at Cassidy, waving his index finger at her. "I just need a couple of days. You won't be sorry."

He turned to face Cassidy and poked the red button on his screen. "Oh, hi. Sorry about that. Deadlines."

"Good morning. What are you doing up so early?" She eyed the lanky guy with shaggy hair. She couldn't tell if he had rolled out of bed like that or whether rumpled was the look he was going for.

"I'm always up early. I wanted to catch you before you started your day. I was hoping you'd be able to update me on some of your property's history. It sounded interesting." He ran his hand through his dark hair.

She nodded slowly. "Come on in. Do you want some coffee?"

"Sure. Caffeine's always good." Xander followed her to the back.

She pulled two mugs out of the cabinet and filled the coffee maker with water. "What did you want to know?"

Seemingly bored by the conversation, Elvis climbed into his puffy bed under her desk, yawning widely before settling in for a nap. She hoped her stories of the property wouldn't make the reporter yawn, too. She needed some good publicity.

"What have the Weathermen been up to while they've been here? I was hoping you could give me some insight. Any weird requests or unusual activity? Any visitors you know about? My readers are interested in every little tidbit. They must have done or said something you remember."

"No, not really." She reached for the creamer and sugar packets. "They've been quiet guests. I don't think they've had any visitors, but I don't watch them every minute. I thought you wanted to talk about my property."

"I do. I have a couple of stories in flight right now. I still want to do the one about your place and the saloon you told me about. That would be something different, especially if I could get some good anecdotes. I like that you have concerts now at a place that has deep musical roots." He paused and glanced around the room like he was searching for something. "You sure there's nothing hinky going on with the band? They couldn't have gone this long without getting into some kind of trouble."

"Pretty sure." She wondered where this was going. *So much for talking about the history of the area and getting some free publicity.*

"I heard you were the one who found Johnny Storm. Any details you can share? Come on. A story like this will go viral. It'll get millions of eyes on the story and the mention of your place will be good for your business."

That's really not the kind of publicity I'm after.

"Not really. Elvis and I were out for a walk that morning." Cassidy stared at the reporter's deep brown eyes. "It's an active police investigation. The sheriff's office has the most current information. You should check in with them."

"Been there. Done that. They aren't talking except for their cheesy press release. Come on. I need something. Help a guy out. There's got to be more than you and your dog were on a morning walk." He gazed around the kitchen for a moment. "Got anything to eat around here?"

She rummaged through the snack drawer and held up two power bars.

"Thanks." He grabbed both and unwrapped one. After several bites and a slug of coffee, he continued, "Come on. You've been around them for a few days. They've got to have done something my readers would be interested in. I know they're not choir boys. They revel in rebellious behavior. It's been their schtick forever. It seems odd now that they're old enough to be grandfathers, and they're still trying to be relevant and hip."

"Can't think of anything unusual." She hoped her face didn't reveal the fib.

"Are you sure? You can't think of *one* thing my readers would love to know? They've been scrapping with each other for years. Half of them are bitter they weren't as popular or well-off as the others. You'd think by now they'd rest on their laurels and retire to someplace warm where they could show off their gold records and find a girlfriend or trophy wife, not go traipsing around to every small town on their nightly nostalgia tours. That's a lot of work for a bunch of old guys."

"Maybe they really like making music," Cassidy offered.

"More like making money. They do these festivals and cruises all the time. I can't believe they haven't caused you any trouble. They can't go three days without stirring something up. No fights? They didn't set fire to anything? They used to break guitars on stage until it got too expensive."

When Cassidy didn't respond, he changed the subject. "So, tell me about this place you have here. Where's the saloon? And how famous was it?"

"The saloon was a pretty big deal in its day. It burned down in the eighties. They said it was caused by a kitchen fire. I heard another story about a lightning strike. It was an old wooden building, and they allowed smoking indoors back then. Who knows what really happened? It was over in the woods that way." She pointed out the window. "You can still see what's left of the foundation. The woods and vegetation have kinda reclaimed it."

"Any plans to revive it? It's historic. You could probably have a nice sideline business going."

"Nah. I like hosting a variety of events. I know nothing about running a bar." Cassidy couldn't imagine rebuilding the saloon and opening a musical venue piled on top of all the other things she had to do to keep the place viable. She shook her head to clear her mind so she could focus on the reporter.

"You should think about it." He flashed a lopsided grin. "It'd be cool."

Closing her eyes for a few moments, she tried to stop the dull ache behind her eyes. "The property's been in my family for close to one hundred and fifty years. Before the interstate, the road out there was the main route to and from Nashville. The saloon hosted all kinds of performers. Some really big names stopped by on their travels. It was the place to catch all kinds of live music."

"Sounds like a great tourist attraction with all that history. I'm telling you, you really need to think about this as an expansion opportunity."

"It was before my time, and I'm not sure I can recreate what it was in its heyday. Times have changed. The closure was a big blow to my family. I don't think my grandfather ever recovered from the loss of his building and all the memorabilia."

"Was anyone hurt?" His eyes seemed to sparkle at the prospect of the tragedy and a good story.

She shook her head. "Thankfully, nobody got hurt. The fire destroyed a lot of history and memories. Like I said, the ruins are on the other side of the grotto and cave if you want to take a look. It's kinda spooky now, but it may make for some interesting pictures. Help yourself."

"I took the Crooked Road Tour out in southwestern Virginia once. It was really cool with all the heritage music stops. I liked the old drug store that had concerts at night. You should think about doing something with your family's legacy here."

"If I do, I'll give you an exclusive on the plans." She was growing weary of the conversation. "Do you want some more coffee?"

He took the last bite of the second power bar and shook his head. "I've got to meet someone in town. And I have to finish my stories. Let me know when your friends will be around. I'd like to talk to them about their memories of the saloon. They looked like a fun bunch."

"They are. They all grew up with my grandmother, and they've been so helpful to me since I've taken over the business. It's a lot different here than when I left." She sipped her coffee in hopes that would end the conversation.

"Where'd you go?"

"I ended up in Washington, DC, after college. I did a lot of social media marketing. When my grandmother died, I decided to come back here and see what I could do with this venue. The Pearly Girls jumped in to help. They're like family."

"Funny name. Is that your name for them?" He threw the wrappers into a small waste bin in the corner like he was shooting hoops. Of course, he missed the can. Both times.

"The four of them—Roxie, Ruthanne, Aileen, and Kate—lived near my grandmother, Evelyn Devere Jamison, here in the valley when they were all young. They did everything from church youth group to 4-H together since grade school. They grew up in the late fifties and sixties—you know, the era of Jackie Kennedy and Camelot. Their group wore their pearls as a fashion statement. Back then, people dressed for every occasion, and it became part of their signature look. Check them out next time you see them. They all wear pearls *with everything*. Back in high school, some guy called them the Pearly Girls, and the nickname stuck."

"Well, tell the gals to call me. I should be here for at least a few more days. Your place is nice. I hope it works out for you." He rose and dusted his hands on his jeans. "Thanks for breakfast. Text me if you think of anything related to the Weathermen. Right now, anything Johnny Storm is hot. I'm counting on you to be my inside source."

She raised both eyebrows, not sure she truly wanted the job.

The Pearly Girls had agreed to meet with Xander at the office later in the afternoon. Cassidy made sure they had coffee and tea and a plate of cookies before their discussion started. When they had settled in the conference room, she and Elvis slipped back into the office to review the event schedule for the next few months. She had three weddings, a family reunion, an author's book launch, and a holiday craft show slated for the upcoming months. Bookings were good, but she would really like to fill all the empty weekends. As she thought about ways to advertise, she heard peals of laughter coming through the walls. The giggles and cackles continued in waves. *They must be keeping each other entertained.*

Unable to concentrate, Cassidy padded back to the conference room and stood by the back wall. Xander alternated between munching on cookies and scribbling furiously while the gals took turns recounting stories about their escapades.

"We used to sneak in the back to see the shows. Evelyn's father would pretend not to see us and let us stay. Evelyn was Cassidy's grandmother. She had the best voice, but her parents wanted her to have nothing to do with the music business. Her dad would let us hang out there a lot as long as we didn't tell his wife or our mothers. They would have tanned our hides if they knew we were hanging out in a honky-tonk with the ruffians," Ruthanne said.

"Proper ladies didn't hang around in saloons or drinking establishments during those days. Kind of funny to think about now, since we all eventually grew up during the summer of free love and became hippies and free thinkers, and did all kinds of things that would have made our mothers blush. I'm sure my mother is still clutching her pearls and rolling over in her grave." Aileen's eyes gleamed with amusement as she tucked a strand of hair behind her ear.

"What doesn't kill you makes you stronger," Roxie agreed with a smile. "I've earned every one of these wrinkles as we've traveled on this journey. Think of all we've done and the people we've met. I wouldn't trade any of it. No regrets."

"Y'all remember the night we got to meet Willie Nelson and Waylon Jennings?" Ruthanne squealed. "I still have their autographs."

"You could have heard a pin drop when they walked through the front door. They ordered drinks and watched the band performing that night. Then they joined in after the intermission. What a night! Waylon and Willie, right here in Ivy Springs."

"Rumor has it they signed the bar before they left," Kate said.

"Oh, they weren't the only ones. You could see signatures from Dolly Parton, Tammy Wynette, Loretta Lynn, Patsy Cline, Glen Campbell, and Johnny Cash." Aileen bounced slightly in her seat. "I wish it hadn't burned down."

"Hank Williams was there a time or two before he died. I know his son popped in several times through the years." Kate reached for another iced cookie.

"Oh, he was. Junior signed his name in one of the stalls in the ladies' room," Roxie interjected with a mischievous half grin.

"And how would you know?" Kate raised one eyebrow.

A slight smile crept across Roxie's face. "I don't kiss and tell."

"So, ladies, how did the saloon catch fire? I'm sure its loss was devastating to the family and the community." Xander's pen was poised above a worn-looking red notebook.

"The sheriff at the time told Evelyn's father it was a lightning strike. There was always a lot of smoking and drinking going on at that place, so it could have been caused by all sorts of things," Kate said.

"It could have been a careless smoker or a kitchen fire. That's what everybody said at the time," Aileen added.

"You know how people talk." Ruthanne sipped her tea. "It seems everyone in town had an idea of what started the fire, including it being a group of women who didn't like their husbands boozing it up there. Yep, there was even a vigilante story floating around."

"They were bored, and they talked too much. It happened during a bad thunderstorm late one night," Roxie added. "Most of the building was gone before Cassidy's grandfather woke up and realized what was going on."

"There was nothing left by the time the volunteer fire department got here." Ruthanne patted at imaginary crumbs at the corner of her mouth with a cloth napkin.

Xander continued to scribble notes as the gals talked for almost an hour about the Ivy Springs Saloon and its famous patrons.

"Well, ladies, I could listen to you all day. You have some amazing stories. And it's so easy to see your love for this place. What do you say about going outside and snapping some photos with some of the magnificent views of the property? I have to head downtown at three thirty for another meeting."

"Of course. Turn us into celebrities." Ruthanne giggled while fluffing out her curly hair.

The Pearly Girls pulled out compacts and lipstick for quick touch-ups before following Xander out the door.

"And don't forget to tag Celebrations at Ivy Springs. I'll make sure we share your posts," Cassidy yelled to Xander's back.

He waved one arm in the air and followed the boomers toward the grotto.

Some free publicity couldn't hurt. Maybe I should do something to highlight the musical history of this place. I can't let this be known solely as the place where Johnny Storm died.

Cassidy headed back to her office to check emails as the gals wrapped up their session with Xander. About twenty minutes later, she noticed everything in the farmhouse was quiet. Too quiet.

A tap, tap, tap sounded in the front. Someone knocked again before she and Elvis could get to the door. *The girls must have headed out. That's odd. They usually say goodbye.*

She opened the front door to find Deputy Turner with his back to her. He turned toward her and nodded while finishing a call. "Good afternoon." He pocketed his phone. "I stopped by to see how things were going. Any more issues with the band?"

"Not really. Just the normal stuff. They live in a different world than I do. I'm glad I'm not in the limelight like they are. The press descended on us. That was a new experience I wasn't ready for. I've never seen so many reporters and TV trucks before." Cassidy paused when she heard a scratching sound under the porch.

Leaning over, she tried to catch a glimpse between the slats of anything moving. "I hope it's not a rat or raccoon or something. I'll have to get Levi to check it out."

Deputy Turner nodded and pressed his index finger to his lips as he pointed downward with the other hand. "Might be several large somethings."

Cassidy turned her head and stared downward, puzzled by his comment. When there were no other noises, she returned her attention to the deputy. "Okay. I'm glad the media's interest is starting to dwindle. I've been referring all the calls about Johnny Storm to the sheriff's office."

"I know." A slight smile crept across his mouth. "He was talking about how the volume of calls has increased since the Weathermen have been in town. He even had to take a turn answering the hotline."

Cassidy paused again at what sounded like a giggle and then more scratching sounds from below their feet. Then there was a faint hissing sound. The noises were odd. Not really animal-like. She dismissed the distraction and tried to focus on what the deputy was saying.

"So, nothing odd going on around here. I'm going to walk over to the buses and then take off. Let me—us—know if you need anything." He pulled his sunglasses out of his front pocket and trotted down the stairs. "You may want to check on the critters. I'm sure there are big hairy spiders down there, too."

Cassidy leaned over the railing when she heard an "Ewww" from somewhere nearby. It was hard to see through the decorative lattice. Chalking it up to a bird or a squirrel, she turned to go inside, and then the scraping noise got louder, and she thought she heard whispers. *That wasn't the breeze.*

Bounding down the steps, she hurried around the side to where a piece of lattice was lying in the grass. *I'm definitely going to have to get Levi to fix this. Someone's been messing around here. I hope it's not a vagrant. Where did Deputy Turner go?*

Then Aileen's head popped out from under the porch. "Hi, Cassidy." She wiggled out of the small opening. She stood and dusted herself off as Kate and Ruthanne scooted out behind her.

"You have a cobweb in your hair." Kate brushed it off Ruthanne.

"I hope that's all there is. I got the willies now thinking about all the bugs and snakes that could be down there. I'm going home to take a shower. I heard what the deputy said." Ruthanne wiped dirt off her dark slacks.

"What are you all doing?" Cassidy glanced at the women and the small hole under the porch they crawled out from.

"Nothing really." Kate shrugged. "You've got a loose piece of lattice. You might want to call Levi."

"Roxie left with that fun reporter. She was going to show him some pictures she has at home of the old saloon. And then the cute deputy drove up," Ruthanne admitted.

"We saw him walk up to the porch, and he was on the phone. We snuck around the building and ducked under the porch to see what we could find out." Aileen raked her hands through her hair, checking for more cobwebs or insects. "Maybe he would reveal something about the investigation."

"Was it worth it?" Cassidy asked.

Kate and Aileen shook their heads vehemently.

"He was talking to his sister. He's going to babysit her kids on Sunday afternoon," Ruthanne said. "So she and her husband can go out for their anniversary. That's nice of him."

"It was a quick call," Aileen agreed. "Chitchat. I was hoping for something police related. Or something about Johnny Storm."

"Can't win them all." Kate gave Cassidy a quick hug. "We'll keep our eyes and ears peeled in case we hear anything else. See you later."

"He *is* cute, and now we know he likes kids." Ruthanne wiggled her eyebrows at Cassidy.

The gals waved and slinked off toward the parking lot.

Cassidy rolled her eyes.

Those gals would do almost anything for the latest gossip.

LATE MONDAY EVENING

Cassidy's phone trilled. She rooted around Elvis and the lap blanket to find it. "Hello?" she said, seconds before the call went to voicemail.

"Hey, Cassidy, this is Deputy Turner. Sorry for the late hour. We're short-staffed tonight, and I'm not able to send a car by. Any chance you could go by the buses to see if Beau Cox is there? There was an altercation in town this evening, and we need to reach out to him."

"Sure. I'll see if he's on the property." Cassidy paused to slip on her shoes. "He's not staying with the band, but he's here a lot. I'll let you know what I find."

"Thanks. I owe you one." He disconnected before she could reply.

"Come on, Elvis. You can keep me company on my walk." She attached his leash and then rummaged through the kitchen junk drawer for her flashlight.

The pair picked their way over the path to the grotto and garden. A full moon provided almost enough light to navigate the path without her flashlight. The wind rustled the tree canopies as they headed down the cut-through to the meadow. An owl hooted in the distance, and Elvis froze to listen to the night sounds. Cassidy paused, too. The bird's hoot, and the moon peeking through the trees, created a spooky backdrop. Goosebumps traveled along her arms.

Cassidy's phone rang again. The sound seemed to echo through the darkness.

We're popular tonight. She didn't recognize the number. "Hello?"

"Uh, this is Karl. Karl Schultz. I need a ride back to your property."

"Hi, Karl. Where are you?"

"I'm at a place called Feeling Saucy. A gal named Tina gave me your number. The pizza's pretty good here. I finished eating and now I'm tired. I need a ride to your place, and I can't find an Uber. Stuff shuts down early around here. And it's too far to walk. I'm hoping you can help me out."

"I'll be there in a bit. Look for the white van with the Celebrations logo on the side. I'll pull up out front of the pizza parlor."

"Okay. White van. Celebrations. Got it." He hung up before she could ask any questions.

She let out a heavy sigh and did a quick lap around the buses. "Come on, Elvis. No sign of Beau or the rest of the band. No sign of anyone here. Let's get Karl."

Cassidy pulled out her phone and texted Deputy Turner with one hand as they walked back to the office.

> No one near the buses. Karl called and needs a ride. Heading to town now to pick him up.

She pocketed her phone before he could fire back a bossy reply. "I did my duty. I told him what was going on. I don't need him fussing at me right now. I'm in no mood for another lecture. Come on, Elvis, let's go for a ride and find out what's up with Karl."

After getting Elvis settled into the van's front seat, she sped out the main entrance and made it to the outskirts of town in record time. Missing the town's first red light, she got caught by the second one a few blocks later in front of the sheriff's office. The wait for green seemed to take forever.

As the van slowed in front of the restaurant, Elvis put two paws on the dashboard and scanned the empty sidewalk. The red neon Feeling Saucy sign flashed on and off. Patio lights twinkled at a slower beat creating a festive atmosphere even with all the empty tables. Several late-night diners sat inside behind the large plate-glass window. Scents of oregano and garlic wafted outside from the restaurant and drifted on the breeze. The smell of hot pizza made Cassidy's stomach growl.

Scanning the faces of the restaurant patrons, she didn't see Karl. She stared through the windshield at the empty sidewalk. After several minutes, she redialed Karl's number.

Four rings. No answer. No voicemail either.

Where is he?

Cassidy rolled down the windows an inch or so and shut off the engine. "You guard the van. I'll be right back." The little dog wedged his nose close to the opening in the passenger window, sniffing the pizza scents seeping in.

The tiny brass bells jingled when she opened the door. Sal's son, Pete, who was flattening dough on the counter near the door, called out a greeting. "Hey, Cass. How's it going? You want a pie or a slice?"

Cassidy smiled at the now grown-up kid she used to babysit. "It's good to see you. One of the guys from the festival called and said he needed a ride back to my place. You haven't seen him lately, have you? Like in the last fifteen minutes? Kind of a stocky guy with longish brown hair and a gray goatee."

"One of the guys from that band was here earlier. I know because he told everyone he was famous and played bass for the Weathermen. He wanted to give everyone an autograph." Pete rolled his eyes and continued to pound the dough with his fists. "He had a shiner, but he didn't want to talk about it. He was here for a long time. Might have been a bit tipsy." Pete lowered his voice. "I was hoping the food and the three Dr. Peppers would sober him. Rockers really do party hearty—even on Mondays."

A half smile crept up Cassidy's face. "They're a lot wilder than I'm used to, and they keep interesting schedules. Any idea where he went?"

"Nope. You didn't see him outside?" He looked toward the door.

She shook her head, and he wiped flour on his apron. "Hey, Jamal. Jamal!" he hollered.

A rangy teen stuck his head around the corner and popped out his earbuds.

"Do me a favor. Check the men's room and see if that stocky guy from the band is in there."

"The old guy that was sitting near the door?" Jamal asked. "The Dr. Pepper guy?"

When Pete nodded, the young man wiped his hands on a towel and then tossed it onto the counter. "Gotcha. Be back in a sec."

"Sorry to put y'all to all this trouble. I tried calling him, but there was no answer." Cassidy's stomach knotted. Something didn't seem right. Karl should be there.

Jamal popped his head around the corner again. "Nope. No one's back there. He's ghosting you."

"Thanks. If you see him, tell him Cassidy drove over to pick him up." Pete shook his head then turned to Cassidy. "Sorry for your trouble."

Jamal saluted with two fingers and returned to wiping tables.

"I'm going to check outside again. Thanks for all your help. Hopefully, I can find him before he gets into any more trouble. See you later," Cassidy said. "Tell your mom and dad hi for me."

"Come back soon. It's always good to see you."

Cassidy slipped behind the wheel of the van. "See anything worthwhile?" she asked Elvis. Without answering, he curled against the passenger seat. "Karl wasn't inside either. I wonder where he ended up. And Pete said he had a black eye. I'm curious to find out what happened to him. There's no telling with these guys."

She pulled out her phone and tried his number again.

Still no answer. Cassidy sank back in the seat. *Where did he go?* Pushing down the rising panic, she toyed with the idea of calling Beau.

A sharp knock on the driver's side window caused Elvis and Cassidy to jump. She let out a little squeal and Elvis growled. The pair stared at a disheveled Karl who leaned against the van. "Sorry. I couldn't find you," he mumbled. "Hope you haven't been waiting long."

"Come around." She moved Elvis into her lap.

Fumbling with the passenger door handle, it took Karl several tries to open it and even longer to step into the van. "Seat's up close." He fiddled with the lever to adjust it.

Because it's Elvis's seat. When he finally got settled, she asked, "Are you okay? What happened?"

He closed the door and slumped back in the seat. "It's been a long night. I want to go to sleep." Karl tilted his head back and closed his eyes.

"Okay. I'll get you to your bus." She started the engine and glanced at the aging rocker. "Seat belt."

Karl didn't move.

Cassidy cleared her throat, and Elvis snuggled into the space between her and the center console. "Karl, you need to put your seat belt on."

His eyes flew open. He sat up, reaching for the belt. "Oh yeah. I was resting my eyes. It's been a busy week and a long night. I'm ready to pack it in." Karl stared out the window and rubbed his eyes. "Jack, Beau, and I decided to come into town. We went to some wine bar and listened to a jazz quartet. They were pretty good. Then Jack and Beau wussed out. They wanted to go to bed. I told them I would find my own ride home. I wasn't ready to call it a night. I met some girls. We hung out for a while and had some drinks, but they took off when I was in the bathroom." He sank back in the seat again. "I thought there was a bar in town, but my phone said the nearest one was a lounge in some motel. I walked and walked and finally found this sleezy fifties-looking motel. There was a piano player and this woman who couldn't sing. Some entertainment. It was awful. I told them so."

Cassidy made a face and hoped he couldn't see her in the dark. She pulled away from the curb. "Then what happened?"

"They didn't appreciate the critique from a professional and famous musician. Can you believe that? I was a judge on *Sing Like You Mean It* for two whole seasons. I know what I'm talking about." His words were slurred. "That woman was terrible. She couldn't carry a tune, and she was overdramatic. No stage presence at all. No wonder she was singing in that dump. She thought she was some kind of opera singer. Just awful." He touched his cheek gingerly. "The pianist was good. But the chubby woman couldn't sing. I told her that." Karl absentmindedly stared out the window.

Cassidy rolled her eyes. *I'm sure that's what she wanted to hear.* "What happened?"

"She ran at me. Who knew a portly woman could be fast in a long dress and heels? She was on me like a dog on a bone. She kept hitting me with her song book. And no one did anything to stop her. Actually, the audience laughed and clapped. They kinda cheered her on. In ten seconds, she turned into some kind of lady wrestler." He paused, and Cassidy hoped he wasn't looking for sympathy. When she didn't say anything, he continued, "And when I went to shove her off me, she punched me in the eye. I mean, full-on roundhouse. Where did a chick learn to punch like that?" He rubbed his cheek again and winced.

"And how did you get back here?" Cassidy asked, hoping to change the subject.

"I walked. I'm definitely getting my exercise this trip. Ha, probably more than I've had in the last three years or so. Yep, I walked back, and the pizza place looked good, so I stopped in for some drinks and chow. When I was ready to head back, I couldn't get in touch with Beau or the others, so somebody gave me your number when I told them who I was and what I was doing in town. Can you believe some of them had never heard of the Weathermen? Do you guys have cable up here? It seems a bit backwoodsy. The younger generation knows nothing about classic music."

"Yes, we have cable and the internet." She swallowed the rest of her snarky comments as she pulled into her driveway and followed the maintenance road to the meadow, afraid to let Karl stumble through the woods in the dark. "There you go." She stopped next to the C-shape arrangement of dark buses. "Back home safely."

"Good. I need to call it a night." Karl climbed out of the van but stopped the door from closing. "Thanks for the help." He firmly shut the door after several failed attempts. As she backed up to head home, Elvis reclaimed his shotgun seat. Hopefully Karl would get some sleep and stay away from critiquing other singers in the future.

Returning to her spot in the parking lot, she reached to grab Elvis. "Come on, baby. It's time for us to turn in, too."

Before she could get her key in the door, her phone buzzed, sounding a lot louder than it probably was. Elvis took advantage of the distraction to sniff around the patio.

"Just a news alert." She frowned, pocketing the phone. "Come on, pup. I've had enough excitement. I don't need to know fog and a chance of rain are on the way."

Elvis let out a low wolf growl and lunged at a shadow. Cassidy tried to corral him and to pull him closer to her. Who was skulking around her home at this hour? If it was Karl, she might not be so polite this time. He had caused enough drama for one evening. What was he doing?

A flashlight beam directed at her face startled her, causing her to groan as she held up one hand in an attempt to block it. "What is going on?"

"Sorry." Deputy Turner lowered the flashlight. "I didn't mean to startle you. I saw your van pull in and spotted you two out here.

I thought I'd swing by for an update."

"Thanks for the heart attack." She tried to calm her heartbeat and the swooshing sound in her ears. "What can I do for you, Deputy?"

"I was checking on Karl and wanted to ask a few questions if you have a minute." Before she could answer, he continued, "So he called you for a ride this evening?"

"Did you talk to him tonight?" She glanced at the time on her phone.

He shook his head. "No. No answer at any of the buses."

"He called me right before I texted you. And he wasn't where he was supposed to be when I arrived, but we eventually connected. I dropped him off at his bus a few minutes ago."

"How was he? His speech, gait, et cetera?" he prodded.

"He'd definitely been drinking earlier this evening. He was talkative when he got in the van. He said he did a lot of walking to and from town tonight. And he stopped at Feeling Saucy for some late-night pizza."

"And Dr. Peppers," the deputy added. "Jamal told me. What else happened?"

Cassidy paused. It seemed odd Deputy Turner would respond so quickly. *I don't see his cruiser anywhere. How long has he been here? I just dropped Karl off. Isn't there anything else going on tonight at the sheriff's department? It seems like he's spending a lot of time around here.*

"There really wasn't much to it. Pizza parlor. No Karl. Then he showed up. We chatted, and I drove him here. End of a long night." Cassidy shrugged.

"What did he tell you?"

"That he, Beau, and Jack started off at a jazz thing at Planet of the Grapes, that new wine bar in town. When the other guys bowed out, he ended up at one of Sid Proctor's places out on the highway. It seems Karl had words with the entertainment there. He said something about providing the singer with a critique from a professional," she said.

"Oh, he did." The corner of the deputy's mouth twitched upward. "And the singer was not happy about his comments."

"Karl said she attacked him and punched him. He had a pretty good black eye as a souvenir." She tried not to giggle. The idea of some lady slugging the washed-up rocker was somewhat comical.

The deputy attempted to stifle a slight chuckle. "Karl hightailed it out of there after the piano player and the bartender dragged her off him. I answered the call from the motel manager. The singer admitted she probably lost her temper with him. Since Karl had left the motel bar and was nowhere to be found, I was trying to contact his manager earlier when I got your text. I stopped here to check on Karl and get his side of the story. I need to finish my report. He didn't answer my knock."

"He's probably sleeping it off." She cracked a smile, too. "He may not be all that willing to talk about what provoked his bruised eye. Or how the lady clobbered him. Probably not the best publicity move. I saw him head to his bus. Whether or not he stayed there, I have no idea."

"It's probably best he sleeps it off. I'll try to catch him in the morning. I need to know if he wants to press charges in the bar altercation. Have a good evening. I'll make sure you both get inside before I leave." He patted Elvis.

"Of course. Safety first. Good night." She locked the door behind her.

"Elvis, what an evening. How many days left of this concert tour? Remind me of all this if I have the big idea to schedule another one anytime soon. What else could go wrong?"

TUESDAY MORNING (NOT TOO EARLY)

Cassidy couldn't wait for the office coffee maker to finish her espresso. She was running on fumes this morning. Her talks with Karl and Deputy Zac had kept her up past her bedtime, and then replaying the encounters in her mind had her tossing and turning for hours. All the issues with the Weathermen kept piling up. Her thoughts on how to pull together something for Johnny Storm took over. *Maybe I should put up some kind of plaque or monument near the garden in his honor. What would be a nice tribute without looking like a crass marketing opportunity?*

Shaking off the thoughts, she spooned sugar into her coffee, creating a little whirlpool as she stirred.

Before she could begin on her routine tasks, the back door flew open. Ruthanne blew in. "Hi, Cassidy. I'm so glad you're here. Have you checked your email yet? I know you'll know exactly what to do. This has been the most fun and the biggest fiasco, all rolled into one." Ruthanne paused for a beat to load a pod in the coffee machine. "I need some more coffee."

I'm not sure she needs any more caffeine.

Cassidy smiled, pulling out her phone and scrolling through emails. Her smile faded as she began to read. "Oh, no. Oh, no. I hadn't seen this. Thanks. I probably need to think of something to say. A little warning from the town council might have been nice."

She sank down further in her chair and tried to keep the headache forming behind her eyes at bay. She reread the email again. Chuck Radcliff, the town manager, had called an emergency meeting to talk about Johnny's death and whether or not the Groovin' through the Decades concert needed to be canceled.

As the coffee maker sputtered steam, Ruthanne let out a huge sigh of relief. "I knew with all of your marketing and publicity experience you'd know what to do. Have you talked to the promoter or anyone else? Why would they want to cancel it? Nobody else seems to be in any danger."

Cassidy shook her head and opened a Word file to document some talking points. "I have about an hour and a half to get ready. I need to run upstairs and change, too. Somehow, I don't think my pink hoodie and jeans will project the best image, especially if I'm trying to calm some of the hotheads on the council and make a case for why the show must go on."

"I've already texted the gals. We'll be your posse and cheerleading squad. We've got your back, girl, especially if Sid 'Pro Quo' and his cronies start mouthing off. Roxie and Kate will give them their comeuppance. And one of us may elbow him if we need to shut him up." She balled her fist and punched her other hand several times for emphasis.

"Thanks. I can always use the support. I'm going to add some numbers to my notes here, and then I'll take Elvis upstairs with me. I think today calls for a business suit and heels." She tapped some more notes in her document as hundreds of disparate thoughts bounced around in her head like lottery ping-pong balls awaiting release from the cage.

After dashing off a draft of her ideas and giving it a quick proofread, she grabbed the pages off the printer and slid them into a Celebrations at Ivy Springs glossy folder. "See you at the meeting. I've got to go warm the curling iron."

"Don't forget the pearls. And wear bright colors," Ruthanne yelled after her. "Perfect for every occasion."

"I'll have to see what goes with the outfit. With all those baby boomers—no offense—staring at me, I want to make sure I look like I know what I'm doing. They always look at me like I'm twelve. I'm glad I have you all in my camp. Y'all don't act like the others who advocate for no change in this town. They act like technology and the internet are going to bring about the end of civilization."

"They're not as groovy as we are." Ruthanne raised both hands to the ceiling and danced around the desk. "We'll talk some sense into those old fogies—or at least shame them into keeping their snarky comments to themselves."

"See you at the meeting. Come on, Elvis." Cassidy sprinted up the stairs.

After a quick change of clothes and fluffing her hair, Cassidy put on more makeup and jewelry than normal. She found her Celebrations company pin and attached it to her lapel. "There, Elvis. I think that's as good as it's gonna get on short notice. Wish me luck. I have to go battle the good ol' boys. They can't cancel the concert. That would create even more chaos and massive refunds. I don't need that right now."

Cassidy made it to downtown Ivy Springs in record time. She came to a screeching halt outside of the government center housing the sheriff's office, jail, administrative building, and the library. Parking in the overflow lot, she hiked in her heels to the glass doors of the library. Her sneakers would have been better for navigating the hilly terrain, but the heels added more flare to her strong businesswoman attire.

Before reaching for the door, she took a deep breath to force herself to focus. *You are here to represent your business and all the excellent work your team does to bring tourist dollars to our little part of the Blue Ridge Mountains. Do not let them psych you out. You've got this.* She let out the air slowly and steeled herself for whatever happened next.

Cassidy wended her way around tables, bookshelves, and people until she got to the large conference room at the back. Finding an empty seat in the back row, she scanned the room of familiar faces. Beau Cox, Steve Owens, and Bianca Carpenter sat in the front row in front of the podium. Bianca tapped furiously on her phone. Like matching bookends, Sid "Pro Quo" Proctor and his cronies filled the first two rows on the other side. Sid was the crankiest business owner in town, and he was vocal about everything that wasn't his idea. The owner of two no-tell motels on the edge of town and a realty company spewed his views to anyone who would listen. Normally, his goal was to convince anyone who disagreed with him he was right. Cassidy pushed concerns of the bellicose neighbor out of her head as she could feel her blood pressure rising. *Focus, girl. You need to be able to make your case. Do not let him or his bunch get in your head.*

Before Cassidy had time to chat with anyone, Chuck Radcliff, Sheriff Asa Howell, and Marion Jones—the head librarian and town business council president—stepped behind the lectern. Chuck tapped his college ring on the microphone, and the electronic squeal made the audience squirm in their plastic chairs.

"Sorry about that," Chuck said. "Good morning, all. Thanks for showing up on such short notice. We've had some recent events in town causing some safety concerns, and we're meeting today to determine our next steps."

Cassidy caught movement out of the corner of her eye. The Pearly Girls filed in and stood against the wall near the exit. Ruthanne gave her a little finger wave.

"Y'all tell the folks out in the hall there are a few more seats on this side, and there's room for those who don't mind standing. Can you hear us out there?" Chuck said.

"Yes, we can," a male voice from outside in the corridor boomed.

"Alrighty then." Chuck cleared his throat and took a sip of water before he continued. "We are all saddened by the recent and tragic loss of Johnny Storm who was headlining the Groovin' through the Decades concert out at the Celebrations facility. We're thrilled Cassidy and her folks bring so many tourists to our little corner of the Blue Ridge Mountains, but Asa and I have had a lot of calls about the murder. Folks who haven't locked their doors for ages are on high alert. I'm going to let the sheriff speak in a minute with an update on his investigation. Then Marion will lead the open discussion about what our next steps should be. Our goal is to maintain law and order. And to keep Ivy Springs a safe place for everyone. Asa, take it away." The town manager stepped aside and scanned the faces in the room.

"Thank you, Chuck." The sheriff pulled the microphone closer to his mouth. "I don't know about not locking doors. Safety should be everyone's concern all the time. Be aware of your situation and make sure you're safe. We are deeply sorry for the family, friends, and fans of Johnny 'Storm' Mason who was murdered after a concert last Saturday. Our team is working around the clock, and we've brought in resources from the state police and other localities to assist. We want to assure everyone we're doing everything we can to wade through all the leads that will end in the arrest of the person responsible. If you know of anything helpful, I encourage you to call Crime Stoppers."

"Sheriff, do you think it's just one killer?" Xander yelled from the doorway. All eyes turned toward the reporter in the torn jeans, high tops, and an olive-green hoodie. He sported his signature tousled hairstyle.

"I'll take questions at the end." The sheriff grimaced. The last thing he probably wanted was a nosy reporter exacerbating the situation. "Right now, we're pursuing all leads, no matter how small they seem. And I'm not going to comment on the suspects or the path of our investigation. But we promise to update the public as soon as we have a break in the case. For now, I'd like to reassure the good people of Ivy Springs that there doesn't seem to be an ongoing threat. We're focusing on his lifestyle. The team thinks his murder was related to that."

"What does *that* mean?" Xander interrupted.

Marion and Chuck glared at the reporter. "We'll take questions at the end," the sheriff repeated as he stepped to the other side of the lectern to make way for Marion to address the room.

Marion cleared her throat and adjusted her glasses attached to a beaded chain around her neck. "Good morning. I'm Marion Jones, head librarian and business council president. And like our town manager said, this part of the discussion is to brainstorm our next steps for the good of our community. Murder and crime can damage the good reputation we've worked so hard to create. I'd like to open the floor to discussion. Please raise your hand, and I'll call on you." She adjusted her glasses again and scanned the audience.

Sid "Pro Quo" jumped to his feet, waving one arm in the air.

"Yes, Sid." Marion nodded with a barely contained scowl. "Go ahead and get us started."

"This concert has brought thousands of folks to our area. We've had to increase police activity and trash pickup. What is all this really costing us? And is it really worth it?" He gazed around the room, sank back in his chair, and crossed his arms over his chest. "I haven't seen a rise in motel guests as a result of all this. And as a taxpayer, I'm not too keen on footing the bill."

"It's because nobody wants to stay in your rattrap motels. The days of drive-up motels and roadside attractions are long gone. Welcome to the twenty-first century," someone yelled from outside the door.

"Who said that?" Sid demanded, straining to see.

When no one responded, he jumped to his feet and tried to climb over those seated in his row. "Who has a problem with my quality motels? My places are a fixture in these parts."

"No one." Marion banged her gavel on the lectern. "Sit down, Sid. And for the rest of you, we will be civil, or I'll ask the sheriff to escort you out. Now, are there any more ideas?"

Steve Owens rose. "Yes, ma'am." Marion pointed to the concert promoter.

He cleared his throat. "Hello. I'm Steve Owens from Way Cool Entertainment. We're responsible for the Groovin' through the Decades concert series. When we negotiated with the venue and the town, we included additional security and funds for facilities, trash pickup, and traffic control. Those services were paid for through ticket sales. This event didn't use town resources to fund the support and services provided. The town actually made money from the ticket sales from the way the contract was structured."

Sal Russo leaped to his feet. "And the concertgoers have increased my food sales. It's drawing a lot of people to town, and I appreciate it. The concerts have definitely helped my bottom line."

"Sid's bitter that guests won't stay in his fleabag motels." Whoever was in the hallway apparently wasn't a fan of Sid or his motels.

Sid harumphed and looked over his shoulder at the people outside the conference room.

"Order." Marion turned her head toward the doorway and stared over her glasses. "Whoever said that, do you want to come up front and make a statement?" There was no response from the hallway. "I thought not. I am serious about being civil here. We have rules and standards. If this continues, you will be removed from the meeting."

"Excuse me," Sid interrupted. "Don't I get a rebuttal?"

"Go ahead." A crimson flush gave away Marion's frustration. "Sid?"

The lanky businessman with the comb-over stood. "I run quality, affordable vacation and short-term rentals. I don't agree with the comment that was lobbed at me. My business is doing fine with or without Cassidy's events." He plopped himself down in his seat and crossed his arms over his wrinkled navy blazer. "And I was here long before she took over that place. And I'll be here long after she gets bored and moves back to DC."

Aileen raised her hand to speak. "Good morning, everyone. It's great to see you. I've lived here all my life. We all remember the boom times and the busts. Cassidy works round the clock to plan public and private events to support our community. And if you all think back to the early 2000s, a lot of downtowns were boarded up and people were leaving in droves. The creativity of our council and townsfolk helped us build a community people want to visit. And we have to remember we all depend on tourist dollars. Look at all the places in town that people want to visit. Why do you want to cut off that revenue stream? Raise your hand if you profited from these concerts."

Applause and cheers rose.

When the noise settled to a dull roar, Marion asked, "Any more comments or thoughts?" She paused to look at the faces in front of her. "Well then, by show of hands, who thinks we should pause the music festival out of caution for the safety of our community?"

A handful of arms shot in the air. Marion took a moment to count. Sid Proctor waved his arm around and then turned in his seat to see who else agreed with him.

"Okay. Who thinks the shows should continue as scheduled?" Marion asked.

Three-quarters of the room stood and cheered. Marion's eyes narrowed to mere slits.

"Okay, okay. We definitely heard you." Chuck moved back behind the podium. "The show goes on. Thank you all for coming out. Are there any questions for any of us before we close this out?"

"Me! I have questions." Xander pushed his way into the room from the hallway.

The shuffle of people gathering their things drowned out Xander's rapid-fire questions. As the room emptied, Cassidy watched the reporter rush the lectern to corner Chuck and Asa.

Flipping her purse strap over her shoulder, Cassidy moved with the crowd toward the exit. She quickened her pace, trying to catch the Pearly Girls. On her way out, Cassidy received a host of thanks and shoulder pats. The attention made her feel warm inside. Sometimes it seemed no one noticed all her efforts, and it really *was* her intention to bring visitors to the area who would spend money and enjoy the mountains and the other amenities as much as she did.

Without seeing any of the Pearly Girls on her way out, she hiked back to the van and kicked off the shoes pinching her toes. Her stomach rumbled, reminding her it was lunchtime. She detoured into town and found a parking spot on a side street next to Feeling Saucy. Pizza was what was needed to celebrate the little victory today. Cancellation of the concerts would have blown a crater in her bottom line. She was counting on that money to finance some improvements to the property this fall. *I'm glad we dodged that bullet.*

Breathing a sigh of relief, she opened the restaurant's glass door.

"Hey, Cassidy. Great work. And thanks for all you do. What can I get you?" Sal motioned for her to choose a table. "I appreciate all of the businesses in town who supported me and make this a great place to live."

She settled in a red vinyl booth in the corner. "I think I'll have two slices of sausage and a Coke. You make the best pizza." Her phone pinged, alerting her that perfect weather for the next three days was on its way.

"It'll be there in a flash." The meatball of a man with the white apron disappeared into the kitchen. Cassidy skimmed her email, filled with several thank-you notes from local business folks. A dark shadow crossed her table, causing her to look up.

Deputy Turner stood next to the table. "Hello. You got some good news at the meeting. Mind if I join you?"

She nodded and he slid into the seat across from her, setting his uniform hat on the bench next to him.

Cassidy hoped she didn't look surprised at his attempt at friendliness. Usually, he was prodding for information or making some surly comment instead of starting a conversation. "How are things going?"

"I'm sure you heard the sheriff's update. We've been working round the clock on the Johnny Storm murder. The sheriff is putting a lot of resources on this."

When Sal approached with Cassidy's order, he greeted the deputy. "Hi. Good to see you, sir. What can I get for you?"

"Thought I'd get a jump on lunch before the crowd rolled in. I'll have a small pie with everything and a root beer."

"One junk pizza coming up. Be back in a sec." Sal pressed the round tray against his side and disappeared in the back.

The deputy encouraged Cassidy to eat her pizza before it grew cold.

Cassidy stared into the deputy's deep green eyes, not knowing what to think of this kinder, friendlier side of the man. *Who is this guy and what does he want? I usually only get 'tude from Deputy Zac. He must be looking for something. We've never had a friendly convo before. Or lunch for that matter. Maybe we're turning over a new leaf.*

Taking a bite and chewing slowly, she formulated what she wanted to say. Perhaps, if he was in a chatty mood, this could be a great opportunity to get some information. She lowered her voice even though no one was near enough to hear their conversation. "So is it true you're focusing on the people in Johnny Storm's life and not someone from town or a random serial killer running around on the loose?"

"It was only one murder, so no, no serial killer." His tone shifted slightly. "And yes, we're focusing on his past personal and business relationships. There are several suspects with motives. It takes a while to sift through all the interviews and calls we've had. The tipline has been on fire."

Cassidy took a bite of her pizza. Peeking through her eyelashes, she caught him staring at her. She grabbed her napkin and wiped her lips, hoping there was no sauce on her face.

He looked away and a slight flush reddened his cheeks. "We have to take everything seriously until we can discount it. A murder investigation is not like what you see on TV. It is a long and methodical process."

"I feel better knowing there's not a murderer out there stalking his next victim, especially since I live so close to where it happened. I feel like I'm always looking over my shoulder."

"The killer's still running around out there. Everyone needs to be vigilant." His words dampened her sense of relief.

Cassidy pursed her lips. "I know, but it's kinda nice to know it probably isn't a neighbor or a friend. I couldn't think of any reasons why a townie would want him dead. Most who are old enough to remember the band were starstruck they were here in Ivy Springs."

Sal edged to the table and put the deputy's pizza and drink in front of him. "Here you go. Youse guys let me know if you need anything else. I'll be in the back prepping for the lunchtime rush. Enjoy your food." Sal winked then hustled toward the kitchen.

The deputy nodded and dug into his meal. The conversation faded as they ate. Between bites, Cassidy stole glances at the attractive deputy.

Not able to let go of the notion of pumping the deputy for information, Cassidy tried another angle. "Any idea on the murder weapon? I heard the investigators talking about a garrote. And I saw the wire around his neck that awful morning." She wrinkled her nose and took a sip of her drink.

"We found a drumstick in your flower bed with some indentations in it and another in the pond with the body."

"Indentations?"

He picked up a fork and held it in front of him, pretending to wrap something around it. Then he picked up a spoon and held it in the opposite hand. "There's a handle on each end." He wiggled the spoon and fork. "When they used it for leverage to choke someone, the wire or the string cut into the wood of the drumstick. Hence the indentations." He pretended to pull tightly on his imaginary weapon and made a scrunched-up face.

"The wire was a guitar string, right?" When he nodded, she pressed further. "Do you think the materials used were chosen on purpose?"

"Could be," he mumbled around a mouthful of pizza. "They may belong to the killer, or they could have been used to frame someone." He shrugged his shoulders, swallowed, and then took another bite of his overloaded pizza.

Cassidy's eyes widened. "Sounds awful either way. Do you think it was planned like the setup you mentioned? Or do you think it was random like someone grabbed things that were handy in the heat of the moment to make a weapon?"

Realizing he may suspect she was still investigating on her own she avoided mentioning she had researched the history of the garrote, if for no other reason than to stave off another lecture.

He furrowed his brows. "It probably took some time to make the device, so I don't think it was something that happened on a whim. It also takes a bit of strength to wrap and bend a thick guitar string."

"So, it was probably someone with the band who had access to wires and drumsticks," she whispered, leaning forward. *That should let Roxie off the hook.*

Deputy Turner stared intently at her for a few seconds. "By the angle, it probably was someone taller than him. They'd have to be able to subdue the victim and choke them with a guitar string, even using a garrote. There was no indication the body was dragged to your garden. The medical examiner is pretty certain it happened there. And there were no signs on the body that he had been bound or tied. It looks like the killer attacked him in your garden. We'll know more when the autopsy's completed. And it makes sense the victim probably knew his killer."

A tingle shot through Cassidy. Dirk had drumsticks. Jack, Karl, and even Johnny had access to guitar strings. *I guess anyone with the band could get hold of equipment easily. They are looking at his acquaintances.* On the one hand, she was relieved it wasn't someone she knew and trusted, but now she would constantly be looking over her shoulder while the band was on her property. "Drumsticks and guitar strings."

"Or a wire," he corrected.

Too late. You slipped. You already said it was a guitar string. Beau mentioned it, too.

Cassidy decided silence was the best policy before she dug a deeper hole for herself with the observant deputy.

He didn't press for more from her or accuse her of doing what he had repeatedly told her not to do—investigate on her own. "Keep an eye out and call us if anything looks weird or you have any more dustups."

"The band members definitely do lead more hectic lives than I'm used to." Cassidy glanced across the table. She racked her brain for something to keep the conversation going without making it look like she was prying for information. "So, what do you do for fun when you're not chasing the bad guys?"

He returned her stare.

I hope I didn't just cross a line. This is awkward. With my luck, I just killed the gabby thing we had going.

He recovered quickly from his surprised look. "I run, and I referee lacrosse and football when I can. My work schedule doesn't leave a lot of free time." He took a swig of his drink and set the plastic cup down with a thud. "What do you do for fun?"

"Me?" A flush rushed to her cheeks. "I grew up here, but I moved away for college and my first job. A lot has changed, and some things never do. My grandma died, and I took over her business, so I haven't had a lot of free time either. I like hiking and kayaking. And I love hanging out with Elvis. And music. I love all kinds of music."

"You stay busy. Your family owned the legendary saloon everyone talks about." He pushed his plate away.

She nodded. A light went on for Cassidy. He knew more about her than she realized. "That's before my time, but yes, the remnants of the old place are still there. I hike back there sometimes. It's near the cave on the property."

"Sounds like it was a popular place during its day. Asa has a lot of tall tales from his honky-tonk days."

"Where did you grow up?"

"Waynesboro. After college, I joined the Marines. The War on Terror was in high gear, and I did three tours in Afghanistan and Iraq as an MP. When I got out, I took a job with the Charlottesville PD."

"How did you end up here?" she asked.

"There was an opening. Not much was happening careerwise in C-ville. All the next-level promotions were filled by guys who weren't going anywhere anytime soon." He stared at Cassidy for a beat. "When I interviewed with Sheriff Howell, he kept telling me it was a much smaller department, but I could do lots of different things. I was kinda pigeonholed in the other job. And here there's a path to moving into a detective slot."

"That's good. It's a nice area. Do you live here? I mean, I never see you around town." Heat rose in her face the longer he stared at her. *I hope he doesn't think I'm stalking him. It was just an observation. It's a small town. And I'm curious.*

"Outside of town on Route 156. I rent an apartment over a lady's garage. She's widowed and retired and doesn't mind having a police car in the driveway."

Cassidy grinned. Having a cop cruiser in your front driveway could definitely be considered a good thing to ward off criminals. "The people are friendly here, and there're lots of things to do. It's mountain country."

"Your cave sounds cool. You'll have to give me a tour of it sometime."

The butterflies inside her awakened and bounced around.

She nodded, but before she could comment, he pulled out his wallet as Sal approached.

"No charge. We're celebrating the music festival." Sal waved off his attempt to pay.

"I can't let you do that," Cassidy and the deputy said in unison.

"Then leave a tip. A big tip. A giant tip. I'm celebrating today and looking forward to more concerts and events. See, I have the poster in the window." He cracked a smile and shuffled toward the back.

"Thanks for lunch." Zac stood, grabbing his hat off the bench. "It was nice to sit at a table for a change. I usually eat in the cruiser or at my desk." He dropped money on the table to cover his meal. "See you around."

She stared at the back of his tall frame in his black uniform. The polyester shirt stretched across his back and arms. He had the physique of a weight lifter—broad shoulders and a cinched waist. She shook off the weird feeling and added more money to the pile on the table.

"Thanks, Sal," she called as she hurried out the door. The deputy's cruiser pulled away from the curb. When he passed, he saluted with two fingers. She returned a quick wave and hurried to the van. She needed to get back and do some more research now that she had a new focus.

17

TUESDAY EVENING

Cassidy spent the afternoon searching the internet for anything remotely related to Johnny Storm's death. However, she did get a bit distracted for a few minutes on the Ivy Springs Sheriff's Office web page, which led to some poking around. According to the staff page, Deputy Turner ran track and played football, soccer, and lacrosse in high school and college. He had a whole list of professional commendations and certifications in law enforcement. Not learning anything new about the deputy, she searched for him on social media. *Figures. He's flying under the radar with no social media presence except LinkedIn, and he hasn't posted anything there in a year.*

After a couple more Google searches, she found several online articles about his high school accomplishments and sports awards and one about his Marine Corps promotion. She smiled at the younger pictures of him in a football jersey and his dress blues. Lately, he'd made attempts at being friendlier, but he always reverted back to his all-business, scowling self. Sometimes, he was hard to read.

Chiding herself for spending so much time checking out the deputy, she did another search for the Weathermen. "Now that's interesting." Elvis lifted his head. When he didn't see any snacks, he rolled over in his bed. "Well, *I* think it's worth noting." It seemed at the beginning, there was another bandmate, Phillip Peters. He had multiple stints in rehab, and the rest of the band voted him out in 1975. He spent most of his time bad-mouthing the rest of the guys. "Maybe that could be a motive? And he kinda looks familiar. Have I seen him recently?" Her brain replayed memories of the recent concerts and people she talked to.

"Probably not." Roxie blew in, dropping a shopping bag and her green Michael Kors purse onto the other desk.

"Hey, I didn't even hear you come in. How are you?"

"Good. And I'm stealthy. Just looking for a couple of things. I'm having drinks with my book club in town in a bit." Roxie's smile almost resembled the Grinch's in the cartoon classic.

"Why don't you think I could've seen Phillip Peters recently? He looks a little familiar, but I can't place him."

"Keep researching. He died in the early eighties from a drug overdose. Rumor has it he was blackmailing someone in the record industry. He had been blackballed and was sponging off anyone who would take him in. He fell hard. Ruthanne liked him, and she was disappointed about how it all turned out. Another sad rock-and-roll tale."

"Tragic. Rats. I thought I might have a lead to check if he was skulking around town. Another guy affiliated with the band also overdosed..." Cassidy skimmed through her notes. "One Eddie Merritt." She skimmed her notes.

"Yep," Roxie said. "He took Phillip Peters's place. It was short-lived. And it was an interesting time in the seventies and eighties. There were a lot of drugs, and AIDS had arrived on the scene. Kind of scary. Anyway, the band decided to stick with Johnny, Jack, Karl, and Dirk after that. Hey, a foursome worked for the Beatles and the Monkees. Sorry to burst your bubble. You'll have to find some new leads." Roxie pulled out a sketchbook from a pile on her desk. "I wanted to work on some designs tonight. TTFN. See you tomorrow." She breezed out the front with a wave over her shoulder.

"Well, Elvis. I guess it's back to the old drawing board."

The front door opened. Elvis yipped and tore into the front room.

"You back already? Did you forget something?" Cassidy followed the dog's path.

"Uh, no." In the foyer stood the concert promoter, Steve Owens, with his trusty sidekick, Bianca, behind him, engrossed in whatever was on her phone.

"So sorry, I thought you were my colleague. She left seconds ago. How can I help you?"

"Didn't see her." Bianca didn't even lift her head. Steve rolled his eyes at his young assistant.

"Just wanted to touch base. I'm glad the town decided not to shut us down. I brought you the updated schedule." He turned toward Bianca.

She finally glanced up and shifted around for something in her messenger bag. She pulled out several loose sheets of paper and handed them to Cassidy. "Here you go. Hot off the printer. Well, sort of."

"Thanks." Cassidy flipped through the pages. "It doesn't look like there were too many changes."

"Nope. We had to switch days for two of the bands. One of them had some bus trouble in Ohio. Glad it's nothing major. Everything good on your end?" Steve checked his watch.

Cassidy nodded. "We're ready to go and glad we get to stick to the plan. Sometimes, the traditional factions in town like to flex their muscle and lodge protests about any kind of progress. I'm grateful they were outvoted this time."

"Well, keep up what you're doing. You have a lovely place here. Even with the, uh, unpleasantness. I'd like to talk to you about doing something else next summer if you're interested. I'll call you in a couple of weeks to talk about another tour. Your ticket sales were good."

"Sounds like a plan." A jolt of excitement bounced around inside, turning into butterflies in the pit of Cassidy's stomach. *Yes! Just what I need to boost revenues. And it keeps the music connection to the past alive and well. My grandfather would have liked that. See, I can do traditions with a modern twist!*

As the promoter plunked a pair of aviator glasses on his nose, Cassidy decided to probe for some information. "Any word from the sheriff or the medical examiner about Johnny Storm?"

"Nope." He shook his head and strode toward the door with Bianca following along in his wake. "But I doubt I'd get any updates. Nothing other than that he was strangled in your garden. I heard his ex-wives and family members are all bugging Beau about the will. Mr. Storm seems to have socked away a pretty nice nest egg. And the creditors are calling, too. Even after Johnny's death, Beau still has his hands full cleaning up all Johnny's dirty work."

A moment before his hand turned the doorknob, Cassidy stopped him. "What dirty work?"

Bianca giggled, then blushed when Steve glared at her. "Let's say Johnny had no restraint. If he saw something he wanted, he went after it. He bought anything and everything. He was pretty generous, too. He'd buy lavish gifts and take extravagant trips with entourages. And Johnny never worried about consequences or costs. He kept Beau and his accountants busy paying for excesses and tidying publicity messes he always managed to create. My guess is the estate isn't as large as everyone thinks. When the dust settles and all the bills are paid, what's left may not be worth fighting over. Who knows? We'll have to wait and see how all this shakes out. I'm sure the tabloids will have a field day. See you around. Reach out to Bianca if you need us." He turned and his magenta-haired assistant followed him to the porch.

Cassidy tapped the tip of her index finger to her chin. "Interesting." She zipped in the back and added the new factoids about Johnny to her spreadsheet.

Standing and stretching, Cassidy glanced at the schedule Bianca had provided. "No concert tonight. We're going to have to entertain ourselves. Come on. Let's see what we can scrounge up for dinner."

Elvis scurried to the back steps to be admitted into the residence. Flipping off the downstairs lights, Cassidy grabbed her laptop and followed the dog upstairs. "Another easy commute." She patted the Chihuahua mix on the head.

Not finding a wide variety of dinner options, she looked at the little dog. "Nothing's grabbing me here. Wanna see what we can find in town?" Elvis yipped and ran to the door as she flipped her purse strap over her shoulder.

Cassidy parked the van on a side street a couple of blocks from the main drag, and the pair hopped out. "Elvis, what do you feel like for dinner? Ivy Springs is a happening place tonight."

The small dog strode along the block like he was a boss with his head held high and a determined step. He followed the scents from the nearby eateries and paused outside a wrought iron fence surrounding the patio for Meat and Greet, a bistro and hangout for the hip crowd in the valley.

"You like the name, huh? And you're also trying to tell me I need to mingle more. You and the Pearly Girls. Okay, let's find a seat." The pair located a black metal table near the edge of the sidewalk where they could people watch.

Before Cassidy had settled herself on the cold metal chair, the waiter materialized and handed her a menu. "Hi, I'm Tim. Can I get you one of our drink specials this evening?"

"Hi." She glanced at the menu. "I think I'll have your barbecue slider plate with iced tea."

"Are you okay with the fusion coleslaw, baked beans, and hush puppies that come with it?" Tim hadn't even bothered to write down her order.

"No coleslaw. But everything else is fine."

"Be right back with it and a treat for your friend here." Tim pivoted on his heel and quickly disappeared.

Elvis's ears perked at the magic word, and Cassidy patted him on the head. She scrolled through her emails and social media feeds while her dog lay facing the fencing, so he could get a good view of anyone passing by.

The Chihuahua mix let off a string of yips and danced at the edge of the patio. He was small enough to squeeze his head between the wrought iron bars. Cassidy looked up as Karl dodged people on the nearby sidewalk. He peered over in her direction, then abruptly turned and jaywalked across the street. "That was odd," she said aloud.

"Everything okay?" Tim set her drink and plate in front of her.

"Yes, I thought I saw someone I knew, but maybe it wasn't him. Thanks."

"Be careful. That plate's hot. I'll be back in a few to check on both of you." He bent over and placed a bowl of water next to Elvis, handing him a bone-shaped treat.

Cassidy dug into her meal. It had the right mix of savory and sweet in the barbecue sauce. Mmmm. They did barbecue right.

Movement across the street caught her eye. Karl paced in front of the gift shop and stopped next to a tall blue statue of a chubby bear with a hat. Deputy Turner approached and said something to the bass player. Karl scowled and waved his arms around as Deputy Turner continued to talk.

Cassidy wished she were closer so she could hear what they were saying.

Then Karl threw his hands in the air and stomped off. The deputy watched but didn't follow. He eventually blended in with the crowd headed in the opposite direction.

That was interesting. I'd really like to know what was said. I wonder if the deputy asked him about his altercation and souvenir black eye.

Shaking off the mysterious encounter, Cassidy finished her meal and handed Tim her debit card when he returned with the bill.

"I hope everything was good," he said, looking at her empty plate. The waiter scanned her card on a handheld device and placed her card and receipt next to her. "Come back and see us."

"It was very good. Thanks."

Not ready to head home yet, Cassidy led Elvis across the street to the gift shop. She picked up the dog and wandered in. Tiny brass bells on the door jingled to announce her entrance. Berry and vanilla scents tickled her nose. The shop was filled with every type of gift imaginable, and all the bright colors and shelves were a bit overwhelming to the senses. So much to look at.

"Welcome to Bearly Collectibles." A woman with long silver curls waved to her. "We've got every kind of gift you could possibly want. Holler if you need any help. Cute dog."

"Thanks. This is Elvis. I'm Cassidy Jamison. I own Celebrations at Ivy Springs up the road."

"I love your place. I went to a friend's wedding there last spring. What a magnificent view. I'm Deannie, by the way."

"All the bears are great. I saw one of my guests come by here a few minutes ago, and I decided to hop in and check out your store." Cassidy browsed a glass shelf full of stuffed bears.

"Kind of short, stocky guy with long hair?" Deannie wrinkled her nose.

"That's him. He's one of the performers from the concert tour at my place."

"I know. He told me at least three times. He wanted to buy Zeke." Deannie pointed toward the large glass window.

Cassidy stared out the window and furrowed her brows.

A slight giggle slipped from Deannie. "Zeke's my enormous bear out front. He's kinda my mascot for the store. Anyway, the guy kept telling me about his bear collection at home and how Zeke would be perfect for his man cave. He spent twenty minutes trying to convince me. I don't care what band he plays with; Zeke's not for sale. That guy was kinda pushy. I'm glad he finally got the message and moved on."

"Glad it all worked out. Zeke looks perfect out front."

"Look around and let me know if I can help with anything. A lot of the items are made by local artisans." Deannie moved behind the front counter.

Cassidy and Elvis browsed several displays and stopped at the one full of Christmas ornaments. As they moved to the funny card rack, a muffled crash sent Deannie flying toward the front door. "What do you think you're doing?" she yelled, yanking the door open.

Cassidy clutched the wiggly Elvis closer to her and rushed out behind Deannie who waggled a finger at Karl. "I told you Zeke wasn't for sale. He better not be broken." The five-foot wooden statue lay on its side across the sidewalk.

"I was just looking at him. He must have fallen over. Maybe it was the wind. This is kinda dangerous. It could have hurt someone. This is a hazard. Hey, you could sell it to me, and I'll take care of it for you."

Deannie's cheeks flushed red. "I told you before. He's not for sale. He's part of my store. My branding!" The petite woman leaned over and hoisted the bear back up to a standing position. Then she circled the statue to assess any damage.

Deputy Turner navigated his way through the growing crowd spilling off the sidewalk into the street. "Folks, we can't block the road. I need for you all to move back before we impede traffic."

"I didn't damage your bear. He's fit as a fiddle." Karl pulled out his wallet. "Here's thirty-three bucks for your trouble. Sorry to bother you." He pressed the money into Deannie's hand and disappeared in the crowd.

"Everything okay here?" Deputy Turner turned to watch Karl.

"It is now. Zeke had a little spill, but I don't think he's any worse for wear." Deannie patted the big blue bear.

"Good." The deputy nodded at Cassidy and made his way along the sidewalk to where Karl had retreated a few seconds before.

"Bye." Cassidy waved to Deannie and hugged Elvis closer to her as she headed for the van.

Once settled inside, she snapped her seat belt in place. Elvis had claimed his spot in the passenger seat. "Well, thanks for being a fun dinner date. That whole Karl thing was a little weird, wasn't it? I wonder if the deputy caught up with him?"

Not interested in the deputy, Karl, or Zeke the Bear, Elvis turned around twice in the seat and plopped down for a quick nap.

Cassidy pressed the accelerator, making a beeline for home and her kitchen table. She spent the rest of the evening poring over fan pages and blogs about the Weathermen. Some resulted in bits of information that might be useful. She added the new items and Karl's bear adventure to her spreadsheet.

A little after ten, Elvis yipped and bolted to the door.

She counted off her key findings in her head as they descended the back stairs. "Okay, okay. We both need a break. I have way too many thoughts bouncing around in my head. Johnny and Jack did well for themselves. Between the two of them, they wrote all the bigger hits the band had. I couldn't find out much on Dirk. He seemed to fly under the radar and didn't appear on the gossip sites. Karl had financial and addiction problems. Phillip and Eddie are out of the picture. I wonder about Beau, but he seems devoted to the band. He's always taking care of the guys. Maybe it could be one of the roadies or security guys? I'm going to have to find some way to talk to them and get their names. Might mean more walks for us!"

When he heard one of his favorite words, the little dog's ears shot upward, and he double-timed his steps.

"I'll take that as agreement." She clipped on Elvis's leash, and the pair headed outside toward the grotto. Fanning her phone's flashlight ahead of them, she shuddered when she got a glimpse of the koi pond. This part of the property used to be her favorite, but lately, it brought back gruesome memories. Shadows bounced around and created an eerie setting, making her shiver despite the warm evening. Somehow, her serenity garden was anything but peaceful. The flitting shadows spooked her now.

Easing Elvis away from the pond, the little dog took the hint and trotted toward the rocky area near the cave. Sniffing the air, Elvis tugged and tried to pull her toward the opening. As they got closer, the coolness exuded by the cave caressed her skin, causing goose bumps to erupt over her arms. The inky darkness and the shape of the cave made the evening sounds bounce around and echo. It was hard to tell where the noise was coming from. Hugging both arms around herself, she tried to shake off the chill and the freaky feeling she was being watched. Suddenly, all of Deputy Turner's warnings flooded into her consciousness. "Okay, Elvis. Time to go."

The little dog strained against his collar and pulled closer to the mouth of the cave.

"Come on." Cassidy tried to keep her voice from shaking.

Cassidy heard a moan. She paused and listened. Chalking it up to a tree frog, she took a couple of steps, but stopped when she heard louder moans coming from the cave. This time Elvis growled and lunged toward the opening.

A faint, "Help...help me," danced on the evening breeze. She scooped Elvis into her arms and took a couple of steps closer.

"Hey, who's in there?" she yelled.

"I need help. I'm back here. Come and help me."

Cassidy shined the beam from her phone around until she spotted a pile of something looking like denim and clothing near the side wall.

"I need an ambulance. You gotta come help me. Don't leave me here." The figure tried to sit but fell back in a heap. Deputy Turner's warnings about being careful got louder and louder in Cassidy's head.

"I'll call for help. Stay still." She backed out of the cave.

The echoes from the moaning grew. *All that's missing is the scary horror movie music and a guy with a chainsaw. Don't be silly. You need to find out who he is and how badly he's hurt. Get a grip.*

Cassidy jumped when the voice spoke again. "Somebody attacked me. I saw someone messing with the equipment bus, so I followed him here. He snuck behind me and hit me in the head. I don't feel so good. Please help me."

More violence.

An icy sensation jolted through Cassidy. She shivered again and tightened her clutch on her phone.

LATE TUESDAY NIGHT

Cassidy took several deep breaths to calm the jitters and then tapped 9-1-1 on her phone. She needed to help the guy, but all of Deputy Turner's admonishments made her skittish. *What if it's a trap? I'll let the police sort it out when they get here.*

As soon as the call connected, she blurted, "Hi, this is Cassidy Jamison at Celebrations at Ivy Springs. I'm at the mouth of the cave at the back of my property, and there's an injured man inside. I'm not sure who it is or how badly he's hurt. He's groaning a lot, and it doesn't look like he can sit. I need an ambulance and the police here quickly."

"Okay. Are you hurt?" The dispatcher's voice was matter-of-fact, yet soothing to Cassidy's frayed nerves.

"No. I was taking my dog for a walk. I own the property. We heard a noise. He's inside the cave."

"Are you safe?"

"I'm fine. There's nobody nearby." Cassidy glanced around to verify her own words.

"Can you see the type of injury?"

"No," Cassidy said. "I didn't go inside in case it was a crime scene. He was talking a little bit. He said someone was messing around the buses on the property, and he followed whoever it was. Then he said he got hit from behind. He's moaning a lot."

"Okay, so you said it's on the back of your property near the cave. Where the other body was found?"

"Uh, sort of. The other situation happened in the garden." Cassidy let out a long puff of air. *Great. Now my property is notorious for multiple acts of violence.*

"And it's a head injury?"

"Yes, I think so." Cassidy's heartbeat pounded in her ears.

"Did you see the attacker?" the dispatcher asked.

"No. There's no one else here. I think there's only one person in the cave, but I don't know for sure. It's just my dog and me here. I didn't see the attack. I'm not really sure who the injured guy is."

"Okay. Police and rescue are on their way. When they get to the front gate, what should they do?" There was the faint noise of fingers tapping furiously on a keyboard.

"The front gate is open. Tell them to go to the left behind the parking lots. The maintenance road runs up the mountain. When the asphalt turns to gravel, they're almost there. There's a fence post with a No Trespassing sign. That marks the path through the trees to the cave."

"Okay. I'll pass that on. They are about three minutes or so away from your property. I'll stay on the line with you until they get there." The dispatcher didn't say much else, but knowing she was on the line while Cassidy waited made her feel slightly safer. If someone jumped out of the bushes now, at least the dispatcher would hear her screams.

The minutes seemed like hours. Finally, faint sirens broke the ominous quiet. "They're almost here. I can hear them. I'm going to hang up now, so I can wave them this way. Thanks." She pocketed her phone and hugged Elvis tighter.

After a few minutes, the sirens died. All Cassidy could hear was the wind through the trees, then footfalls pounded through the fallen leaves. A pair of EMTs jogged down the path carrying large orange tackle boxes, and a third one followed, pushing a gurney.

"He's in there. I'm not sure who it is or how badly he's hurt." She pointed inside the cave.

The first EMT pulled out a high-powered flashlight that lit most of the front of the entrance.

Cassidy stepped closer to the mouth of the cave to see what was happening. She whipped around at the sound of sticks crunching and feet pounding through dried leaves. Deputy Turner and Sheriff Howell ran down the path from the woods and joined the small group gathered near the cave.

"What's going on, Cassidy?" The sheriff paused for a second to catch his breath.

"I don't know. Elvis and I heard groans. The guy inside said 'help me' a couple of times and tried to sit. When he fell back, I called you all. I'm not sure who it is."

"What are you doing back here in the woods so late?" If Deputy Turner's tone was any indication, Cassidy was in line for another lecture. So much for a détente. "Elvis and I went out for his evening walk. He heard something and darted over here."

Before the deputy could reply, Sheriff Howell patted her shoulder. "We'll figure it out. Stay here in case we have any more questions."

The flashlight beams from the EMTs and the police bobbed around the inside of the dark cave giving it a disco strobe effect on the walls.

Cassidy caught her breath when they moved the injured man. It was Jack Simon, the other guitar player. *Who is targeting the guys in this band?*

Cassidy sank down onto the cool ground, and Elvis curled up in her lap. She fired off a series of texts to her security, the band's manager, and the Pearly Girls about what they had found.

The EMTs worked on Jack for what felt like eons. Cassidy scanned her social media feeds to pass the time.

"So how did you find him?" A voice boomed in front of her, causing her to jump.

Deputy Turner grinned. "Situational awareness. Always know what's going on around you. Sorry. I didn't mean to startle you." When she didn't say anything in reply, he continued, "Are you okay?"

"Just a little shaken. I didn't expect to find another body. Thankfully, this one is conscious. But you sneaking up on me didn't help."

He ignored her comment. "Okay, can you walk me through how you got here tonight?" He pulled out a small notebook and pen from his front pocket.

Cassidy stood so he wasn't towering over her. She looked at him and took a step back. He was almost a foot taller than she was.

I've never noticed how tall he is. But he's not going to hover over me.

Cassidy cleared her throat. "Elvis and I were out for an evening walk, and something caught his attention. When I calmed him down, I heard a noise inside the cave."

"Did you go in?"

"No. I didn't know what was going on, so I called y'all. He could have been hurt, the bad guy could still be around, or maybe it was a trap. And I didn't want to contaminate your crime scene if it turned out to be one."

A slight smile crossed his lips. "Okay, good. Did you talk to him?"

"A bit. He called out for help several times. Then he said someone attacked him from behind. Is he going to be okay?" A sense of dread weighed on her shoulders.

"They'll take good care of him. He'll be transported to the hospital for tests and observation. Have you notified anyone else?" He gave her a pointed glance.

Cassidy nodded. "I sent a message to security, the band's manager, and my team."

He raised an eyebrow. "Word will be all over town soon. Any word from the manager?" His stare bored into her.

She scrolled through her email and texts. "Nothing yet. Jack said he saw someone messing with one of the buses, and he followed them here. Uh, Beau, the manager, isn't staying with the band. He's over at Sid Proctor's motel."

"Okay. So, no one else was around? You didn't happen to see who attacked him?"

Cassidy shook her head. "Nope. We didn't see anyone else."

"Okay. I'm going to look around and then head over to the buses. I'll call you if we have more questions." Deputy Turner turned and began walking along the path. After multiple passes, he expanded his search into the woods.

This isn't like it is on television at all. Police investigations are a lot of waiting and watching. And I didn't have a chance to ask him if he found Karl after the altercation at Deannie's.

By the time the EMTs carted Jack off, a forensics team had arrived with all kinds of lights and gear. The lights on stands illuminated the darkness almost as bright as daylight.

A crash and then some muffled swearing came from the woods. Before she could alert the sheriff, Beau Cox stumbled out of the underbrush and dusted off the knees of his dress pants.

"Hey, Cassidy. Where's Jack?" Beau glanced around him, taking in the scene.

"Are you okay?" she asked.

"I took a little tumble back there, but I'm fine. Is Jack still here? What's going on? Did they take him somewhere?" Beau rubbed his elbow and stared into the cave.

The sheriff approached. "Mary Washington Hospital in Charlottesville. I know you want to get over there quickly. I'll walk you back to your car, and we can chat. I have a few questions."

Finding herself alone with the forensic techs who scurried in and out of the cave, measuring and snapping photos, Cassidy picked up Elvis and gave him a slight squeeze. The temperatures had dropped into a chilly range from the afternoon's warmth, and her fingers and toes had started to tingle. With not much going on and no one else close by to talk to, she decided to call it a night.

"Come on, Elvis. We'll take the garden path back." The pair headed toward the grotto. Elvis, excited to be moving again, believed it was playtime. He cavorted and sniffed everything in sight until she guided him back to their apartment for hot tea and her fuzzy blanket.

Too wired to sleep, she opened her spreadsheet and filled in what she had learned tonight. Then her phone pinged with a barrage of texts from the Pearly Girls:

Ruthanne: Is he okay?

Aileen: Oh, my stars, what happened?

Ruthanne: Are you okay? Do you need us to come over?

Kate: I'm in my jammies, but I'll come. Heck, I may throw a coat over them. I need time to change my shoes. Do you need me to drive over?

Roxie: Did he die? Please say no.

Cassidy: No, he didn't die. And I'm fine. No need to come over tonight. He didn't see his attacker. They took him to the hospital. Forensics is still here.

Roxie: We want details tomorrow.

Ruthanne: Nighty night. Call if you need us.

Kate: I'll check with my friends at the hospital for the 411 on Jack.

Aileen: I'll check in tomorrow to see what you uncover. I'm gonna watch the news and then head to bed.

Roxie: Headed out for a late date. See you after lunch tomorrow.

Cassidy smiled, feeling warm and tingly inside. She had a great support team. The gals always had her back, even if they did tend to smother her from time to time. They meant well, even with all the lectures and opinions. It was nice to not feel so alone.

TOO EARLY ON WEDNESDAY

A buzzing sound assaulted Cassidy's ears, jarring her awake. She covered her head with her pillow, but the pesky noise didn't go away. The annoying alarm finally pushed its way to the front of her consciousness. Fumbling around until she found her phone, she mashed the button to stop the offensive noise. "Hey, Elvis. Time to get a move on. We need to see what the sheriff's team uncovered." The little dog burrowed deeper under the covers to continue his nap. "Yep, I'd stay in bed, too, but we have things to do. These late nights are killing me." She padded into the bathroom, hoping a steamy shower would improve her mood—and the crick in her neck.

Pulling on jeans and a lavender shrug over a white T-shirt, she slipped on her sneakers and headed for the coffee maker. A double espresso lifted her spirits as she rummaged around for something for breakfast. Grabbing a banana and a yogurt, she packed her messenger bag. "Come on, puppy. I'll fix you breakfast downstairs after your walk."

After a quick lap around the backyard, Elvis stood guard in the office kitchen until his food and water bowls were filled to his satisfaction. While he chowed down, Cassidy flitted around the office, turning on lights and booting up her computer. *Today is going to call for more caffeine. I can tell already.*

Before Cassidy could head back to the workroom, someone rapped on the glass window of the front door. *Who needs something this early? I'm going to need more coffee to get going.*

Deputy Turner.

"Good morning, Deputy. What can I help you with?" She pulled open the heavy door.

"I'm glad I caught you before you started your day. Do you have a minute?" He held his hat in his hands.

"Sure. Come in. Can I get you some coffee?"

"That would be nice. It was a late night." He looked around the lobby and followed her to the back where Elvis yipped a greeting but stayed focused on his kibble.

After the coffee maker made its last few gurgles, she handed Deputy Turner his mug and pushed the tray of creamers and sweeteners toward him.

"Black is fine, thanks." He savored a few sips before continuing. "This is good. Nice and strong." He set his mug on the table. "Jack Simon is being held for observation. He has a slight concussion and needed a few stitches. They'll probably release him sometime today if they haven't already."

"That's good news. I wonder if he'll perform tomorrow. I'll have to check the schedule." Rummaging around on her desk, she found the folder and ran her finger down the list of shows. "The Weathermen aren't scheduled again until Friday and Saturday. That's good. Maybe he'll have time to rest after his ordeal." When he didn't respond, she continued. "I'm still a bit concerned about the attack. First Johnny and now Jack. I always seem to be looking over my shoulder lately, and it's unnerving." Her voice trailed off as she watched to see if Deputy Turner's facial expressions gave anything away.

He's got a pretty good poker face.

"Always be aware of your surroundings. Take your phone with you. Check in frequently with family and friends." He walked around, inspecting the windows and doors. "Don't take unnecessary risks. You've got good locks here. Always be vigilant and keep the doors locked when no one is here or when you're by yourself."

She nodded and let out a slight puff of air. *I know he's trying to be helpful, but this whole situation makes me want to go buy a weapon. I don't feel safe on my own property.* "I try to be cautious, but sometimes we get too comfortable and don't always pay attention to security. I'm trying to be alert to what's going on around me, especially when there are guests on the property."

"We've stepped up patrols around here. We also have additional officers from other jurisdictions helping out." He flipped the latch to lock one of the far windows. He pointed to the lock. "Did anyone else on your team see or hear anything related to the attack in the cave?"

So much for small talk. He's back to business again. Let's see how long it takes for him to lecture me about the unlocked window.

Cassidy struggled to keep her facial expression neutral. "No. I was the only one from my team on the property last night besides the contract security. Have you checked with them? The guys from the band are staying in the buses. Was Jack able to provide any more information? Maybe he remembered something important."

The deputy shook his head. "Only what he told you and us at the scene. It was dark, and he didn't recognize his attacker. He didn't recognize the voice either. He said the guy spoke in low tones."

Her phone pinged an alert. Mateo Domingo's name flashed on her screen. "Just a minute. This is my contract security guy."

She held the phone to her ear and turned away from the deputy. "Hey, Mateo, what's up?"

"Good morning. I wanted to give you an update from our rounds. Late last night, one of my guys chased someone off your property in the woods."

"Wait a sec. Deputy Turner is here. I'm going to put you on speaker. Mateo Domingo, president of Domingo Security, this is

Deputy Zac Turner from Ivy Springs Sheriff's Office. Mateo, can you repeat that?"

"Hey. Late last night, one of my guys chased someone in the woods behind Cassidy's place. My guy was patrolling the perimeter of the property, and this guy in a black hoodie came snooping around near the tree line by the wedding garden. When my agent called out, the guy took off running into the woods. He chased him for about a quarter of a mile before he lost him near a road."

"If it's where I'm thinking, that's down mountain about a mile and a half from Cassidy's place," the deputy interjected. "Did he get a look at the guy?"

"Nah, not really. A black hoodie, which covered most of his face, and black pants. He took off running so fast there wasn't time to get a better look. He's not sure if the guy went deeper in the woods or ducked out on the road. By the time my guy hiked back, the forensic team and the police were finishing their work at the cave. My guards didn't spot anything else unusual. The rest of the night was quiet. Life around the buses was peaceful. Not a peep out of anybody."

"When did this all happen?" Deputy Turner recorded the highlights in his small notebook.

"The guard spotted the trespasser coming out of the woods about one fifteen," Mateo said. "He got back to the property after the chase about two thirty."

Cassidy chewed on her bottom lip. "That backs up Jack's story about an intruder on the property. He told me someone was skulking around the buses and the band's equipment."

"Thanks for the update, Mateo. If your guard thinks of anything else, let us know." The deputy frowned while he reread the notes he'd jotted down.

"Will do. I'll send you both a copy of the incident report. Hey, Cassidy, I appreciate all the work for my team. Keep it coming." With a click, Mateo disconnected the call.

"I'm headed over to see if Jack is back yet. Maybe what the security guard saw will jog some memories. If you think of anything else, let me know." The deputy rinsed his mug in the sink and strode out the back door.

Cassidy sank into her office chair and did a couple of breathing exercises until Elvis hopped in her lap and settled beside her for his morning nap.

Cassidy was sorry Jack was injured, but maybe that attack would take the spotlight off Roxie.

She petted the smooth hair on Elvis's head. "Hey, baby, you've got the right idea about relaxing. A lot has gone on here recently, and it all revolves around this music festival. I forgot to ask the deputy about whether or not he had a chance to talk to Karl again. His behavior has been a little odd lately."

She scanned through the camera feeds around the perimeter of the property. After watching Beau and herself come and go in separate cars, there wasn't any other movement or people sightings. She spotted the ambulance and police when they drove through the front gate. No hoodie guy. And no chase by the security guard. She let out a deflated breath. "Darn, Elvis. I thought maybe one of the cameras might have caught something. I need to invest in more cameras for around the garden and the farmhouse."

She added what Mateo's guard witnessed to her Weathermen notes. "Does this mean it's a random stranger who keeps coming back to the property? Why would someone with the band try to break into their own equipment bus? Wouldn't they already have access? I know it doesn't make a lot of sense, but I still have a gut feeling it's someone related to the band or their business. What am I missing?"

"I have no idea." Kate dropped her purse and oversized beach bag onto the table. "Thought I'd stop in and check on you and give you an update." Her blouse—a swirl of aqua, white, and navy blue—fluttered behind her as she strode toward the coffee maker.

And report back to the Pearly Girls on the latest news. Cassidy smiled. "What did you hear from your contacts? Anything good?"

"I talked to my friend who's an ER nurse at the hospital. She couldn't give me too many specifics on Jack Simon's case, but I was able to find out that he has a mild concussion. He got clobbered from behind, and he needed a few stiches. He had some scratches on his neck and hand, and his clothes were covered in dirt. And my friend didn't even know he was famous." Kate rolled her eyes. "She said he was nice, polite, and handsome for someone her dad's age. They released him in the wee hours when he refused to stay longer. She said the manager picked him up."

"Interesting. That matches what Jack told me. I was wondering why the hoodie guy was poking around their equipment. What was he looking for?"

"I don't know, but my friend did have a tidbit of gossip." Kate flashed a mischievous half grin. "She said Jack talked a lot while they were checking him out. He fussed about this tour and all the bad luck they've been having. He made some comment that no amount of money was worth continuing with touring, and he's done with all the hassles and the constant traveling. He said he'd go back to Florida and figure something else out since the royalty checks couldn't even buy him a coffee these days."

Cassidy tilted her head to stare at her friend while continuing to stroke Elvis's fur. "You'd think with all the hits and success they had they'd be set for life."

Kate shrugged. "Some of the artists and actors back in the day didn't have all the clauses in their contracts that benefited them. Most were so anxious to get a deal or a gig they signed anything. Sometimes they didn't own the rights, or the money wasn't as good as it could have been. You hear stories all the time of popular stars from the fifties and sixties going broke. It happened to a lot of stars and athletes because the studios and management got most of the money and controlled everything." She paused and then quickly added, "They spend too much, live the high life, or get mixed up with unsavory people and habits. It's amazing how much money they can blow through in a short amount of time."

Cassidy glanced up. "Money is a pretty typical motive for murder. Either there's jealousy at someone who has it, or there's bitterness about not getting one's fair share. But that doesn't explain the guy in the dark hoodie who disappeared into the woods. And if he is Jack's attacker, who is he? I'd feel better if it was someone targeting the band and not some marauding serial killer who could be after us, too. I guess it's a killer either way, but one of the scenarios makes me feel like I don't have to worry much about being next because this is centered around the Weathermen."

"At least they'll be gone in a few days, and we can get back to normal." Kate dug through her desk drawers. "Normal would be a nice change. And for what it's worth, I do think it's all centered around the members of the band."

There's not much time left. This murder could take months to solve. What if they leave, and we never find out who did it?

"There you are!" Kate exclaimed. A puzzled look crossed the Pearly Girl's face. "I was looking for some swatch samples the other day to see what was available for ribbons and sashes for the wedding. I was thinking mauve or champagne, and I couldn't find the sample books. They were in the bottom of the cabinet under the coffee maker. I don't know how they got over here. I'm sure I left them on the counter. Anyway, I hope they'll give me some inspiration. I need to check in with Roxie to see what kind of flowers she's thinking about using. It's a sunset wedding. I want it to look magical. Maybe we could go bold with oranges, reds, and purples. There's a thought. Bright and beautiful."

Cassidy nodded, still lost in all the varying motivations for killing Johnny Storm. And was the attack on Jack Simon another attempt at murder or something else? She blinked to push the dark thoughts out of her head. "I can't wait to see what you come up with. This is going to be a lovely grotto wedding. The bride and her mother will be in next Wednesday for more planning."

"It's on my calendar. Roxie and I are going to have a couple of different idea boards made up for them to see the samples in several color palettes." Kate flipped through the swatches, holding them up to the light.

"That'll be good. Let me know if I can help with the software." It wasn't the most glamorous side of event planning, but it's what Cassidy knew she was good at.

"Roxie's going to take a crack at it. I'm sure she'll call you if she can't get the thing to work. It looks like Pinterest, so it shouldn't be *that* hard. For now, I'm going to focus on the swatch books." Kate slid them into her beach bag. "Time to head out. I'll let you know if I hear anything else. The gals and I will be in tomorrow, and we're planning to go to the show." She gave Cassidy a reassuring pat on her shoulder. "Don't worry. It'll get solved, and things will get back to normal, boring, everyday pretty quickly. But think of the stories we'll be able to tell."

THURSDAY MORNING

With a steaming cup of tea and a bagel slathered in peanut butter, Cassidy settled in the office. After riffling around her desk drawer, she found the elusive bottle of aspirin and promptly popped two in her mouth. "Elvis, these late nights remind me of college. In fact, I haven't done this much research since those days. I feel like there is something I'm missing. I have all kinds of notes and disparate facts. But there are still too many missing pieces. Too many unanswered questions." *Maybe I'm kidding myself that I may be able to figure this out.* As a kid, she was good at puzzles, and had always wanted to be either Nancy Drew or Batgirl.

She opened her notes and entered what she found on the gossip websites. "Well, pup, I know more about the personal lives of the Weathermen than I could have ever dreamed of. It's interesting to read the articles from the early days." Their images were carefully managed, and they were all portrayed in the best light—even Eddie Merritt's death and Phillip Peters's drug arrest and addiction were downplayed. When the seventies and eighties came along the Weathermen seemed to do their best to show they were bad boys of rock and roll. The epic stories and scandals were everywhere. Cassidy thought they must have gotten rid of the publicist. Drugs, women, and wild parties seemed to be common denominators. There had been no attempt to keep them squeaky-clean in the media. It was almost like they were trying to one-up each other with the next scandal.

Elvis stuck his nose in the air and pranced off to find a napping place. *Obviously, he doesn't care about the band's wild ways or my research.*

"I found some stuff on money woes and lawsuits. Maybe these little tidbits will fall into place and create a bigger picture with some answers if I keep searching." Cassidy clicked on a link leading to the band's catalog of songs. "Hmmm. I didn't know a BJ Taylor wrote a lot of the lyrics. That's odd. Who is this person? I thought I read earlier where Johnny wrote most of their stuff." She searched through her notes but couldn't find a confirmation to validate it.

Her curiosity piqued, Cassidy spent the next hour searching for BJ Taylor online. Lots of B. Taylors, but she didn't find anyone famous or in the music industry. And none of the names in the search results were for songwriters, singers, or music producers.

Pulling up three different streaming sites, she checked for songs by the Weathermen. All three showed BJ Taylor's name. "Okay, who are you? And does it even matter?"

Still not interested in her searches for this BJ person, Elvis danced at the back door.

"Okay, okay. You're right. It's a good time for a break," Cassidy said. "Let's see what's happening around here. The gals should be in shortly. Tonight's concert night. There's a funkadelic seventies band and a B-52s cover band on tap tonight. Sounds like fun, right?"

Elvis dashed outside and bolted to the garden as soon as she opened the door. Cassidy stood near the small pergola with the mountain view. The flowers and spectacular vista made this place magical. The upcoming wedding would be beautiful with the bluish-green backdrop of the valley, the mountains in the distance, and all of Levi's carefully tended flowers. Fairy lights would make the whole event even more ethereal. She made a mental note to check on the cost of the strands. Twinkles would add some pizzazz. The little white lights changed the whole ambience of the barn. It was now perfect for indoor weddings. Why not add some to the garden?

Her phone vibrated, echoing in the stillness of the grotto. Despite not recognizing the number, she clicked to accept the call. "Good morning. This is Cassidy at Celebrations at Ivy Springs."

"Good morning, Cassidy." The voice was faint, but recognizable.

"Ruthanne. Is that you? Where are you? Is everything okay?" Concern made Cassidy's voice rise several octaves.

"I'm fine. We're all fine. We're tired. Can you come and pick us up? We need a ride."

"Sure. Are you sure everything's okay? You don't sound like your bubbly self."

"Fit as a fiddle. We're at 101 N. Main Street in Harrisonburg. Could you get us as soon as you can?" Ruthanne whispered.

"No problem. You'd tell me if something was wrong, right?"

"It's as good as can be. We're not in any danger. We'll explain everything when you get here. It's been a long night, and we're all tired. Thanks, Cassidy. See you in a bit."

"I'm headed your way now." Cassidy hurried Elvis toward the office. "Come on, boy. I need to retrieve the gals from Harrisonburg. You guard the place, and I'll be back as soon as I can. I have no idea why they spent the night in Harrisonburg, but I'm looking forward to their tale. With them, it's always an interesting story."

After typing in the address in her GPS, she pulled out her sunglasses. "I'll find out why the Pearly Girls are hanging out in Harrisonburg. Here's to an unexpected road trip."

The normal ninety-minute trip was closer to two hours after hitting traffic on I-81 and two stops—one for gas and another for an iced coffee. Cassidy finally pulled into downtown Harrisonburg and navigated the streets around James Madison University.

The GPS announced, "You have arrived at your destination." Cassidy looked up and down the street. No sign of the Pearly Girls.

She scanned the sidewalks at the nearby government buildings and the shops across the street. According to the matching address, the gals were either visiting the fire museum or the city's public safety building.

The coffee she'd had on the road turned sour in the bottom of her stomach. Knowing the gals, they weren't learning about the history of fire safety.

After a five-minute search for visitor parking, she flipped her purse strap over her shoulder and hurried to the main door of the public safety building to stand in a short line queued in front of the glass window. When it was her turn, she told the deputy with powdered sugar on the front of his uniform that she was there to pick up Ruthanne Carmichael.

A slight smile crossed the deputy's face. "She and her friends are down there. They've been waiting for you. And they'll be happy to see you." He pointed to the hallway to Cassidy's left.

Nodding her thanks, Cassidy headed in the direction he pointed. Her sneakers squeaked on the industrial floor. The more quietly she tried to walk, the louder the squeaks got. To Cassidy it sounded as loud as a basketball game on a gym floor. Shrugging off the concern that she was making too much noise, she hurried to find the gals.

She heard the chatter before she rounded the corner. The four Pearly Girls sat in a waiting area with several vending machines and an oversized coffee maker. The normally put-together women were rumpled and appeared worse for wear. Tendrils of Ruthanne's hair had escaped her ponytail. Aileen looked like she hadn't slept in days. No one had touched up their usually impeccable makeup.

"What happened?" Cassidy rushed toward them.

"We're glad to see you." Kate jumped up to hug Cassidy.

The four surrounded her for a group hug, and all of the sexagenarians greeted her at once.

When they stopped squeezing her, she stared at the disheveled group. "What's going on?"

"Let's get out of here," Roxie linked her arm with Cassidy's and started walking. "We'll tell you in the car. That is, after we stop for breakfast. The service in this place stinks."

"They don't have room service," Kate glared at her friend, but with a half grin as the tiny band tromped down the hall. None of the gals ever stayed angry or frustrated with each other for longer than a minute.

"That deputy made it a point to tell us that," Ruthanne said. "He was nice about it, but he reminded all of us it was called jail for a reason."

Roxie rolled her eyes. "I'm hungry and a little bit cranky. So, breakfast and lots of coffee are first on my list. Then we can share details."

"Bye, Roscoe." Ruthanne waved to the deputy behind the glass window.

"Bye, Ruthanne. Bye, ladies. It was nice to meet you. I'll make sure to check out your place the next time I'm in Ivy Springs." He grinned. The gals must have regaled him with stories to stay on his good side.

"Come on." Roxie nudged Ruthanne. "I've had enough of this place for a while. This was not one of our finest moments."

It took a few minutes for the Pearly Girls to get settled in the van. As the others piled in the back, Kate reluctantly took the front seat next to Cassidy, making a point of staring out the side window. The silence was deafening. No one made eye contact with Cassidy's glare in the rearview mirror. And no one was talking.

"There's a coffee shop," Roxie yelled. "Up there on the left. Get over. This is an emergency."

Cassidy switched lanes and found parking on a side street. The Pearly Girls hopped out of the van before she could ask any questions.

How in the world did they get to Harrisonburg with no car? Steeling herself for an epic tale, Cassidy ordered a giant iced mocha and a piece of banana bread.

The little group huddled at a metal table on the patio with their orders.

"What a beautiful day this turned out to be." Ruthanne stirred sweetener in her dark coffee.

"Always Pollyanna." Roxie took a swig of her chai. "In hindsight, this might not have been our best idea."

Kate harrumphed her disapproval, then blew on the steam rising from her coffee cup. "Well, you weren't complaining when the opportunity presented itself."

"We were trying to be helpful," Ruthanne added after brushing blueberry scone crumbs from her lips.

Aileen nodded. "And if I remember correctly, Roxie, you figured out how to get in. And that caused all of this. We probably should have gone home instead of breaking and entering."

Cassidy nearly spit out her iced coffee. *Breaking and entering?*

"There was no breaking. Just entering. I can't help it if they don't lock their windows." Roxie shrugged.

Feeling left out and more than a little confused, Cassidy interrupted. "Okay, spill it. I drove two hours to get you all after staying up all night doing research. And we have another long ride back home. Y'all are being super vague, and I have no idea what you're talking about. So, tell me what's going on."

"Okay, Miss Crankypants," Roxie said. "For someone your age, you should be out having fun. You work too hard. And you've been tired and grouchy lately from too much work. Lighten up. We need to hook you up with some people your own age."

"But we love you and are so proud of you." Ruthanne patted Cassidy's hand.

"I'm still waiting and getting crankier by the minute." Cassidy frowned at the Pearly Girls.

Suddenly becoming interested in stirring her coffee into a tiny vortex, Ruthanne clammed up and stared inside the cup.

"Okay, okay. I need some clean clothes and a hot shower. If it'll get us back on the road and home faster, I'll fill you in." Kate set her drink on the table and took a moment to swish away invisible crumbs. "Yesterday, we went over to talk to the guys in the band. They were having cocktails by the buses, and they invited us to join them."

"We thought it would be a good opportunity to ask them some questions. You know, to help you with your research," Ruthanne added.

"Anyway, we had some drinks and brats with the guys, met the roadies, and learned way more about their private lives than we wanted to." Kate stared across the street.

"Like I said before, we should have gone home, but we had no idea at the time things would go so wrong." Aileen glanced at the other gals with her lips pursed as if waiting for someone else to drop the big news.

"Dirk doesn't talk much, but we heard about the demons Karl's been battling for years and his women troubles. And about how much Jack wants to get back in the studio to work on a new album." Kate picked at her croissant.

"Karl is one hot mess," Aileen muttered.

"But he's loveable, and he asked Aileen out after the concert tonight after regaling us with his long list of bad breakups and scandals." Ruthanne giggled.

Aileen gave her a side-eye. "He really didn't make an excellent case for himself. He needs to learn how to read a room. Not sure why I attract the needy ones."

"It's your wild hair, and he's better than Sid Pro Quo." Roxie's comment earned her a nasty look from Aileen.

"I think that will be a hard *no* for both of them," Aileen added. "Anyway, back to the story. Beau talked a lot about the tours. They do it to keep the revenue coming in since they haven't recorded anything new in a while. We heard about every city they've visited in the last three years. And it was a lot."

"And he said how much they would all miss Johnny. They'd have to meet and decide how to proceed after this tour. He was waiting to see what happens with the murder investigation and the will. That could affect royalties and such." Roxie sipped her drink before pointing her finger at no one in particular. "Money is always a motive."

"Interesting. They definitely have a lot of baggage. The more I dig, the more motives I find for a bunch of people to want to do harm to the band members. Unfortunately, no big red arrows point to one person." Cassidy blew out a puff of air.

The gals fell into an unusual silence. All seemed to be preoccupied with their drinks or phones or watching the traffic pass by the small patio area. They still had yet to answer the most pressing question.

"Okay," Cassidy made a point to make eye contact with each woman as if she were interrogating a group of kindergartners on the playground to see who pushed little Suzie off the swing. "Before we head out, you didn't get to the part about how you ended up here. Well?"

Again, all the gals looked around, suddenly busy with staring at the sky, their feet, or their coffee cups.

"I'm not getting back in the van until you tell me. I can sit here all afternoon if that's what it takes, but we'll miss the show."

"You're being capricious," Roxie frowned. At least it was a better worded comeback than a kindergartner would have used.

"She did drive all the way up here to get us," Ruthanne said.

Aileen cleared her throat. "After the party broke up, the band guys went into town with Beau. And we decided to head out since none of us wanted to go with them. We took the long route to enjoy a walk around your property."

"It was a lovely evening," Ruthanne interjected, as if that made the story all the better.

"And Kate wanted to look at the garden to bounce some ideas off the group about the wedding." Aileen nodded. "So, we were *technically* doing research."

"Ivy is the hot new thing." Ruthanne continued to stall. "It'll go well with the lilies and roses. And it's the namesake of our beloved town."

Cassidy flashed each of them a death glare. The sun was warming up the temps, and they were nowhere close to wrapping up this story.

"But back to the story. After the guys left, Roxie had a brilliant idea." Aileen nodded to Ruthanne to nudge her to pick up the story.

What is with them? This is maddening!

"We were circling the buses to see what we could see before we headed home," Ruthanne added. Roxie glared at her over her sunglasses but didn't interrupt.

"Roxie pointed out an open window on Johnny's bus." Kate tapped her foot against the table leg.

These women really don't want this story to come out. It must be a good one!

"Anyway." Aileen picked up the proverbial ball. "When no one was looking..." She glanced at Ruthanne.

"I was the lookout," Ruthanne interjected. "To make sure no one snuck up on us."

"Like I said," Aileen repeated. "When no one was looking, Kate hoisted me up, and I wiggled through the window. Then I opened the door and let the others in."

"It's because you're petite," Ruthanne added. "I stayed outside to make sure nobody approached. If they did, I was going to do some bird calls to warn the gals." Ruthanne crossed her arms over her chest.

Who do they think they are? Charlie's Angels?

"We wanted to see if we could find anything. Maybe there was something there we could use to uncover the murderer. It was like we were Jessica Fletcher. The opportunity fell into our laps."

Now Cassidy really knew they'd lost all good sense.

"And we took it," Roxie said with pride.

"And it was exhilarating," Ruthanne added with a wicked grin.

"After the police had already been over the scene?" Cassidy stared wide-eyed at the Pearly Girls. The whole story was preposterous.

"They miss stuff." Roxie rummaged through her purse. "Like this." She pulled out a day planner and waved it around. "It's Johnny Storm's calendar and phone list. I was hoping you could find something useful in it." She pushed it across the table to Cassidy. "If there's something there, I know you'll find it."

Cassidy stared at the leather book like it was going to bite her. "But how did you get to Harrisonburg?" she asked for what felt like the tenth time.

"I'm getting to it," Aileen snapped. "After our search, it was getting dark, so we slipped out of the bus. On our way to the parking lot, we literally ran into Karl. Well, Kate did. She crashed into him, and they landed in a heap on the grass."

"I got a couple of bruises, but at least Karl broke my fall. He thought I was flirting, so I had to put a kibosh on that." Kate rubbed her elbow.

"Anyway, he really was one hot mess. He'd had a bit too much to drink, and he said he needed to head up the road to see someone. He was fumbling around in his pockets for car keys. Well, we couldn't let him drive, so we went with him." Aileen picked up her cup for a sip, realizing too late it was empty. She set it back on the table.

"Who was he going to see?" Cassidy was still trying to picture Kate elbowing an amorous Karl to get him off her.

"We never found out," Roxie said.

"Huh?" Cassidy shook her head. All of that, and they didn't even know who it was Karl met? "And whose car was it? Do we need to go back and get the car? Where is it?"

"It's a long and complicated story." Kate shook her head and rolled her eyes. "Karl told us it belonged to one of the roadies, and he gave Karl the keys. And it was okay to borrow it, so off we went with Ruthanne driving since she only had a ginger ale at the party."

Ruthanne nodded primly before Kate resumed the story. "He gave us some address near northern Virginia. If we had known it was going to be an all-night road trip, we may have talked him out of it. Anyway, it was too late, and we were already in the car and on the road. When we got to Harrisonburg, we pulled off because we needed a tinkle break, and Karl needed some coffee to sober up."

"We went into a McDonald's," Aileen added. "We all needed a break from Karl and his constant chatter, and I wanted a Coke. He talked nonstop for two hours. He rivaled the motormouth skills of the preteens in my eighth-grade English classes. Mr. Chatterbox."

"And he didn't even say anything worthwhile." Ruthanne scrunched up her nose and whispered as if it was some big secret. "He whines and complains a lot."

Aileen nodded her agreement. "After we all took turns in the bathroom and we got our drinks and Roxie's french fries, we couldn't find Karl. I mean, the restaurant wasn't big, and he had just disappeared. We all went outside, and still no Karl. There were some police cars in the lot, and a couple more pulled in. We didn't think much about it. We were trying to remember if anyone had Karl's phone number."

"And when we climbed in the car to wait on Karl, the police swooped in on us like a flock of vultures." Roxie threw her hands up for dramatic effect.

Cassidy's eyes widened. "Where is Karl?"

"We don't know. We got busted with a stolen car and thrown in the pokey." Ruthanne's voice quaked. "He disappeared into thin air. And he never came back to help us. Sheesh. He's definitely on my bad list now."

"I bet he saw all the police presence and skedaddled," Kate said.

"How am I going to tell my kids I was arrested and spent the night in jail?" Ruthanne whimpered, her lips pulled down in a childish frown. "We have records now."

"Ask Roxie. I'm sure she's got lots of stories from her run-ins with the law by now. She's a pro with police relations." Kate shrugged, lifting her chin as if to declare it was all Roxie's fault for having lived a more cavalier life.

Roxie glared at her over her sunglasses. "Go big or go home, I always say." She waved her hand dismissively. "What doesn't kill you makes you stronger."

Aileen squirmed like a kid in the front row of class who had the answer. "The car was impounded, and we were hauled in for hours of questioning. We didn't see each other again until they put us in the tank to cool off. We didn't even get a phone call until this morning. They didn't give us much direction about what's next. Only a bunch of papers and a court date."

"I didn't have a chance to call my lawyer." Roxie stared at a chipped nail, apparently unfazed by her latest run-in with the law.

"Okay." Cassidy picked up her trash. "We need to get on the road. We've got a concert to host tonight. And you all probably need a hot shower and a nap."

"Jail wasn't what I thought it would be like." Ruthanne frowned. "The bench was hard. There were no pillows or blankets, and we had to share a bathroom, if you could call it that. I don't think any of us got any sleep."

"But they did have a TV. We watched ESPN all night." Aileen threw up her arms. "Oh joy."

Kate rolled her eyes and started gathering the trash.

Confession lightened the mood. The gals chatted like nothing had happened all the way back to the van.

"Cassidy, here. You forgot this." Roxie waved the day planner at her. "This may make this whole fiasco worthwhile. It could be the break you need."

THURSDAY AFTERNOON

Cassidy pulled into the front lot of her property. The gals' cars were parked nearby. As they climbed out, she remembered something she'd wanted to ask them before all their legal troubles. "Hey, have any of you heard of a BJ Taylor?"

"No. Who is that?" Aileen hopped out onto the asphalt.

"Should we have heard of him? Her?" Kate extended a hand to help Ruthanne out of the back.

"I came across the name in some research on the Weathermen. I couldn't find anything on him. He has some writing credits on their songs. It piqued my interest when I couldn't find anything on him or her. So, no BJ Taylor that you know of affiliated with the band?" Cassidy frowned. She'd really hoped they'd know something about the mysterious BJ.

Kate flipped her purse strap over her shoulder. "Nope. I have no clue."

"I'll look through my scrapbooks," Ruthanne offered. "I kept every bit of stuff I could find on them from the early days. I'll let you know what I have. But the name doesn't ring a bell with me either."

Before finally climbing into their own cars, the gals waved, hugged, chatted in the parking lot, and promised to be back in time for tonight's show.

Cassidy headed to the office to spring Elvis for some R and R. The beautiful afternoon and the buzz of activity drew the pair like a magnet to the amphitheater where staff in all black moved equipment and lights around on the stage. "Be on the lookout for black hoodies and Karl," she whispered to Elvis.

They watched the beehive of activity for about twenty minutes until the pile of uncompleted work tickled at her thoughts and demanded her attention. "Come on, pup. We have to finish our work before we can play anymore today. And I'm kinda already behind because of the unexpected road trip." With a reluctant-sounding whimper, Elvis followed her toward the farmhouse.

As they rounded the corner of the stage, Karl approached and froze in his tracks when he spotted her. She opened her mouth to ask him how he was doing, but he turned and bolted in the other direction.

Stunned, Cassidy wondered what had provoked that reaction. Ignoring the impulse to chase after him, she led Elvis back to the office. *Suspicious or maybe guilty? What is Karl's story? How did he get back from Harrisonburg? And why did he run out on the gals and away from me?*

Cassidy hadn't been at her desk for more than fifteen minutes before the front door opened.

"Hello!" she yelled from the back. "I'll be right there."

Not hearing a response, she hustled to the front, trying not to trip over Elvis, to discover Beau standing there, his gaze ricocheting around her waiting area like he was casing the joint.

"Good afternoon. Do you have a minute? I need to straighten some things out, and Karl owes an apology to your team." He stared at the sea glass in the vase on the coffee table.

"What do you mean?"

"Let's say when Karl gets an idea, he tends to fixate on it. When it's music or song lyrics, he's pretty successful. But some of his real-world ideas haven't turned out as well. Harebrained is how his bandmates describe most of his brainstorms. Let's just say he's impulsive. And it often causes trouble for him and those around him."

"I'm not sure I follow you." Cassidy stepped closer to the sofas and guest chairs, wondering if this had anything to do with Karl's erratic behavior earlier.

"The other night, Karl got it in his head to meet someone he met online who was this superfan with a podcast and a music studio. This guy had some get-rich-quick scheme Karl had to get in on. One thing led to another, and he decided since we didn't have a show he was going to meet this person and see where it led. Did I mention the guy was two or three hours away? Anyway, your friends came to his rescue when he was not able to drive. He borrowed one of our roadie's cars. And by borrowing, I mean he lifted the keys out of the guy's jacket."

Cassidy pursed her lips but remained silent.

Beau cleared his throat a few times and stared at his feet before continuing. "Lizard, the car owner, didn't know your friends were with Karl. When he realized Karl and his car had disappeared, he reported it stolen to teach him a lesson. Lizard feels really bad. And now he has to figure out how to get his car out of an impound lot. He had no idea the police would arrest four seniors in a McDonald's parking lot and hold them overnight in the lockup for stealing a car and taking it on a joyride."

She tried to stifle a smile. The Pearly Girls had a knack for being in the middle of some strange adventures, worthy of a sitcom. "I had to drive up and get them this morning."

"I'm so sorry Karl caused all this trouble. With the mess with Johnny and Jack, I haven't been paying much attention to him. He needs more supervision than a seventy-three-year-old man should. I talked to Lizard and our lawyers, and they contacted the police. All charges have been dropped against the ladies. Again, I apologize for this misunderstanding. If there's any other fallout, please let me know. We don't want anything to happen to their reputations, especially when they were only trying to help Karl. We'll take care of what we can."

Best I don't mention they climbed in the window of Johnny's bus and stole his day planner. They're not as sweet and innocent as they look. "Thank you so much. I'm sure they will be thrilled to hear the news." She flashed him what she hoped came off as a reassuring smile.

"And I'll have Karl apologize to them when he feels better," Beau said.

"Where did he go? Ruthanne said they couldn't find him when they stopped in Harrisonburg. I ran into him a little bit ago, but he didn't speak. He must have been in a big hurry."

The manager's cheeks flashed a tinge of pink. "When they stopped in Harrisonburg, he went outside to smoke. He saw all the police vehicles around the borrowed car. And since Lizard had blown up his phone with texts that escalated from warnings to mild threats, he figured he should get out of there before causing another incident. He didn't want another arrest on his record. He slipped out the back of the restaurant and walked to a bus station where he bought a ticket to Staunton. I had to pick him up from there. Again, my most sincere apologies for any misunderstandings. Please tell the ladies we'll make it right at the concert tomorrow. Karl and the guys want them to be the band's special guests. And you can come, too."

"Thank you. That is very nice. I'm sure the Pearly Girls will love it. How is Jack doing?"

"Better. He still has a slight headache, but he's determined to finish the tour. See you all tomorrow at the show. We'll have reserved seats up front for you. The guys will definitely make it up to you, especially Karl."

Before Beau could scoot out, she decided to take advantage of his chattiness to see if she could pull any other information out of him. Plus, if he was still apologizing for Karl, then maybe he'd be more inclined to answer some questions. "Uh, do you mind if I ask you a question before you leave?"

Beau flashed a toothy grin. "Of course, what can I do for you?"

"I'm curious. I was reading some of the Weathermen's history last night, and I came across some names. Maybe you could tell me who they are. One was a Phillip Peters, and another was an Eddie Merritt, and the last one was a BJ Taylor."

Beau cleared his throat. His smile faded. "Eddie was one of the earlier members of the band. He was a darn good guitar player, but he couldn't cut it. Phil was also an early member of the band who caused more trouble than he was worth. I've never heard of a BJ Taylor. Where'd you hear that name?"

"I don't remember. I looked at so many articles and fan pages. I thought I saw somewhere where someone credited him with writing a lot of their songs."

"Nope. Sorry, can't help you. Johnny wrote most of the songs. Dirk and Jack—well, and even Karl—wrote a couple of the others. Not the big hits. Those were all Johnny's. I'm not sure who said someone else wrote them, but if you find it, let me know. We should get that corrected. I've got to go check on the guys. See ya." He rushed out, not bothering to properly close the door behind him.

"Well, Elvis, that wasn't helpful. Did you notice he went from Mr. Nice and Smiley to Mr. Serious in less than three seconds? And if this guy has writing credits on their songs, shouldn't the manager know about it? I mean, isn't protecting the clients' rights the top priority of a manager? His response was a little weird," she said, closing the door.

Elvis stood and did several yoga-like stretches.

"Okay, let me go check on a couple of things, and then we can go for a long walk."

Before she could get to her desk, her phone pinged several times in quick succession with a group text alert.

Ruthanne: Woo hoo! I'm not a criminal. Glad I didn't tell the kids I was part of a ring of car thieves. No police record. No life of crime for me.

Aileen: Ruthanne, you weren't in the ring, you were the driver of a stolen car.

Roxie: Drive it like you stole it. Despite the ending, it was kind of a fun adventure.

Kate: How so? We spent the night in jail, and we weren't guilty.

Roxie: We were all in it together.

Aileen: We were all involved. You can't claim innocence.

Ruthanne: Like *The Fast and the Furious.* I can always use an adventure.

Roxie: You need a nickname now. You drove a stolen car.

Kate: I don't know about you, but I've had enough excitement today. I may skip the shows tonight. I need some me time.

Aileen: You have to go to the funkadelic one. Come on, you can head to bed after that. Don't be an old fogy.

Roxie: I'm staying for the B-52s's cover band. But suit yourselves. See y'all tonight. Off to get a mani-pedi. Cassidy, did you find anything interesting in the planner?

Cassidy: See you all tonight. Still working on my research.

Ruthanne: I hope the purloined book provides a clue to this whole mess. Ciao.

"Elvis, why didn't you remind me about Johnny Storm's planner?" She rummaged through her bag and pulled out the leather-bound volume. "Let's see what's in here."

After hours of scouring through the notes, and two coffees later, she didn't have much to show for her efforts. She flipped through the current month's calendar and stepped back month by month to January. Lots of dates and meetings. Johnny neatly printed the name and time of each in the little squares.

At first glance, most meetings were with Beau or someone in Beau's office. Coming in second, she counted forty-two entries with different women's names since January for evening or weekend appointments. All of these were in red ink. This would keep the police busy for days if they followed up with all these women.

The only appointment that seemed different said, "Call AE." The message appeared in January, April, twice in May, and the week before the tour. And all of these entries were in blue ink. Who was AE? This was the only entry with initials and no name anywhere. It could be nothing, but why did it seem so odd next to the other ones? Because it was different from all the rest. It was the only one with initials. Cassidy flipped through the addresses in the back of the book. No AE in the "E" section. *That would have been too easy.*

"Aha!" She nearly jumped out of her chair. "Maybe this isn't a dead end yet." Johnny Storm had entered his contacts by first name, and then he jotted notes about the connection next to each listing. She cringed when she read comments like, "hot redhead," "smoking body," and "always ready for a good time."

"Elvis, there are four names with the initials AE." The dog lifted his head and snorted, apparently unimpressed with her discovery.

After photocopying the pages, she pulled out her phone and dialed the first number. Both it and the second number had been disconnected. Feeling slightly dejected, she moved on to the next one.

A young woman with a soft voice answered on the second ring. "Carlson, Emerson, and Hollis. How may I direct your call?"

"Uh...uh, Avery Emerson, please," Cassidy sputtered, hoping this was the right AE.

"Ms. Emerson is unavailable today. Would you like to leave a message?"

"No, thanks. I'll try back in a few days." Cassidy disconnected and sank back in her chair.

A quick Google search led her to the law firm's website. Avery Emerson, a graduate of Stanford, specialized in media rights and public relations. Cassidy guessed the attorney was in her mid-forties. She dressed *lawyerly* in her tailored gray suit and pearls. Flipping back to Johnny's calendar, she noticed the "AE" entries had no notes like most of the other appointments and no comments about appearance or interests.

Taking a deep breath, she punched in the last number for Amber Ellis. Just as Cassidy was about to hang up, she heard a clipped female voice. "It's me. Speak."

"Ms. Ellis? This is Karen Baker. I'm a freelance reporter, and I wanted to talk to you about Johnny Storm." Cassidy cringed at her own lie.

"Not much to tell." Her words were slurred like she was chewing on something. "He's dead. I saw it on TV."

"I'm sorry for your loss. How did you know Mr. Storm?"

"What do you think you know?"

"I'm checking with some of his past connections to see if I can get a different angle for a story on his life. You know, like a special interest story no one else has."

I hope I didn't lay it on too thick.

"Sorry. I can't help you. I haven't seen him in years, and I probably wouldn't have spoken to him even if he had called. I don't have anything pleasant to say about him. He's not the guy his fans think he is."

"Everyone has a story." Cassidy bit her lip, not knowing how much she could push this person.

"There's no story here. Can't help you. I don't want to talk about him." The line went dead.

Cassidy googled Amber and found five pages of different

women who shared the name. There were way too many to find out which one she talked to. *Sleuthing looked much easier on TV.* Feeling deflated, she added her notes to her spreadsheet. A wave of dread washed over her. How was she going to give the planner to the sheriff without incriminating the Pearly Girls or herself? Plus, she had touched it without gloves.

She pinched the bridge of her nose to fight back the ache building behind her eyes. "Elvis, Veronica Mars makes it look so easy. I need to figure out how to get this to the police anonymously." She slid the planner in her desk drawer. A problem for another day.

THURSDAY EVENING

After an entire afternoon of worrying about what to do with Johnny Storm's day planner and how she was going to get it to the police without arousing suspicion, Cassidy pushed the rocker's death out of her mind and decided to escape to the show instead. Too bad she didn't think about inviting anyone to go with her. It could have been a fun girls' night out.

Trying not to feel sorry for herself about her lack of a social life, she wandered the row of food trucks. The mixture of scents floating through the air made her stomach growl as she eagerly checked out all the food vendors and their brightly colored trucks. The variety covered everything from fusion tacos and sushi to barbecue and hot dogs.

After she purchased two shrimp tacos and a peach tea, Cassidy found a spot near the shed that was used as the stage's control room. She leaned against the rough wooden wall and took a bite, lettuce spilling over the edge of the paper. Today, several men and women stood behind the big window in headsets and dark outfits and monitored all the sound equipment the promotions people had rented. They stared at the screens and occasionally said something to someone backstage.

After she devoured her tacos—she hadn't realized until then just how hungry she was—she balled up the wrapper and took one last swig of her tea before heading to the trash can. Mixing in with the crowd, she walked the perimeter to check on things. Not much was out of the ordinary. Guests meandered to and from the concessions to their seats. Nothing was out of place. Relaxing a bit, she decided to do one more lap around the amphitheater before finding a good seat for the show.

Blending in with the growing crowd around the food trucks, she whipped around when she felt someone lightly tap her shoulder. At first, it felt like a crowd bump, but when it happened again, she turned to see who was trying to get her attention.

Deputy Turner stood behind her in his all-black uniform and mirrored sunglasses.

"I didn't mean to startle you. I wanted to check in when I saw you walk past," Deputy Turner said. He rocked back on his heels and put a hand on each of his hips.

She chuckled softly in an attempt to appear nonchalant, and not surprised, by his sudden appearance. "How are things going in your investigation? Any more leads?" The day planner crept into her head.

"It's slow and steady, but the team feels we're on a good path. Things are falling into place. It's kinda nice to be outside for a little while this evening. We've been in that war room for days, following up on leads. We spend a lot of time on the phone or on the computer. It makes for a long day."

She stared at him, hoping he'd divulge more information, but she was disappointed. Perhaps he needed a nudge. "Spending your time looking for crooks and murderers. Any good suspects?"

Deputy Turner pursed his lips and seemed to search somewhere off in the distance for his answers. "We've ruled out a few with solid alibis, but we're still looking at folks who were with him the night before."

A jolt of anxiety flooded through her. Were they still looking at Roxie? They couldn't be. She didn't have anything to do with the attack on Jack. She closed her eyes for a couple of beats to quell the worries about her friend.

"You okay?" He took her hand, then let it go just as quickly.

Her eyes fluttered open. *Did he just grab my hand?* "I'm fine. I was thinking about all the things I need to get done before we wrap up this festival." *I don't want to mention Roxie and the gals. No sense giving him any new ideas.* She spotted Roxie and Ruthanne near the stage. "If my team can help with anything, please let me know. I'm going to go sit with the gals before the show starts."

He nodded and scanned the crowds near the food trucks as Cassidy made her escape. She chided herself for not having a snappy comeback about it not being Roxie. She had panicked when it sounded like the police still had her on their suspect list. Roxie did a lot of wild and crazy things, but she'd never kill anyone. Shaking off her conversation with the deputy, who always made her feel like she was under surveillance, Cassidy picked up her pace to put some distance between them.

Relieved to have spotted the Pearly Girls, Cassidy slid onto the bench next to Ruthanne. "Hey, there. It's good to see y'all."

"I'm excited to be here. It's so nice to be a free woman again." Ruthanne waved her arms in the air. "I'm not made for jail or camping. I don't look good in orange or striped jumpsuits."

"I'm glad we're sprung, and all the charges were dropped. I don't look that great in orange either." Roxie winked.

"Where's the rest of the gang?" Cassidy looked around.

"They wimped out and decided to rest up," Roxie harumphed. "Too many adventures for them lately. But they'll be here tomorrow for the big show. We're expecting the VIP treatment after Karl dumped us and let us take the rap."

"I thought he was a nicer person than that." Ruthanne sipped some pink cocktail with a pineapple wedge. "He's on my list now. I can't believe he left us to face the charges when the whole thing was his idea. And we were just trying to help him."

A drumbeat echoed through the amphitheater, and strobe lights flashed across the stage. The band, made of up five older guys, took the stage in pink-and-purple-sequined jumpsuits with big collars. The lead singer had bedazzled sunglasses and a purple-feathered boa.

The drummer pounded out the first number and the crowd roared. They must have recognized the song. Cassidy enjoyed the funk and disco numbers, even though she had to google some of the references and jokes the band made.

During the intermission, Roxie and Ruthanne returned with a funnel cake and frozen margaritas to share. "I gave the guy in front of me in line your office email." Roxie winked. "His name is Josh, and he's new in town. He's looking to meet people."

"She also told the nice bartender about you, too. Josh looked like a preppy with rumpled hair and a five-o'clock shadow. What I'd call the scruffy look, but his clothes were nice. But if it were me, I'd pick Reed the Margarita Maker. He had blond highlights and cute dimples. And his ice-blue eyes sparkled."

"You both are incorrigible," Cassidy whispered. "Thanks for the input and encouragement, but I can find my own dates."

"But you haven't, so we're helping." Roxie shook her finger at Cassidy. "A girl your age should be out every night. You work too hard, and you're always hanging out with us. It's time to make a move. Your business is stable. You can slack off a bit and enjoy life."

"Exactly. My hairdresser's nephew is new in town, too. He works at the wine bar on Main Street," Ruthanne added. "We want you to have some fun. Hey, what about that cute deputy? He's been hanging around here a lot lately. And we saw y'all talking again earlier." Ruthanne wiggled her eyebrows. "Maybe he'd like to go to dinner."

"He's investigating a murder." Cassidy's cheeks warmed. "And I was asking him some questions. I was trying to get information out of him. Nothing more."

"Is she protesting too much?" Roxie raised one perfectly sculpted eyebrow.

"He is cute," Ruthanne said. "You should ask him out."

"No. He's not my type. He's all business. Plus, he's always lecturing me about something. So not interested." She wrinkled her nose.

"Uh huh, me definitely thinks she protests too much. You should ask him out. I bet he's fun when he's out of his uniform." Roxie flashed a mischievous grin.

Much to Cassidy's relief, the conversation faded as the trio dug into their snacks. Cassidy stuffed her mouth with funnel cake so she wouldn't have to talk any more about Deputy Turner. When the announcer introduced the next band, the crowd noise was too loud to carry on a conversation.

The high-energy B-52s cover band kept the crowd on its feet for most of the show. Cassidy recognized some of the hits from the eighties and joined Roxie, Ruthanne, and most of the audience as they danced in the aisles.

Later, after waving goodbye to the gals, Cassidy headed home. *Maybe I should let the police handle the investigation. My research isn't making any progress. I should spend my time doing something fun instead of constantly thinking about murder.* A gloomy mood seeped into her consciousness. Taking a deep breath, she continued her walk around the edge of the property near the woods before turning toward the farmhouse. Most of the crowd had disappeared. Maybe it was time to get more involved in town things and meet new people. It couldn't be healthy to spend every waking moment at work. Okay...new resolution to make a point to be more social. *But what should I do? A craft class? Dance lessons? A book club? Online dating?*

As she trekked around the property, the stalled murder investigation crept to the forefront of her mind. Could the sheriff's team still suspect Roxie? There was no way she had anything to do with Johnny Storm's death. They needed to look at the forty or so women he ranked in his calendar as part of the suspect pool. Her gut told her there were more like Amber Ellis who weren't Johnny Storm fans. She cringed when she remembered the planner. How was she going to turn it over to the sheriff without explaining how she obtained it? Deputy Turner would be all over it with a million questions.

Lost in thought, she didn't hear the footsteps until they were right on her. Someone in all black rushed past her and into the woods. Her heart raced and panic arced through her entire body. She took a breath, attempting to calm her nerves. Not sure if it was a man or a woman, she made a split decision to follow whoever it was to see what was going on. The sound of crashing footsteps disappeared under the dark canopy of the leaves.

Is this the same guy as before?

Several yards into the woods, it was so dark even the beam on her phone's flashlight didn't help much. Cassidy paused to listen to any noises to give her a clue to the runner's location. She dashed off a quick text to Mateo Domingo in case his guards were nearby.

A stick cracked and broke up the debate she was having in her head about whether to contact the sheriff's office. An icy feeling surged through her veins. She held her breath and listened. Someone was nearby.

Another twig snapped. Was it closer to her? Or farther away? She counted to ten and let out a long breath through her nose.

Then the musical ringtone for her security contact echoed through the woods. In the quiet forest, the music was jarring.

Fight-or-flight instincts battled it out. Flight won. She tore off through the woods, trying not to trip on any roots or ruts in the ground. Ignoring the branches and underbrush tearing at her skin and clothing, she ran like she hadn't since her soccer days in high school.

She didn't stop until she made it to the patio behind the office. Catching her breath, she fumbled with the key. After several tries, it slid into the lock until it clicked. When she finally got the door open, Elvis jumped on her legs, begging for his evening walk. She sputtered, "Okay, buddy. But it's going to have to be a quick one. We need to stay near the house tonight." Unconcerned about potential intruders, Elvis headed out the door as soon as she cracked it wide enough for him to slip out. Cassidy, on the other hand, flipped on the floodlights and stepped out only a few feet from the porch. Her head turned at every night sound, and she couldn't relax until they were both locked inside her apartment.

Then she remembered to check her voicemail from Mateo. Again, his guys didn't find anyone prowling around the property. Two of the guards walked in the woods for several yards, but there was no indication of a trespasser.

I know what I saw and heard.

"Elvis, I'm not sure that makes me feel better or worse. Somebody ran into the woods. Again."

She fired off a text to Mateo to thank his team for checking and asked the overnight crew to watch for any trespassers. Perhaps it really was time she beefed up security at her place—more cameras, at least.

Heading toward the patio, a tall figure waving both arms trotted toward her. "Cassidy! Cassidy!"

Still gun-shy from her earlier encounter, she hesitated. Some of the panic subsided when she realized it was Deputy Turner.

"What's up?" She tried to keep her voice from quaking. Elvis launched himself at the deputy's shoes. The dog was determined to get the law enforcement officer's attention and stall for more outdoor time.

"I talked to one of your guards. Any sign of the person you saw in the woods?" He patted Elvis.

"No. He or she hightailed it into the forest. The person was really tall from what I could tell, so I'm guessing it's a *he*. Anyway, he tore into the underbrush. I followed but couldn't catch him."

He shined his flashlight on her and pulled a twig out of her long, curly hair. "It looks like you ran quite the race there. You're all scratched up. You better go take care of that."

She nodded. "There wasn't really a path in the woods."

"And of course, you decided to follow instead of calling us. Because that's what Mrs. Fletcher or Miss Marple would do. I think someone watches too many detective shows."

Cassidy clenched one hand at her side, bristling at being scolded yet again. "I called my security guards. I didn't know if it was police-worthy yet." She stared back at the imposing deputy, daring him to lecture her.

"With all the craziness around here, err on the side of caution and call it in," he said. "It's our job to figure it out. We want to make sure everyone is safe."

She continued to stare at him without saying a word. There was no way she could remain civil if he talked to her like a child again.

"I'll make sure you get inside safely. Lock your door." He motioned for her to go ahead of him toward the patio.

Her heart was still pounding from her race through the woods, and from being startled. She was pretty sure she'd be sleeping with a baseball bat tonight.

Shutting the door behind her, Cassidy brushed aside the feeling of guilt about not telling him about Johnny Storm's planner. She soothed her conscience by telling herself that if the professional forensics team missed the planner in their search, but the Pearly Girls found it, perhaps she had the better detective team. At least they were better snoopers.

FRIDAY MORNING

It was the last big weekend of the Groovin' through the Decades concert series, so Cassidy treated herself and Elvis to a longer than normal walk after breakfast to soak in some of the solitude of the mountains before they dove headfirst into planning for the next round of events.

As they cut through to the meadow, guys in black were packing up the outside gear. Beau sat on a camp stool off to the side and scrolled through his phone.

"Good morning." She repeated the greeting more loudly when he didn't look up the first couple of times she spoke.

"Hey, good morning. Ready for the last big hurrah? I hope you and your friends are ready for some VIP treatment. I had Bianca save you some really good seats."

"That will be fun. I'm sure Roxie, Kate, Aileen, and Ruthanne are looking forward to it. They've been fans for quite a while."

"And you need to come, too," he said. "Karl owes all of you a debt of gratitude. I'm glad you're still fans after all his antics. Sometimes, he can be too much."

"Uh, do you have a minute? I have a music question. I'm curious about how things work in your industry." Cassidy tried to come off more carefree about it so he wouldn't suspect why she was asking.

"Sure. I'll try to answer your questions. The lawyers and accountants take care of the big stuff like rights and contracts. But I know a couple of things." Beau set his phone on his thigh and stared at her.

"Do all the band members get an equal share of the royalties? Or would someone get more or less, and when would that happen? And who decides all that?"

His eyebrows furrowed until they formed a giant *V* above the bridge of his nose. "It depends. Some bands make a pact, and it's in their contract to share everything equally. Sometimes, the songwriter gets the biggest cut. Sometimes, the original members get a larger cut than newer folks. Sometimes, it's the lead singer. It depends on how they set up their contracts. There are a lot of bands who don't write their own music, so that gets into all kinds of lawyerly things. There're a lot of factors. Everything depends on the set of particular circumstances. So, I guess the answer is, it depends."

Cassidy did her best to keep her expression neutral but inquisitive—without coming off as overly curious. It wouldn't do her any good if he became suspicious and clammed up. "I'm curious and fascinated with this music world. It's all very interesting. I didn't have any clue about the ins and outs and what goes into writing a song and getting it on the radio."

"There are a lot more ways for musicians these days. The internet opened up some avenues that had been controlled by the music industry for a long time. It's good for the indies, but if folks want to really make it with a wide distribution, then they need a crackerjack management team to look out for their best interests." His chest puffed out a bit as he straightened his back and raised his nose in the air.

"I am amazed at all the talent and all the stuff behind the scenes."

"You don't know half of it." Beau chuckled, then glanced down at his phone when it pinged an alert. "There is a lot of wheeling and dealing no one ever sees."

"I thought I read somewhere Dirk actually wrote most of the band's songs." Her stomach knotted up. What if she pushed the conversation too far and he suspected she was grilling him for information related to the case instead of just an ordinary interest?

"Huh? No. He wrote a handful. Karl wrote a few, but eighty or eighty-five percent—especially all their hits—were written by Johnny."

That's not what the online streaming sites say. How do I press for more information? "So, what happens with the band now that Johnny Storm is, well..."

"It depends on who his heirs are and what they want to do. They'll get his part of the royalties. The band and their label haven't talked to determine what the next steps are. I'm guessing the guys, based on their circumstances, will want to continue touring." He made a face but didn't add anything else.

Beau glanced at his phone several times. Sensing he was tiring of the conversation and the barrage of questions, she decided she probably wouldn't get anything more out of him. "It was good to talk to you. Thanks for explaining the process to me. I'm looking forward to the show tonight." Cassidy waved and walked away.

Setting her phone on the desk, she pored over sites about the Weathermen again. "Elvis, I know I saw places where that BJ person was listed as the songwriter. Something seems fishy." She searched several other music sites where BJ Taylor was listed in the writing credits. Printing copies of all the pages, Cassidy slid them into a folder.

Something isn't right. Why are all these changed? This doesn't make sense after what Beau said. And who changed them from Johnny to this BJ person?

The issues with the songwriter nagged her. She searched each album by name on several different sites and created a spreadsheet listing all the songs and who received writing credits for each.

Her head started to throb, and her neck was stiff. To relax, she stood and did several yoga stretches. "Okay, Elvis." She addressed the dozing dog who barely opened one eye to acknowledge her. "By my count, that BJ person wrote all the songs Beau said Johnny wrote. This doesn't make sense. As the manager, wouldn't he know what was going on?"

She saved her spreadsheet and printed a copy for her folder. "That's enough for today. We need to get ready for the show." Elvis sprang from his bed and circled her desk.

Seeing Johnny's day planner in the drawer, she picked up her phone and dialed before she lost her nerve. After nearly hanging up several times, she left Deputy Turner a message. "Deputy, this is Cassidy. I have some information on Johnny Storm for you. Can you meet me in town sometime tomorrow?"

A tinge of excitement spread through her core. *Stop it. It's not a date. It's not even a social call. Yes, he's tall and handsome, but he bugs me to death with all his Dudley Do-Right talk and lectures. I'm going to hand over the planner and what I found online. The deputy can do what he wants with it. I want to clear Roxie. Plus, Deputy Turner did say to report anything I find. So here it is.*

Brushing off the nagging feelings about how to explain precisely how she came to be in possession of the planner to the by-the-books deputy, she shut off her laptop and the office lights. "Come on, Elvis. It's time for your dinner."

After filling Elvis's bowls to his satisfaction, she reheated some leftover spaghetti for herself.

She fluffed her hair, freshened her makeup, and changed her shoes to a pair of strappy sandals. Unable to remember the last date she'd been on, she made a promise to herself to do more things not revolving around work. This business had been all-consuming lately, and she hadn't kept in touch with friends. Envious of the Pearly Girls, she craved some fun and adventure.

With Elvis busy devouring his dinner, Cassidy pocketed her keys, phone, and debit card, and slipped out the door.

She heard the crowds before she rounded the corner near the entrance. Hundreds of people filed in through the front gates. Johnny Storm's death hadn't hurt the band's popularity. Somehow, his murder had created a surge of interest. A lot of the crowd appeared younger than their previous audiences, too.

"Yoo-hoo, Cassidy! We're over here." Aileen and Kate waved from dead center in the front row.

"We have the whole row. Roxie left to see if she could find anyone else to join the party." Ruthanne wiggled in her seat like a teenage girl at her first concert. "This is going to be so much fun. Anybody you want to bring up here? We have plenty of reserved seats. I feel so special."

"I don't think Levi's interested. He's not into the music scene." Cassidy realized her network of social acquaintances, much less friends, was decidedly lacking. Yet another sign it was time she made time for friends and parties.

Before any of the women could continue their conversation, the lights on and around the stage started flashing, and the band members found their places on stage. Beau trotted out and grabbed the microphone. "Good evening, folks. I'm Beau Cox. The Weathermen are excited to be here even though we've all suffered a recent loss with the tragic death of Johnny Storm. Let's take a moment of silence to remember him."

After what seemed like ten minutes but was probably only a minute or so, Beau continued, "But he would want us to celebrate, and that's why we're here tonight. Before we get started though, I'd like to introduce you to some amazing ladies. In the front row, right there, we have Aileen, Kate, Roxie, Ruthanne, and Cassidy—the lovely owner of this amazing property. They made this great venue available for our enjoyment. Let's show them some love with a big ol' round of applause."

When the noise died down, Beau motioned to someone just off stage. "I have a present for you lovely ladies to say thank you for your help and hospitality this week." Two roadies with armfuls of bouquets ran out and passed one to each of the women. Roxie stood and gave the crowd a queenly wave. The audience erupted in cheers again. It was nice to see the Pearly Girls enjoying their fifteen minutes of fame.

Camera flashes exploded all around Cassidy causing black dots to dance in her line of vision until her eyes adjusted.

"Thanks for everything." Beau clapped for the gals. "What a way to start off this celebration. And now, I present to you all, the Weathermen! So, sit back and enjoy the show."

The concert, with its multiple encores, lasted until about ten thirty. Cassidy, along with the rest of the crowd, was on her feet for the last forty-five minutes. The guys put on a good show.

Somehow, it felt like a last hurrah for the remaining bandmates.

"Come on, gals. Jack told me earlier we were all invited to their shindig backstage. Sam, that hunky roadie over there with the earpiece, will show us where to go." Roxie shooed the rest of her friends toward the stage. "Come on, Cassidy, that means you, too. Come on before all the champagne's gone."

Cassidy traipsed behind Ruthanne and Kate to the steps leading to the area behind the stage. Long tables laden with appetizers and a makeshift bar lined one side. The band and their team heaped food on paper plates and headed for the self-serve bar.

"Hey, ladies." Beau swooped in flapping both arms like some kind of crane. "Welcome. Get some food and your beverage of choice. I know Karl wants to talk to you all."

"This should be good." Roxie's smile faded.

"He better apologize." Kate balled her hands into fists and planted them on her hips.

"He's still on my bad list. That was a terrible thing to do to us," whispered Ruthanne. "I don't like being the patsy."

The gals mingled with the band and some reporters who found their way backstage. Cassidy sidled up to a group Dirk and Jack were tag-teaming with tales of funny escapades.

Someone tapped her shoulder. When Cassidy turned, Beau motioned for her to follow him. Behind some speakers, Karl leaned on a large black box. The Pearly Girls, Cassidy, and Beau formed a semicircle around him. A panicked look crossed the bass player's face.

When no one spoke, Beau finally made the first move to nudge Karl along. "Karl, the ladies are here to see you. Isn't there something you want to say to them? You know, about Harrisonburg." The manager stepped closer.

Karl flinched. "Sorry. I thought Lizard knew we had his car. I didn't mean to cause all that trouble." Karl stared at his feet. "When I saw all those cop cars, I spazzed. I could hear Beau and Johnny in the back of my head, warning me not to get arrested again. I freaked out and took off. Sorry I got you all in trouble. I had no idea they would take you in. I swear I thought the cops would let you go."

Ruthanne stepped forward and patted his shoulder. "Well, that's not what happened, but I guess we understand. Everything's been sorted out now, so let's enjoy the evening. No harm done since Beau got all the charges dropped. I'm so excited we've gotten to meet the band. And I love my flowers."

Roxie rolled her eyes and swallowed whatever comment she was going to make.

Kate opened her mouth but closed it again.

Karl reminded Cassidy of a fish out of water. He used the first lull in the conversation to escape the ladies.

After more chitchat about the band's exploits over the years and some photos, Cassidy said her goodbyes. Heading home, the music still rang in her ears. She enjoyed the night sounds of the woods. Lights across the valley twinkled in the darkness. Peace and harmony had returned to her little corner of the world. Now, if they could bring Johnny's killer to justice, then all would be right.

Beau's comments about the songwriters kept worming into her head. Something wasn't right on the business side for this band. *Do*

Johnny's meetings with AE, the attorney, have something to do with this BJ person? And did some kind of behind-the-scenes scheme lead to his murder? What have I uncovered?

LATE SATURDAY MORNING

Cassidy dragged herself out of bed and downstairs to the office. Elvis had no problem in the perkiness department today. He zoomed up and down the stairs twice before she made it halfway down. A double espresso helped her tackle the fall event schedule, her socials, and newsletter. Glancing at the vase of flowers on her desk, she smiled. It was nice of Beau to thank the Pearly Girls publicly, especially after all the trouble Karl had caused. Despite the issues and the tragedy, the shows were fun. She hoped to bring more events like this to the valley.

Footsteps on the porch sent Elvis into DEFCON 4. It took a minute to calm him before she could get the door open and greet the new arrivals.

Dirk blocked the doorway with Beau close behind him. Elvis continued to let out a steady growl every few seconds.

Uh oh. This can't be good. What now?

The two men continued to stand in silence on her porch. "Good morning. Won't you both come in?" She scooped up Elvis to calm him.

"Hey, Cassidy. Sorry to bother you. We're having another issue with Karl. We think he's hurt. Can you come with us? We need you now." Beau squinted and his mouth twitched like a tic.

"Is everything okay?" She set Elvis down.

No one said anything, which sent the tiny hairs on the nape of her neck to full attention. Dirk stared intently at her like he was telepathically trying to send a message. Not picking up on the meaning of his weird stare, she shrugged. "Let me get my phone in case we have to call for help."

"No time. Come on. Now." Dirk grabbed her arm and pulled her through the doorway and away from Beau.

Trying to keep her balance, she closed the door and followed the men down the steps toward the woods.

"Come on. Pick it up." Dirk nudged them along from behind. "We need to hurry. Who knows what he's done this time?"

Beau glared at Dirk and swallowed whatever retort he had.

They were almost jogging when they reached the garden. Cassidy's nerves were fraying. None of this seemed right. "How much farther? Where is he? Should we call an ambulance?"

"He's near the cave," Dirk said. "I'm afraid he might harm himself. We need to hurry."

"Yeah, let's see what we can do first before authorities and the press get wind of this." Beau wiped his brow with the back of his hand. "Maybe we can take care of it. I hate to make it a bigger deal than it is."

"And what's wrong with him?" Cassidy was concerned they needed an ambulance.

"Dunno." Dirk just kept walking straight ahead without slowing his pace. "He was acting weird, even for Karl. He was moaning and mumbling to himself. I got a strange feeling, and I want to make sure he doesn't hurt himself."

"What makes you think he'd do that?" Beau hesitated, shifting his weight from one foot to the other.

"His behavior has been erratic." Dirk's tone became more agitated. "I didn't know if he was on something. He kept whining about not having anything and this wasn't how he was supposed to end up. He was upset about Johnny. He complained his family doesn't talk to him. He said he was better off dead, then he ran off in the woods. Come on. We have to find him before it's too late."

Beau nodded slowly. "You can never tell with him. He cries wolf so much. It's hard to know when there's really a problem. And I think sometimes he only does it for the attention, or to see how people will react. He's always wanted more of a lead role with the band. I think he's always resented being in Johnny's shadow."

Cassidy slowed her gait for a moment. Could Karl have wanted Johnny out of the picture bad enough to kill him? Was all his weird behavior related to that? And if he wanted more of the spotlight, then why was he upset now? Guilty feelings?

"Come on. This way." Dirk nudged her arm.

Cassidy and Beau hurried through the garden with Dirk on their heels. Cassidy gasped. Seeing the koi pond again triggered a flashback to Johnny Storm's lifeless body floating among the lily pads. *Could Karl really have strangled his friend because of jealousy?* An icy sensation flooded through Cassidy. Trying to dispel the morbid thoughts, she took several deep, cleansing breaths. She paused and closed her eyes for a minute. *Relax. There's nothing to indicate anything horrible has happened to Karl. You're on edge. Relax. You will figure this out.*

"Hurry up." Beau now tugged at her arm. "We need to find him."

They hurried past the rocky grotto and slipped around the wooden fencing blocking the entrance to the cave.

"Karl!" Dirk yelled into the cave's dark mouth.

They paused and listened.

"Was that a moan? I heard something." Beau took a step toward the cave but stopped.

"Shh!" Dirk ordered. "Listen."

Cassidy nodded furiously. "I heard it, too. It sounds like it's coming from in there."

Flipping on the flashlight app on his phone, Dirk stepped into the edge of the inky darkness. "It might be an echo. It's hard to tell. Karl, are you in there?"

Beau rushed behind Dirk and tugged on his arm. "I don't think it's coming from that direction. That way. It definitely came from over there. Come on." He pointed to the craggy rocks. "He might have fallen or something. We've got to find him."

Beau and Cassidy climbed over the rocks and headed into the overgrown wooded area. As they trudged deeper into the woods, covered by a thick canopy of leaves that blocked out most of the sun's light, the temperature dropped several degrees. Cassidy made her way over the craggy ground, keeping an eye out for roots and downed trees. The three became separated as they searched for Karl. Every once in a while, she'd hear one of the guys yell out his name. Their calls mixed with the birds and other forest noises.

I hope there are no ticks or giant spiders back here. Shake it off, girl. You need to find Karl before something else happens.

The trio searched through the brambles for what seemed like hours. There were no signs to indicate Karl had ever been back here.

A crash echoed through the woods, followed by a string of curses. Then silence.

"Dirk? Dirk, where are you? Are you okay?" Beau yelled. "Dirk, are you hurt? Karl, is that you? Who's there? Somebody answer me."

Cassidy scrambled up a large rock to get a better view. She couldn't see anyone. No motion. No other voices. "Beau? Dirk? What's going on?" The only sound was the pounding of her own heartbeat. "Beau! Dirk!"

A crack rang out. Several birds shot out of the nearby trees with a lot of caws and flapping. Cassidy jumped down and ducked behind a tree.

Was that a gunshot?

Before she could decide what to do, Beau yelled, "What are you doing, man? Cassidy, Cassidy, run! Run now. He's got a gun. Dirk, what is wrong with you?"

Adrenaline coursed through Cassidy. She ran back toward the cave, her clothes and bare skin slashed by rocks and low-hanging branches that she tried to dodge.

A few seconds later, Beau crashed through the underbrush and shoved her inside the cave. "Be quiet," he hissed. "I don't know what happened out there, but I think he's shooting at me. We've got to take cover now. We need a place to hide. Don't make a sound. I'm sure he's following me. We've got to take cover and figure out what to do. Maybe he hurt Karl."

The pair pushed deeper into the cave with no light. Cassidy grabbed Beau's hand. With her other, she felt along the craggy wall. "This way," she said. "It goes back to a large chamber about twenty feet inside. Then some tunnels feed off the main area." The pair inched along the cave's stone wall in the murky darkness. The cool stillness created an eerie sensation giving her goose bumps and making her think of every possible creepy crawly that could be lurking in the dark.

"What if there's something in here? This could be dangerous. But I don't want to be a sitting duck when he comes for us," Beau took uneven, ragged breaths. "He could do us in and leave us here to rot. It could be weeks before they find us." He let out a heavy sigh. "I guess we'll take our chances. The odds aren't that great right now."

"I think Dirk and his gun are scarier than anything that would be in here." She continued to scoot along inside the cave. "I used to play in here as a kid. There are other exits. If we keep moving, we'll find them. And bears don't hibernate this time of year. Foxes are scared of us. The worst it could be is bats." She shuddered but kept inching along the wall.

The pair edged slowly into the cave's cooler interior.

Cassidy's foot bumped into something. She tripped and fell forward, almost pulling Beau with her. Something soft and warm broke her fall. Whatever she landed on started to groan. *It can't be a bear. Relax and don't be silly. That groan sounds almost human.* She jumped up to get away from whatever moved. Catching her breath, she checked her hands and knees for injuries. No pain in her arms or legs.

"What happened?" Beau's baritone voice boomed in the cave. "Is everything okay? Cassidy, what happened?"

"Uhhh... Help me." A weak, but somewhat familiar voice came from the direction where she'd fallen. "He tried to kill me. Get away from him. He'll try to kill you, too. He wants it all. You have to get away from him before it's too late."

"Karl, is that you?" Beau asked. "It's me and Cassidy. Dirk was chasing us in the woods. We're hoping we lost him. We've got to find a place to hide. He's coming for us. He has a gun."

"Huh. You gotta get away. What? Beau? Not Dirk...my head hurts...and I dropped my phone. It's got to be somewhere around here." Karl's voice faded in the darkness.

"Stay still. We'll get help for you." Cassidy dropped to her hands and knees. "Beau, help me find his phone."

The two of them felt around in the darkness of the cave. She tried not to think too much about what she was crawling around on and all the little critters that could be waiting to bite her fingers. "Beau, head to the other side and work your way back. When he dropped the phone, it may have skidded further back. We've got to find it before Dirk figures out where we are. This is a relatively small space. We can find it."

Their painstaking search stretched on unbearably long for Cassidy's already frayed nerves. *How long has Dirk been gone? If he can't find us in the woods, he'll know we ran into the cave. It's a matter of time before he figures it out. We've got to get out of here and get help. But what did Karl say about Dirk? Is he confused in his addled state? We've got to find that phone, our only link to help. It's here somewhere. I hope it still works.*

Cassidy tried to calm the butterflies flapping around in her stomach and focus on her search. *Slow and steady. Keep going. We've got to find that phone. If we try to run out of the front of the cave with an injured guy, we'll be targets. The phone will help us find the other exits and contact help.* She pushed forward. "The phone couldn't have bounced far. We're going to find it. Karl, hang on. We'll get you out of here."

Karl groaned again. "I can't believe he'd turn on us all... squabbled and fought over the years...he stole from us... took what was ours... Johnny figured it out."

"Karl, be still," Beau ordered. "Save your strength."

The bass player moaned again and rustled. "Cassidy... got to get away from him... now."

Karl's voice came from Cassidy's left.

Still on target. I'm so afraid of getting turned around in here. The darkness and the echoes make it so disorienting. Take a deep breath, girl. You can do this. That phone is around here somewhere.

Cassidy's foot bumped against something that didn't feel like a rock. It skittered across the floor. She scrambled to see what it was. If it was his phone, she prayed she hadn't jut broken it.

Feeling around with both hands, she landed on something that was not rock nor dirt. The coldness of the plastic and glass felt like a million dollars. She touched the screen, and the light illuminated the space like a beacon of hope. "I found it! Karl, what's your password?"

"5-2-7-5. It spells Karl." His voice was weaker than minutes before.

There were no bars on the screen. They were too deep in the cave to make a call. Crossing her fingers, she racked her brain for the sheriff's number. Remembering Deputy Turner's, she banged out a quick text and said a silent prayer when the "delivered" note appeared under it.

"Here, give me that." Beau reached for the phone.

"There's no service here. Help me with Karl. We need to head that way and then through the tunnel. There are exits on the other side of the garden. I'll use the phone as a flashlight, but I need you to help me keep Karl on his feet. We've got to get out of here before Dirk finds us."

"We should go for help and come back and get him. He'll be okay. Come on. We need to get out of here." Beau grabbed her arm. She tightened her grip on the phone.

Karl moaned again. "Don't leave.... He'll come back and kill me, or he'll leave me here to die. You shouldn't be out there with him... try to kill you too...can't trust him." Karl gasped and collapsed onto the stone floor.

"We need to take him with us. Grab him on one side. I'll take the other." Cassidy tried to hoist Karl to a standing position, but he was too heavy for her to lift and hold the light at the same time.

Beau reached over and pulled the bass player to his feet. "Man, Karl. You've gained weight. I'm struggling here. Come on, help me a little. Work with me."

"Everything hurts, and I'm dizzy," Karl whined. "I want to go to sleep. Leave me alone. I'm going to die here anyway. You said so yourself."

What did Karl just say?

They raised Karl up. He made a feeble attempt to hold on to their shoulders. Cassidy grabbed his waist with one hand and pointed the phone's flashlight to shine in front of them. "Come on. There are tunnels back here. Both lead out to the other side. We can find a way to escape and call for help."

"Let's go before Dirk realizes we're in here. This may give us a chance." Beau pulled Karl forward. "He won't know about the other exits."

Several yards ahead, tunnels forked off in a Y shape. "Which one?" Beau asked.

Cassidy squeezed her eyes shut for a moment, reaching back into her memory of this place. It had been a long time since she'd been here. She and her grandfather used to explore the area when she was younger, looking for relics from cavers from days gone by. They had found cans and discarded camping equipment. One of the walls had some graffiti on it dating back to the 1920s. She always wondered who the other visitors were. Family lore told of a relative's bootlegging operation here during Prohibition. It was the perfect place to hide the illegal hooch. The underground climate was the right temperature for storage, and it was out of the way of prying eyes.

Cassidy shook off the memories. "The right one. If I remember correctly, the opening is bigger, like a door, and we don't have to climb up and out of the exit. It'll be easier for Karl."

Karl moaned more as they moved through the tunnel. The roofline sloped upward slightly, and the walls narrowed. The three barely fit standing shoulder to shoulder.

The walls seemed to close in on them. The floor sloped uphill, and light streamed in from an opening ahead. Cassidy blinked several times for her eyes to adjust to the brightness ahead of them.

"We made it." Beau let out a small puff of air. "We're safe."

Cassidy and Beau dragged Karl the remaining few feet to the opening. Outside, they helped the injured man to a seated position on a large rock near an oak tree. He moaned and leaned forward, grasping his head. "We've got to get away from him now before it's too late." He moaned again. "I'm gonna be sick."

"Take some deep breaths. We'll get help for you soon." Cassidy tapped on Karl's phone.

"Hey, wait. Y'all be quiet. I hear something." Beau stood on a nearby rock and scanned the wooded area. "I definitely heard something. Maybe we need to go back inside the tunnel. What if it's Dirk? We need to be quiet," he whispered.

She tapped out 9-1-1 on the cracked phone screen. The call connected quickly. "This is Cassidy Jamison over at Celebrations on Ivy Ridge Road. We've got an injured person here on the back of the property near the cave and the gardens. It's Karl Schultz. Also, there's someone after us. He has a gun. Please send someone fast. And make sure to let Sheriff Howell know. The victim is related to his murder investigations. Please hurry."

"Who are you talking to?" Beau took a menacing step toward Cassidy. He balled both hands into fists and stepped closer to her.

Her face must have registered shock at his outburst because even Karl paused his groaning to stare at the pair. "I was letting the ambulance know about Karl. He needs help now."

Beau's friendly features melted into a menacing sneer. Beau took another step closer, then another until they were mere inches apart.

"Ma'am? Cassidy? Who is with you? Are you all okay? Police and rescue are on the way. Please let me know you're there and safe. Cassidy? Cassidy?" The dispatcher's voice became more frantic.

Beau and Dirk. Beau and Dirk. What was Karl trying to tell me? An icy chill rocketed through Cassidy when the realization hit her. Dirk wasn't chasing them to kill them. He was trying to help. Random facts started fitting together. The giant puzzle was slowly coming into focus. The murderer was here in plain sight all along.

Money. It all revolves around money.

Before Cassidy could react, Dirk crashed through the underbrush and skidded to a stop between Beau and Cassidy.

"Run. He's got a gun!" Beau yelled as Karl let out a noise that sounded like a wounded animal.

Dirk kept one hand in his jacket pocket. "I found you. You can't hide. You're going to pay for what you did," he hissed.

SATURDAY

"I can't believe what you did," Dirk sneered. "I'm not letting you get away with this."

"What are you talking about? It's you who's going down for all of this." Beau stepped closer to Cassidy's side.

Karl looked up, his face lined with confusion. "But you're the one..."

"Shut up. All of you," Beau growled. "And put your hands where I can see them. I've had enough. I am done with you all."

Dirk slowly pulled his hand out of his pocket and put both palms upward. "This is far from over. You have my word on it. You won't get away with this. You may run, but you will pay for what you did."

Thoughts zoomed through Cassidy's mind. Those puzzle pieces were clicking into place almost faster than she could process. It wasn't Dirk after all. Beau was the one cheating them. Johnny had to be neutralized when he found out about their manager's deeds. Beads of sweat popped on her forehead, and her hands quaked slightly. Remembering the phone, she hid it behind her and kept the line open. She could hear the dispatcher faintly calling her name.

"Beau, Dirk, Karl, what is going on here?" Cassidy spoke loudly, trying to provide information to the dispatcher. "Karl is hurt. I can see that. But the rest of us can help him back to the office. It's a long hike to the maintenance road, but we can make it back if all three of us pitch in and help Karl get away from this cave."

Beau's and Dirk's heads jerked toward Cassidy at about the same time they realized someone was still on the line.

"Tsk. Tsk. Too bad for all of you. No more stalling. And we're not going back. All of you inside the cave. Now." Beau shoved Dirk. "And give me that phone before someone gets hurt."

Karl, Dirk, and Cassidy stared at the manager whose wild hair and beet-red face gave him a crazed look, so unlike the normally polished, fast-talking, perfectly styled professional they knew.

"Enough, I said." Beau pulled out a gun from his belt and waved it around. "You all have been too busy messing around in my business. And lucky for me, I have you all in one place. I can take care of this before anyone gets here. Now turn around and march. Back inside the cave. And give me that phone." He lunged for Cassidy.

Not wanting Beau to grab the phone, she threw it as hard as she could inside the cave. The phone crashed into the wall and made a cracking sound as it bounced on the rocky floor.

"That was stupid. But at least nobody will be using it now. All of you get a move on. Inside. Now." With his finger on the trigger, Beau waved the gun around. "I'm tired of playing with you all. I have things to do. You're wasting my time."

"What about me?" Karl tried to stand, but he toppled over in the dirt.

Cassidy turned to help him, but Beau pointed the gun in her direction. "Leave him for now. He's not going anywhere. I'll take care of the two of you and get him later."

"Beau, you've been cheating us for years, but this scheme was low even for you. And Johnny found out, didn't he? And you killed him." Dirk shook with fear or rage, or perhaps both. "Despicable."

"Yeah, why? What were you thinking?" Karl looked around, his eyes wide and his gaze unfocused. At the very least, the poor man had a concussion. "Why, man? What did he ever do to you, except make you rich? We were your gravy train for a long time." Karl slumped back. "We're all going to die here like Johnny." He whimpered, reminding Cassidy of Elvis when his favorite toy got caught behind the sofa and he couldn't reach it.

Beau swung the gun around and stepped closer to Karl. "He, like the rest of you, never appreciated anything I've ever done for you. I have given up my life and my family to be at your beck and call for almost forty years. And not once were any of you grateful for the opportunities or everything I did. I made you what you are. And Johnny was going to toss it all away. I spent countless hours getting you out of jams and keeping your stupid antics out of the paper. And for what? By the time you added up all the hours, I was working for less than minimum wage and losing way too much sleep. This job and all of you destroyed my life and my health. It was time to take care of *me*. And I'll be set to enjoy the rest of my time on earth without even thinking of you ever again."

"But why kill Johnny?" Dirk shook his head. "We were getting ready to go in the studio for another album."

"The writing was on the wall." Beau waved the gun around carelessly. "Johnny was tired of traveling and performing. He wanted out. There was no new album. He was done."

"But you said you had had enough. If it was over, you should have let us go. We all would have still had the royalties," Karl whined.

Dirk glared at Beau. "Not us. Just Beau. He made sure of that by killing Johnny."

"It was an accident." Beau lowered his voice. "We were arguing, and things just got out of hand. It was all a big mistake, but it turned out for the best. Your albums have been selling like gangbusters since it happened." A weird grin crossed the manager's face.

"But that wasn't the whole story," Cassidy interjected. "Johnny found out you were skimming and rerouting the band's royalties. You were telling them their sales were down, but actually pocketing the money."

Beau ran his empty hand through his silvery hair and glared at Cassidy. "It worked for a long time. And then people started sticking their noses in my business and asking stupid questions."

"Yep, we're those meddling kids." Dirk sneered. "We trusted you. You were part of our family. And this is how you treat us? I am going to be in the front row every day of your trial. The band's going to do every interview, blog, and podcast we can find, so everyone knows the truth about you and what you did."

"There won't be a trial. They're going to find your bodies in the cave in a week or so, and I'm going to do a teary press conference about how Karl was hopped up on drugs. It'll be something like a robbery gone bad. When he realized what he had done, he took his own life. You said yourself he'd been acting weird lately. Easy." Beau shrugged his shoulders. "I may even help all the volunteers look for you all." His crooked smile made Cassidy shiver.

"I'm not killing anyone," Karl growled, and then pushed himself off the ground where he'd fallen. "You can't pin this on me. Not cool." Karl lunged but fell forward into the leaves and dirt.

Cassidy moved over to help him, but Beau waved the gun at her again. "Leave him there. He deserves to sit and think about all the things he's done that got him in this jam. And now there's no one to bail him out."

Cassidy took a couple of steps backward, trying to get as far away from Beau and his gun as she could.

"Wait, Karl. I'll take care of it for you," Beau interrupted Karl's litany of groans. "Like I always do. Think of this as the last hurrah. You stay here. I'll be back in a few minutes to fix everything. Now don't go anywhere while I'm gone. Relax. It'll all be over soon."

Adrenaline surged through Cassidy. She had to do something fast. The police were nowhere in sight. They could not go back in the cave with Beau. That would be the end. They had to stay out here and stall until help arrived.

She took a deep breath. Karl still lay prone in the dirt, so she attempted to catch Dirk's eye by tipping her head slightly, but she wasn't sure he understood that she was trying to signal him.

It's now or never, girl. Go for it. And hope Dirk backs you up. You have to try something.

Cassidy let out a wail and lunged for Beau, causing him to lower the gun to try to catch his balance when all 110 pounds of her slammed into him. Dirk followed suit and piled on like a linebacker trying to get a loose ball. He landed on Beau, who knocked Cassidy over. As the two men scrapped in the dirt, Cassidy crawled out from the melee and scrabbled for the gun.

Grabbing the cold metal of the gun, she trained it on the tumbleweed of arms and legs. As their wrestling match continued, she darted into the cave and searched for the phone. Maybe, against all odds, it was still working.

After what seemed like an eternity of searching, she found the phone and hurried back out to survey the damage.

Dirk and Beau continued their tussle in the dirt. It was hard to tell who was winning in the dirt cloud they kicked up in their wake. The person on the top of the heap changed every few seconds.

Turning the phone over in her hands, she stared at the fractured screen. Pressing the button, she said a silent thank-you when the screen lit up.

While Beau was occupied with Dirk, she punched in 9-1-1. The call connected but before the operator could speak, she blurted, "This is Cassidy Jamison over at Celebrations at Ivy Springs again. I need the police immediately. We have been attacked by a man with a gun. Tell the sheriff he's the one who killed Johnny Storm and attacked the others. It's Beau Cox. Please tell them to hurry. I have the killer's gun, but he's still fighting with one of the other guys. I need help now."

"Okay. Who else is with you?" The dispatcher's voice was calm but strained. It wasn't every day the police in this tiny town had anything more than a car accident or a lost dog called in.

"We're outside behind the cave on the property. In the woods. Tell the police officers I have his gun. I'm with Dirk and Karl from the band. And we're trying to subdue Beau, the band's manager."

"Will do. I'm relaying that to them now. You called earlier for an ambulance, right?"

"Yes, Karl needs an ambulance. He's got a lot of injuries."

"They drove around your property and couldn't find anyone," the dispatcher said. "They are still in the area. I'll relay the information for you."

"We need them desperately." She gave directions from the parking lot and tried to describe where they were in the woods.

"Okay, the ambulance and police are headed your way. It's going to be a few minutes. Stay on the line with me."

Dirk and Beau continued to roll around in the dirt and leaves, exchanging punches that sometimes connected with their intended targets.

Someone kicked Cassidy in the leg, causing her to stumble. She dropped the phone but managed to hold on to the gun. "Stop it," she yelled. "Right now."

Dirk flipped Beau over in a WrestleMania move and lay across him, pinning him to the ground. Both men, covered in debris, breathed heavily, gasping and wheezing.

"This is over. The police are on the way. And they'll sort out all the details. I have the gun, so nobody move. I'm a little on edge, and you don't want my trigger finger to slip."

Karl tried to sit up, leading to a string of moans. "Tell them to hurry. I think I'm gonna pass out."

Footsteps thundered through the woods. Sheriff Howell, Deputy Turner, and another deputy Cassidy didn't recognize broke through the underbrush and surrounded the group with guns drawn. "Nobody move!" the sheriff yelled. "Cassidy, what is going on here?"

She lowered the gun and handed it to Deputy Turner. "Beau has been skimming off the band for years. Johnny Storm found out about it. He confronted him, and Beau killed him." She took a deep breath and looked at Dirk and Beau. "Earlier today, Beau told Dirk and me that Karl was hurt, and we had to come and help him. He was hurt because Beau had attacked him. Beau was going to kill all of us and make it look like Karl did it. You know, murder-suicide."

"Are you okay?" The deputy quickly retrieved the gun. He held Cassidy's hand for a few seconds longer than necessary. She was surprisingly warmed by the genuine concern in his eyes.

She nodded as Karl interrupted. "What about me? I'm the one who got attacked and dragged in and out of that cave."

"Rescue is on the way." The sheriff pointed to the third deputy. "Why don't you go flag them down. We'll secure him and the crime scene."

Deputy Turner cuffed Beau and sat him up on a rock while the sheriff checked on Karl. Based on all the dirt and rumpled appearance of both Beau and Dirk, they could've easily said they'd both been wrestling a pig, and no one would have questioned it.

"I'm so sorry," Cassidy whispered to Dirk who stood moving rocks and dirt with the toe of his boot. "Beau was so convincing when he was trying to escape from you. It didn't dawn on me until Karl started talking that Beau was really the guilty one."

"He's like that. He's been a con man all his life. We didn't get wise to him until recently, and it cost us money and cost Johnny everything. Beau will never know how much damage and pain he caused us." Dirk shook his head slowly.

"We'll be over to talk to you in a bit," the sheriff said. "Why don't you both have a seat and wait. One of you over there, and the other across the way on those rocks." He pointed to places far enough away for them not to carry on a normal conversation. "We need to get both of your statements."

"And mine." Karl lifted his head.

"Yes, and yours, too."

Cassidy found her spot and settled in to watch as the three EMTs circled Karl. Another bumped a gurney over the uneven terrain. Suddenly talkative, Karl listed off every possible ailment and every injury Beau had caused.

The EMTs finally strapped Karl to the gurney and rolled him back down the path. When they passed, Cassidy hopped up. "Wait. I have his phone. Thanks, Karl. This saved us." She handed it to the nearest EMT.

"No problem. This thing's seen better days. Glad I could help. Anything I can do to put that jackass behind bars. He needs to pay for what he did to us. And what he did to Johnny. That scumbag even stole my bass chords. He used them to kill my friend. Johnny's death wasn't an accident. That was cold and calculated. He was trying to set me up."

"He tried to set us both up. Your strings and my drumsticks. He turned our trademark instruments into a cruel weapon. Definitely premeditated. He wanted us to take the fall for it," Dirk growled in Beau's direction. "He took sick pleasure in pitting us against each other."

"Are you both okay?" Sheriff Howell approached Cassidy and Dirk. "You look a little worse for the wear. I'd like to get your statements, but we should probably get you checked out while the medical guys are here. Do you feel like walking back to the ambulances?"

Dirk and Cassidy followed the sheriff. The two deputies led the cuffed, and uncharacteristically quiet, Beau to the four police cruisers and two ambulances sitting at angles in the grass near the gravel road. Beau hung his head when the deputies put him in the back of one of the cruisers.

A series of flashes caused everyone to look toward the woods. Xander Mercer stepped forward and photographed Beau in the back seat of the police car. The band's manager tried to cover his face with his shoulder, but the handcuffs made it difficult.

"The media needs to stay back." The sheriff turned toward his deputy. "Get this area cordoned off."

Xander continued to snap away. When the police turned their backs, he moved closer to the ambulances.

"Y'all come over here," a female medic called out to Cassidy and Dirk, while the other EMTs loaded Karl into the back of the vehicle. "Sit right here. Any injuries or pain?"

Dirk shook his head. "I'm fine. I'll probably have a couple of bruises from wrestling Beau to the ground, but it's nothing a hot shower and a couple of aspirin won't cure."

"The same with me. We searched around in the cave, and then I jumped in the fracas when he was trying to subdue Beau. We're filthy, but I don't think anything's broken." Cassidy tried in vain to dust off her jeans, but her clothes were covered in so much dirt and cave gunk they were ready for the trash heap.

The EMT checked her pupils and her blood pressure. After a bit of poking, the medic deemed her healthy. "You seem to be okay. If there's any aches, take acetaminophen. You may want to put something like Neosporin on those scratches. If you experience any headaches or nausea, get checked out. But for now, stay here. The sheriff wants to talk to you."

Before either had a chance to move, Sheriff Howell and Deputy Turner swooped in.

Sheriff Howell took over the questioning while Deputy Turner directed Dirk to a spot a few yards away. "Okay, start at the beginning of today and tell me what happened."

Suddenly self-conscious of how she must look after the cave adventure and the fight, Cassidy tried to smooth her wild hair. "Uh, Beau and Dirk came into the office this morning and said they thought Karl was going to hurt himself. They wanted to find him, and they didn't want to cause another stir in the press. We hiked up the ridge to the cave. Dirk and Beau were acting weird."

"How so?" The sheriff pulled a small notebook and pen from his shirt pocket.

"I dunno. It's odd. They were anxious to find Karl, especially after all the other things that happened. There was some unspoken tension between the two of them. Then when we started searching around the cave, they decided we needed to look for Karl in the woods. We all separated, and I heard a gunshot. Beau ran out of the woods and said Dirk had a gun. We rushed in the cave to hide, and that's where we found Karl and his phone. We eventually followed one of the tunnels to another exit. And then Dirk found us. Karl, Beau, and Dirk started arguing, and I realized Dirk wasn't the attacker."

"How?"

"The argument was about money and how the band had been cheated. Beau got really agitated. I could tell from what Dirk and Karl were saying that they were the victims. Beau was acting squirrely, and then he pulled a gun on us."

"What else?"

"I saw an opportunity, and I lunged for Beau when he was yelling. That started the tussle. I got the gun, and Dirk jumped on Beau. I was able to call you all during the distraction."

"Anything else?"

She shook her head slightly. "Dirk and Karl said Johnny figured out what Beau had been doing. Beau made his murder weapon with the drumsticks and guitar strings to throw suspicion on the band members."

"If you think of anything else later, call me. You'll probably have the media descend on you again when word of this gets out." Sheriff Howell pointed to Xander, who was still snapping pictures of the scene.

Cassidy nodded and started planning her response in her head. When there was a long pause, she realized she hadn't responded yet. "Thanks. I'm going to head back home for a much-needed shower.

Let me know if you need anything. The gates are supposed to open soon for the concert tonight. Are we good to go ahead with it?"

"It shouldn't be an issue. We're going to transport Karl and Beau, and we'll be done here in an hour or so. You need a ride back to your place? I can have one of the deputies take you home." The sheriff tucked his notebook and pen away in his front pocket.

"That's okay. Y'all are busy. Plus, the walk will help me clear my head." She gave a little wave and headed down the path to home and a hot shower.

Deputy Turner smiled when she passed his cruiser. Then he turned quickly and said something to Beau and the other deputy.

Cassidy trekked along the path and cut across the field. The birds and the woodland noises replaced the earlier chaos at the cave. Life at this end of the road was as if nothing had happened.

She was glad they could wrap up the concerts tonight. She hoped the guys felt like performing. At last, Jack, Dirk, and Karl would finally get some closure. She hoped Karl felt up to it. He didn't look that good in the ambulance. She hoped they were able to recoup what Beau stole from them and get on with their lives.

Cassidy glanced at the barn and over in the direction of the amphitheater. In a few hours, it'd be filled for another concert. *And my place will forever be remembered as the place where the band's manager murdered Johnny Storm.*

26

SATURDAY AFTERNOON

A steamy shower turned her fingers pruny. A giant iced coffee made a world of difference. Feeling more like herself, she trashed her shirt and jeans from the morning's cave adventure. She slipped on a comfortable sweatshirt and a clean pair of jeans. She blow-dried her hair into long corkscrews and added a hint of makeup to cover the dark circles under her eyes. The reflection staring back at her from the mirror was perkier than how she really felt.

Locking the residence, she hurried down the stairs to the office. The Pearly Girls, Levi, and Elvis rushed her at the door. Everyone wanted information. Except Elvis. He wanted cuddles, and maybe a treat.

"Where have you been?" Aileen squeezed her so hard Cassidy feared her ribs would break. "We've been blowing up your phone for an hour. When we couldn't find you, we rushed over when all the chaos broke loose. Levi scoured the grounds for you until the police told us to shelter in place. It has been torture waiting for news."

"Sorry about that. Beau and Dirk came by the office and said Karl was in trouble. They needed help. And I left my phone on the desk."

"Well, what happened?" Roxie clasped Cassidy's hand in her own, not letting go. "We've been on edge for hours."

"Give her a second. I'm sure she's had quite an adventure."

At least Cassidy could count on Ruthanne to maintain some semblance of sanity amid the chaos that was the Pearly Girls. "Can I get you anything?" Ruthanne asked.

Cassidy shook her head. If she had another coffee, she'd be wired for a week.

Roxie pulled Cassidy to a chair and gently pushed her into it. "We want details. We saw all the ambulances and police fly through the gates with lights flashing. They told us to stay inside, so we hunkered down here."

Cassidy relayed the story that sounded scarier in the retelling. She paused and scanned the room. Five pairs of eyes stared at her waiting for her to continue. Elvis stared at her too because he still wanted a treat. She quickly added, "We took one of the tunnels out of the cave, but Dirk found us in the woods. There was a lot of fussing, and Dirk said Johnny realized someone was skimming their profits and cheating them. Beau pulled a gun, and then there was a fight. Well, it was more like two guys wrestling, but I managed to get the gun. And that's about when the police and ambulances arrived."

"Beau, the manager?" Kate's eyes widened.

Cassidy nodded. "He's been misreporting and stealing royalties and earnings for years. The other day I noticed some of the music sites listed BJ Taylor as the writer, and some didn't. I asked Beau about it, and he got all weird. He was changing the writing credits and funneling money to different accounts. He pitted the band members against each other and kept things stirred up."

"The chaos kept them arguing and distracted them." Aileen folded her arms over her chest. "And he almost got away with it if you hadn't figured out the financial scam."

"The planner you found led me to a media lawyer Johnny had been talking to. He definitely knew something was wrong." Cassidy was beginning to feel a bit anxious being the center of all this attention.

"See, we make a great team." Roxie smiled.

"And we'll forever be linked to the Weathermen." Ruthanne's face lit up like a teenager.

"None of us would have dreamed of that in the seventies. It's funny how things turn out," Kate said.

"I'm going to go check on things near the cave." Levi gave Elvis a pat on the head, handed him a treat, and then strolled toward the door. "Call me if you need anything. This is way too much drama and excitement for me."

"So, are we having a show tonight?" Roxie clasped her hands in front of her, resembling a child in a candy store with unlimited cash.

"The sheriff said they should be done soon. They took Karl to the hospital." Cassidy reached for the flyer on the coffee table. "Tonight, two tribute bands open for the Weathermen. One is for Billy Joel, and the other is for the Beach Boys. I wonder what they are going to do if Karl can't perform. From what the sheriff said, it sounded like we wouldn't have to cancel because of the investigation. But we don't know about Karl. I guess we'll see." Cassidy wandered to the back and picked up her phone to fire off a quick text to Steve and Bianca. Her phone rang before she had a chance to walk back to the front.

"Hey, Steve. How are you?"

"What is going on up there? Heard you had some crazy action this morning." Steve's voice was tense, but polite.

"The police took Karl to the hospital and arrested Beau Cox for the murder of Johnny Storm." There was no way to sugarcoat the news.

"Holy shamoli. Never in a million years would I have thought it was him. Bianca and I were speculating it was some angry ex-girlfriend or a crazed fan. Wow. That changes everything. That only leaves Jack and Dirk. Let me give them a call to see what they want to do. It's too late to get a sub. Maybe we'll have to just go with the opening acts. I'll call you back. But plan on opening the gates at the normal time unless you hear otherwise from me." The call clicked off before she had a chance to respond.

"What's up?" Ruthanne was biting her bottom lip, expecting the worst news.

"Steve, the promoter, said we're going on as planned tonight. If the Weathermen don't perform, we'll have the two opening acts instead."

"That should be interesting." Aileen shrugged. "I'll be there." The other gals nodded. "Though I'd like to see the Weathermen one last time."

"Cassidy, do you need anything while we're here?" Ruthanne's hands were fidgeting with the hem of her blouse. "Maybe you should go and rest, and we can take care of anything that pops up."

"I'm good. I'm going to work on a statement to get ahead of the barrage of questions we may get about Beau. I'm sure the arrest is going to stir up more interest and more media requests."

"I'm headed home to get ready. Meet y'all back here after five?" Roxie danced out the door while humming a familiar tune.

The gals chattered as they gathered their things. Elvis stood quietly by the couch watching the flurry of activity. In an instant, the gals were gone, and the silence in the office was almost deafening. The only noise was the air conditioning swishing through the ducts.

"Come on, puppy. We need to get some work done before the show."

Cassidy's phone pinged, distracting her. Bianca had texted an update: Karl's been released. The Weathermen are on for tonight.

She responded with a series of thumbs up and heart emoji, then fired off a text to the gals to give them the news. It didn't take long before her screen filled up with responses.

Ruthanne: Oh, yay. I'm so glad they can go on as planned. Can't wait.

Kate: I'm sure it'll be bittersweet, but maybe it will bring closure for them.

Aileen: Glad they decided to go on. A nice way to close out the festival. I know I'll cry.

Ruthanne: Me too. But it's going to be special.

Ruthanne: It's going to be chilly tonight.

Ruthanne: Y'all bring a sweater.

Roxie: Yes, mom. See you all tonight.

Cassidy finished her announcement about the arrest and directed questions about the investigation to Sheriff Howell. She added a line about tonight's concert with a link to purchase tickets for good measure. "Come on, let's go for a walk before I have to get ready." She grabbed Elvis's leash. He didn't need to be told twice.

The pair walked around the patio and the garden. Elvis tugged toward the path to the barn. "What's up with you? Usually, you want to visit your friends the fish."

He continued to lead her to the large red barn. "This'll be the center of attention in a few weeks. We've got two weddings and a big anniversary party scheduled for the barn." The rustic dairy barn held an unexpected surprise when the doors opened. The stalls had been turned into a bar/kitchen area. The loft now had a railing and was a place to view the action with some cozy seating. Originally used to house cattle and horses, the space was large enough for a stage and a dance floor, as well as enough tables to accommodate three hundred. Cassidy had covered the interior with thousands of twinkling lights creating a magical look for any occasion.

Elvis let out a low guttural growl and chased a chipmunk into the tall grass. "Okay, hunter dog. Good job at keeping us safe from the marauding hordes of chipmunks and squirrels. Let's go get ready."

Not wanting to give up on the chase, Elvis reluctantly stared at the grass.

"We have treats at home," she insisted.

The magic *T* word did the trick, and Elvis forgot all about his quest.

After getting him fed and settled, Cassidy rummaged through her closet for a layered outfit for tonight's show. Settling for a white camisole and a long multicolored sweater, she paired it with leggings and her purple Converse Chucks. She retreated to the bathroom to touch up her hair and makeup.

"Okay, Elvis. What do you think?"

The little dog opened one eye from his napping spot on the couch.

"I'll take that as a compliment. You stay here and guard the house. I'll be back soon."

The noise near the amphitheater and the smells from the food trucks caused her to pick up her pace. The crowd size hadn't diminished any with the murder and attacks.

The weight of the world lifted from Cassidy's shoulders. She took in deep breaths of mountain air. What a relief to put this behind them and to know the killer had been brought to justice. Tonight was for celebration and new beginnings.

She greeted people as she made her way along the line of food trucks. Deciding on a chartreuse-colored one covered in cartoon vegetables, she found a place in a short line that moved quickly to the service window.

"Cassidy? Cassidy! I thought that was you." Marion Jones, the librarian, breathlessly approached the food truck line. "Just who I wanted to talk to."

"Hi, Marion. Are you having a good time?" Cassidy shielded her eyes from the late afternoon sun.

"Oh, yes. We have a contingent of library workers over there who are out for a rollicking evening. I love what you've done with the place. That's kinda what I want to talk to you about. We will be having business council elections in November, and we think you would be great for one of the roles. Any interest?"

Cassidy stepped back in surprise. "I hadn't really thought about it. What are we talking about?"

"I'll email you the roles and the responsibilities. We have the four elected board roles and a bunch of committee chair positions we'd like to fill. Think about it. You'd be a great asset to our team. I'll email you, and you can let us know next week. We'd love to have you. It would be a great way to promote your events and to get reconnected with the town business owners."

The man ahead of her moved forward, and it was Cassidy's turn to order. "Thanks. I'm flattered. I'll think about it."

"Good. You're perfect for it. Let me know if you have any questions. See you soon." Marion melted into the crowd while Cassidy ordered her food.

After retrieving her peach tea and a Green Goblin pita with sprouts, spicy beans, and avocado, Cassidy found a spot to people watch and to eat her dinner.

Maybe a committee role would be a good opportunity. She'd been gone for a while, and things had changed. She did need to reconnect with the town folks. Even if she didn't feel ready yet to take on a big leadership role, maybe she could start small.

The first band started its sound check, and she balled up her wrapper and headed for the nearest trash can.

A hand tapped her on the shoulder. Cassidy jumped and let out a high-pitched squeal.

"I am so sorry. I didn't mean to startle you. You didn't turn around when I called your name." Ruthanne's expression registered concern with the fine lines around her eyes and lips more pronounced than Cassidy remembered.

Cassidy let out a heavy breath. "It's okay. I was lost in thought, and I'm still a little jumpy. You look nice."

"Thanks. It felt like a special occasion." Ruthanne held out both arms and twirled to model her sparkly pink blouse. "We're over in that section. Come sit with us. That is, if you don't have plans or a date."

"Sure. That will be fun. I'm looking forward to the lineup tonight. I've always loved Billy Joel and the Beach Boys."

The pair wended their way through the crowd and settled in next to the other Pearly Girls as a singer with jet-black hair and dark sunglasses took the stage. All he needed was a sequined jumpsuit, and he'd look like an Elvis impersonator.

Despite not resembling the Piano Man—at all—the singer did a respectable job of sounding like him. The crowd was on its feet for most of the show. And there were several audience sing-alongs with "My Life" and "We Didn't Start the Fire."

Between bands, Roxie and Kate passed out margaritas for everyone. The adult icy drinks were like Slurpees with a definitive kick.

"How fun," Ruthanne squealed. "Mine's watermelon. Yum."

"The truck back there has multiple slushy machines. We got one of each. Mine's prickly pear. It's got the sweetness of the fruit and a little kick of jalapeño to keep it exciting." Roxie sucked hers down quickly. If she wasn't careful, she'd get brain freeze.

Cassidy sat back and sipped her apple one. Tonight was turning out to be lots of fun. And after everything, she deserved some fun.

The songs from the sixties, seventies, and eighties warmed up the crowd. By the time the three Weathermen took the stage, everyone was standing. Karl walked gingerly to his bass and microphone stand. His stiff gait was the only visible indication of today's trauma.

"Hey, Virginia. We've had so much fun in your beautiful mountains. This place will always be bittersweet to us because of what happened to Johnny, but the view is stunning here, and you guys have been so wonderful. Thanks for packing this place every night to see us. We are humbled by the love and eternally grateful. So, sit back or stay on your feet. We like that, too. We hope you enjoy the show." Jack stepped back from the mic stand and then signaled the band with a dramatic strum on his guitar that resonated in the air.

The Weathermen played until eleven o'clock. The audience still demanded an encore with cheers and applause.

After two more songs and another standing ovation, the Weathermen blew kisses to the audience on their way off stage.

Feeling drained from the day's excitement, Cassidy waved and said her goodbyes, too. "See you tomorrow. Thanks for a fun evening and the drinks."

Ruthanne patted her shoulder. The Pearly Girls planned to hang around to see if the Weathermen would materialize again. Cassidy wasn't sure what mischief the gals had in mind, but she wasn't going to stick around to find out.

Upon collecting Elvis, she realized he had other ideas about turning in for the evening, too. He bounded down the stairs and could barely contain his excitement until Cassidy finally got his leash clipped and the door open. A few remaining concertgoers were making their way to the parking lot while a deputy—but not Deputy Turner—directed traffic to the main road. Now, why did she suddenly care if the deputy were still around? She'd had enough of his lectures anyway.

Guiding Elvis toward the garden and away from the amphitheater, Cassidy fumbled for the flashlight application on her phone. The tiny dog tugged her along to the koi pond to see his fish friends. Peace had returned to her serenity garden.

I'm definitely going to order a plaque to remember Johnny Storm. It would look nice in the gardens as a tribute.

While Elvis greeted his finned friends, she breathed in the night air. It soothed her jangled nerves. The summer scents on the cool breeze smelled like home.

"Come on, baby. It's getting late." Elvis reluctantly followed her home where she changed into pajamas and scrubbed her face.

"Elvis, the bands were good tonight, and Marion asked me to serve on a business council committee. My first reaction was that I'm too busy, but maybe this is the thing I need to be more social and to get involved. I don't have to lead the group. Maybe I can join a committee or something."

Elvis opened his eyes wide, and his eyebrows wiggled.

"I'll take that as a maybe. We'll see what it entails. Right now, I want to get some sleep. This has been a long festival and an even longer day. I'm glad all the craziness is over."

27

SUNDAY MORNING

Elvis lowered his head and let out a series of yaps. When they rounded the corner to return to the office, the crowd in the parking lot stunned both of them. "Oh, wow. They're back. I thought we were done with all this." Cassidy scanned the lot full of satellite trucks representing TV stations from all over. "Guess what's in store for us today?" Elvis ignored the crowd of reporters and continued his quest for whatever scent was in the nearby clump of grass.

She scooped up the Chihuahua mix and jogged to the back door. *No one banging on the front door yet. I guess that's a good sign.*

Leaving the lights off, she booted up her laptop and popped a dark roast pod in the coffee maker. "This may call for lots of caffeine. And maybe chocolate."

Elvis ignored the coffee, the news crews, and the paparazzi. Instead, he snuggled in his puffy bed.

Cassidy scanned her email, deciding not to delete the interview requests. Maybe she could think of a way to use them for publicity. She skimmed Marion's email about the council roles and saved it for later.

The front door slammed. Footsteps, mixed with chatter and giggles, thundered across the hardwood floor.

"Cassidy, you in? The place is all dark. Are you back there?" Aileen yelled.

The gals made their way in, plunking down bags and purses, and taking over the room.

"We're back here. We were trying to fly under the radar, hoping all those reporters wouldn't notice we're in here." Cassidy pushed back from the desk.

"Too late," Kate grumbled. "Roxie waved at them as she sashayed up the front porch steps. Nothing like putting the spotlight on us."

"They're very nice." Ruthanne appeared extra chipper this morning—mascara and a bright pink kimono-esque top made her positively glow. "Very friendly. We stopped to talk to them on our way in. They're from all over. I saw a TV truck from Florida out there."

"We made sure to keep their focus on the wonderful venue we have here and not all the mayhem the Weathermen brought with them." Kate plopped down in a chair across from Cassidy.

"One of the reporters took my card. She's planning a wedding next spring." Ruthanne beamed.

Cassidy nodded slowly, trying to hide any anxiety about the four of them talking to a group of reporters. Before she could continue, the whoop of a police siren sent everyone to the front window to see what was going on. A police cruiser inched through the crowd. Its red and blue lights flashed. The media folks moved back and let it pass.

"What now?" Cassidy groaned, waiting to see why the police were here.

"Oh, look. It's that cute deputy." Kate flashed Cassidy a larger-than-usual grin. "You know the one. Cassidy, he seems very nice. All business, but responsible."

"And definitely cute." Ruthanne squeezed in between Roxie and Aileen to peek out the window. Her lilac perfume tickled Cassidy's nose.

Cassidy hoped she had her poker face on. The gals had been trying for weeks to fix her up with any eligible bachelor in the tri-county area. *Hopefully, something will come along and distract them from all the matchmaking talk. And I'll be glad not to have regular police visits at the office for a change. We're due for some quiet around here.*

Deputy Turner found a spot to park, but he didn't immediately get out of the vehicle. When he did step out, he set his Smokey Bear hat on his head and waded into the crowd of reporters, who flocked around him. For a few seconds, they lost sight of him in the crowd.

Not wanting to be caught staring out the window, Cassidy hurried to the front counter and pretended to be busy. Elvis seemed to consider this a game, so he joined in.

A firm rap on the glass of the front door sent Elvis's yipping into overdrive. Taking her time getting to the door, Cassidy opened it with a flourish. "Good morning, Deputy. Come in."

"Good morning. Quite a crowd you have out there. Oh, and quite a crowd you have in here! I feel like I'm late to the party. Good morning, ladies." He paused to pat Elvis on the head. "I stopped by to get you to review and sign your statement from yesterday, Cassidy."

"Come on back to the office. Can I get you some coffee?" Cassidy tucked a stray curl behind her ears.

"Thanks. Yes. Black, please."

The Pearly Girls and Elvis tromped behind him to make sure they didn't miss anything. Having an audience only made her more jittery. Cassidy made a face at the Pearly Girls, who ignored her.

She pointed to the table surrounded by vintage vinyl chairs and fired up the coffee maker. "Anybody else want coffee?"

The gals all shook their heads and pretended to work on tasks around the office. Roxie, the only one not feigning work, pulled up a chair beside the deputy and waited for his next move.

He took several sheets of paper from a folder, set them on the desk, and busied himself with his phone.

A few minutes later when the coffee maker puffed out its last blast of steam, Cassidy handed him a mug and slid into the chair across from him and Roxie. The other three Pearly Girls listened intently from a few feet away. She was glad they were stationed behind him so he couldn't see them falling all over themselves to eavesdrop.

Reading through the pages, Cassidy didn't find any errors in the transcribed version of her statement about Beau Cox. When she paused, he handed her a ballpoint pen. Their fingers touched for a slight second, and a tingle trickled along Cassidy's spine. *Don't be silly. He only let me borrow his pen. He's gruff most of the time. He's the last person I should be interested in. Plus, I have too much to do around here to be running around crushing on the police deputy—even if he does look good in his uniform.*

Signing her name with the flourish of John Hancock, she pushed the pen and the pages toward him. "I knew someone was cheating the band members. I thought it was Dirk, and yesterday, he *was* acting odd. I couldn't pinpoint exactly what bothered me, but something seemed off. By the time I realized he wasn't the killer, it was too late. Beau had already whipped out his gun and started talking about getting rid of all of us. His plan was to blame it on Karl."

"The doctors said Karl had a concussion and was severely dehydrated. Hopefully, he'll take some time to heal and to work on his other issues." The deputy blew on his mug and took a sip.

"He felt good enough to go on stage last night," Roxie interjected.

Cassidy nodded in agreement. "From what they said at the concert last night, it sounded like they were going to keep the band together. I hope they do. They've got some lifelong fans."

"None of this was ever how I imagined meeting the Weathermen." Roxie relaxed into the chair with a loud sigh.

"It wasn't how I imagined our first meeting either." Ruthanne's cheeks flushed a pretty rose shade. "But what an adventure."

Cassidy closed her eyes for a moment. "I've been thinking about that since it happened. It took me a bit to get over the shock and then the fear my business would always be remembered as the place where Johnny Storm was murdered. I think I'm going to put up a plaque in the garden. He should be honored with a memorial to him here." Her voice trailed off.

Ruthanne clapped her hands. "I think that's a splendid idea. And we could have a nice dedication ceremony." Aileen and Kate nodded in agreement and chattered in hushed whispers. They had already started the planning—or maybe they were plotting their next escapade.

Hopping up from her seat, Cassidy dashed to her desk and rummaged through the drawer for the purloined book. "Here." She held out the book to the deputy. "We found this on the property." *We kinda did. He doesn't need to know all the details of how we came to be in possession of it.*

Roxie raised a perfectly sculpted eyebrow when Cassidy handed Deputy Turner the book, but she didn't offer any commentary either.

"Thanks." He drained the last few drops of coffee. "I've got to get back. Let me know if you have any problems with the crowd outside. They seem to be bored and bummed that there's really nothing happening here. I told them the Commonwealth's attorney and the sheriff have a press conference scheduled for two this afternoon. They should head out by lunch to cover that. I'll reach out if I need anything else."

"Oh, we'll all be here." Kate yelled from the back where she'd disappeared when Cassidy had brought out the planner. "Don't be a stranger."

"Stop by anytime," Aileen added with a little finger wave. "We always love to chat."

The deputy cracked a smile. "I can always count on you to be front and center in whatever is going on around Ivy Springs."

Cassidy and Elvis followed the deputy to the front door. On the porch, he paused on the top step. "You did well yesterday. Thanks to you we caught the killer." The corners of his mouth turned up into an almost-smile.

Cassidy closed the door behind him and let out a long puff of air.

"You should ask him out," Roxie said.

"What? No. He's so not my type. Plus, he's older than me. And bossy." Cassidy shook her head vehemently.

"Firm. No nonsense. Leadership skills." Roxie ticked off his perceived positive traits on her fingers.

"And cute," Ruthanne added. "And I mean *really* cute."

Cassidy's phone rang. *Saved by the bell.*

"Good morning. Celebrations at Ivy Springs. How may I help you?"

"Hi, Cassidy. This is Britt Mahoney. Well, I was Brittany Rogers back in high school. Not sure if you remember me. I was a senior when you were a little ol' freshman. Anyway, I am the chair of the reunion committee for my class, and next year is our big milestone anniversary. Instead of having it at the high school like our prom, we'd like to come out and talk to you about renting your facilities. Kelly—Kelly Mason-Todd—saw your place on the news, and we all thought it would be perfect. We love all that country charm."

"Of course, I remember you all. How have you been?"

"College. Marriage. Three kids. Stay-at-home mom. Full-time beauty blogger and influencer."

"Congratulations. Wow! You've been busy. When would be a suitable time to meet?" Cassidy retreated to her desk.

"How about Monday afternoon? We'd love to tour the place and share our ideas," Britt said.

"How about three o'clock?"

"Sounds perfect. See you then." Cassidy hung up and pivoted toward the canine and human eyes all locked on her. "See, real work. No time to be boy crazy."

Roxie made a tsking sound and waved dismissively. "There is always time for interesting men and adventures."

ACKNOWLEDGMENTS

Writing is mostly a solitary endeavor, but it takes the support of so many family and friends to take it from idea to its final form. Thank you, Stan Weidner, for all your love and support and for always being there; my parents who instilled in me a lifelong love of reading; Cortney Cain for all the five a.m. check-ins; Meagan Van Laeken and Jocelyn Cain, my pop culture gurus; and Bill Cain for always keeping everyone entertained.

I am so grateful for my talented Sisters in Crime, Guppy, and Writers Who Kill friends. Your support is invaluable! Many thanks to Jackie Layton, Sue Minix, Marilyn Levinson, and Ruth B. Hartman for the great early reads.

Thank you to Weidner Photography for making me look good. Many, many thanks to my fabulous agent, Cindy Bullard, for all her guidance and hard work. And a huge thank you to Amanda Chiu, Ashlyn Inman, and the entire team at Turner Publishing. You all are amazing!

I am so grateful for all the mystery lovers, and I can't wait to share Cassidy, Elvis, and the Pearly Girls' adventures with you.

ABOUT THE AUTHOR

Originally from Virginia Beach, **Heather Weidner** has been a mystery fan since Scooby-Doo and Nancy Drew. Through the years, she's been a cop's kid, technical writer, editor, college professor, software tester, and IT manager. As an author, she writes the Pearly Girls Mysteries, the Delanie Fitzgerald Mysteries, The Jules Keene Glamping Mysteries, and The Mermaid Bay Christmas Shoppe Mysteries, and her short stories have appeared in various publications.

She is also a member of Sisters in Crime: National, Central Virginia, Chessie, Guppies, and Grand Canyon Writers; International Thriller Writers; and James River Writers; and she blogs regularly with the Writers Who Kill. She lives in Central Virginia with her husband and a pair of Jack Russell terriers.